I0665085

Tar Heart

THE NEW HAMPSHIRE MYSTERIES
(BOOK THREE)

MIRA GIBSON

Copyright © 2016 Mira Gibson

Cover Design: The Killion Group, Inc.

Mystery Royalty

mysteryroyalty.com

All rights reserved.

ISBN: 978-0-692-66868-9

This is a work of fiction. Names, characters, places, and incidents either are the product of the author's imagination or are used fictitiously. Any resemblance to actual persons, living or dead, events, or locales is entirely coincidental.

PROLOGUE

IT WAS FREEZING, the moonless night deceivingly still except for the stiff wind.

Vacantly, Rose stared at the lake shrouded in darkness, its icy surface, the snowdrift spilling out from the shore, as dread ratcheted up her spine, her heart pumping madly.

As the frigid wind bit into her, she agonized over calling her husband and leaving another voicemail message. She was gripping her cell like a wishing stone, she realized, when the wind changed course, causing her hair to whip into her eyes.

He hadn't picked up when she had tried his cell phone. Dialing his office line had rendered the same result and unnerved, Rose had left a brief, frantic voice message, keeping her point cryptic while urgently demanding he get back to her.

How much time had gone by between her first and second messages? Had minutes elapsed or hours? Anxiety was skewing her sense of time. Her mind was racing like a hamster on a wheel, spinning faulty logic, analyzing their curt exchanges in a favorable light, though she knew she was lying to herself. The hints Benjamin had dropped, the vague answers she had offered to quell the issue, appease her husband, and put the whole matter to bed, amounted to a foregone conclusion.

He knew.

The wind picked up, blowing in from the lake and kicking up snow—needles whipping her face, dampening her light-auburn hair.

Folding her arms, Rose hunched her shoulders. She should've thrown her coat on. A thin sweater and jeans weren't enough to keep warm on a wintery New Hampshire night.

The floodlights over the porch cast just enough light to illuminate the backyard, the natural snow banks, the footprints and fist marks her son had left in his quest to make snowmen and angels. On several occasions he had peed along the shore, intrigued as any two-year-old that the hot stream could melt the snow crust.

He was kneeling where the drift spilled onto the frozen shore. He scooped snow into a powdery ball then chucked it into the wind. Almost before leaving his mittens, the snowball came apart, flurries raining over him. He cackled uproariously and looked at his mother, certain she would find it hilarious.

But she was somewhere else entirely, cradling her phone to her ear, her shoulders rounded in a secretive hunch, as she paced. Her tone, ordinarily melodic and light, sounded guttural, an edge of panic cloying up her throat with every word.

"Benjamin, please," she insisted, her cell phone was ice against her cheek. "If you don't get back to me..." She had nothing to threaten. She didn't even have a convincing explanation for her colossal mistake, one that had been years in the making. "Please, don't do this. Call me."

After hanging up, she switched the cell-setting from vibrate to ring, turned the volume up as loud as it would go, then clutched it worrisomely beneath her chin as if willing the device to ring, only vaguely aware that Tucker was running in circles along the shore.

This life meant everything to her. She wouldn't let it crumble. She refused.

Decisively, she dialed his office line and left yet another rushed, cryptic voicemail message, nervously fiddling with her necklace, its pendant—a relic of the life she had traded for this one—where it rested against her collarbone.

Roughly the size of a quarter, the heart-shaped pendant adorned with a jagged opal was one of her sister's finest. Holly had crafted it from her own design, working late into the night at her studio, determined to make her jewelry dream a reality even at the expense of her finances.

Holly ran hot and cold with her, always had and always would. For twins, they rarely saw eye-to-eye. Each had a tendency to be easily sucked into arguments, going for the other's sore spots, kicking one another when they were down, perpetually raw and on guard whenever the other was near. But there had been periods of calm before each storm. And it had been during one of those rare occasions that Holly had given her the necklace.

Where had it all gone wrong?

And why was she now tumbling down the same pike with Benjamin?

Secrets, she thought, tucking her cell phone into the back pocket of her jeans. Rose had her secrets. It was who she was. She liked them. She needed to lead that second life. The one her husband didn't know about, the one that breathed thrill into her bones with each passing day. Except now he knew. She sensed it. And the house of cards she had built on well-crafted lies and sheer audacity would soon come fluttering down.

She would do anything to prevent its fall.

With shaking hands, she pulled up Holly's contact, tapping quickly against the LCD screen, though her staccato breath obscured it with white plumes of condensation, and sent the call through.

When she glanced up with ringtone blaring in her ear, she saw Tucker padding out onto the ice—ice she knew wasn't safe—and bolted after him, sprinting as fast as she could, her boots punching hard against powdery snow until she reached the icy shore.

"Tucker!"

He turned, doe-eyed and oblivious to the danger he had placed himself in, a big smile on his face.

"Rose?" Holly's voice came strained through the earpiece. "Did something happen? Is Tucker okay?"

She didn't respond as she waded cautiously onto the ice, her son watching her and at times clapping the snow off his mittens with no awareness that the ice was thin enough to crack.

He was ten yards away, standing where freezing lake water had seeped up onto the ice.

"Tucker, honey, come here," she said, reaching out for him to take hold of her hand though he was yards away, a mere shadow in the darkness.

Holly kept saying her name over and over again impatiently, but Rose was fully focused on her son, praying the ice would hold, as he shuffled playfully towards her.

It wasn't until she had Tucker by the arm, a breath of relief rushing out of her, that she returned the cell to her ear.

"I can't get a hold of Benjamin," she said urgently, Tucker skipping and bounding beside her, though he was tethered in her grasp. She ushered him towards the shore. "I'm afraid I messed everything up."

Holly sighed into the receiver, knowing her sister far too well to waste time trying to calm her down. Rose didn't panic except irrationally, and there was often no getting through to her. If Rose believed she had done something to jeopardize a relationship, then Holly trusted she surely had. She had done similar to Holly so many times it had ultimately resulted in their estrangement.

"What do you expect me to do?" Holly asked, at a loss. "It's not like he talks to me. He probably hates me. I thought you did too, for that matter."

"I don't hate you," she murmured distractedly as she helped Tucker through the sliding glass door that connected the porch to the living room.

Confrontational, she asked, "What did you do?" her tone stripped of its prior compassion.

"I can't get into it."

"He'll come home eventually, won't he? You can talk to him then."

"He hasn't been home in weeks," she said in a brittle tone, stripping Tucker out of his winter coat and snow pants, and getting him situated with his Thomas the Tank Engine toys. "I tried his office. I tried the resort. I tried his cell. There are no more numbers to try."

Again Holly sighed and when her voice came through it held an edge of resignation mixed with defeat.

"Are you asking me to come over?"

Debating, Rose made her quick way to the sliding glass door, which she had left ajar and just as she was about to close it, she remembered Tucker's shovel and pail in the yard.

"I don't know," she said, suddenly indecisive now that she had Holly in her ear. She trekked towards the pail, but didn't pick it up when she reached it. "I hate that we don't talk."

Holly let out a sardonic laugh, which relaxed into a carefully measured breath, and Rose expected the usual lecture over whose fault that was. "What are you really worried about, Rose? The police knocking on your door?"

She snapped, "Why would you ask me that?"

"Why do you think? Are you in some kind of trouble?"

"I'm concerned I'm losing my husband."

"I thought you had gotten it together," she said as though she was pained that her twin was heading down a long, familiar, yet sordid road she should've outgrown by now. "You have a son, for Christ's sake."

Rose gazed out across the lake, scanning the darkness as if doing so would free her from every mistake she had ever made. "I shouldn't have called you."

"I can't do this with you anymore. I can't go months without hearing from you then get a call in the middle of the night when you're freaking out. I can't."

Holly continued rattling off the countless ways her twin had disappointed her over the years, which mostly centered on the sad fact that their problems had prevented Holly from seeing Tucker, but Rose was suddenly distracted. The distinct sound of tires crunching over compacted snow followed by a brief flare of headlights blazing across the yard sent her heart punching up her throat. A vehicle had pulled into the driveway.

"Holly," she said, interrupting her sister's tirade. "I think he's here. He just pulled up. I have to go."

As Rose lowered her cell phone, Holly insisted she not hang up, but she didn't have a choice. She ended the call and started through the snow, thoughts tangling over what to say to him, how she might convince Benjamin to stay with her, though every option seemed trite if not manipulative.

Expecting her husband to come through the front door, she rounded the porch, snow crunching under her boots and icy wind stinging her cheeks, but before she could pad up the steps, she caught sight of a figure stalking around the side of her house.

Whoever the figure belonged to, the person was wearing a black ski mask.

"Who's there?" she asked, treading cautiously, terror riding high. When she added, "Get out of here," her voice was a frayed thread.

"I thought we had an understanding," said the masked figure, cocking the gun she hadn't realized was in the person's hand.

Her eyes snapped up and she instantly knew who the person was.

Some secrets were meant to stay buried.

"Don't do this," she begged and then tried to lie. "The police are on their way."

"I doubt that."

Suddenly, her mind felt starkly paralyzed with fear.

Without thought, Rose took off running. Punching her boots hard into the snow and pumping her arms, she dashed with little concern that she was rushing headlong towards the ice. When she reached the lake, charging hard across its frozen surface, she nearly slipped, but righted her balance, and pressed onward.

Whimpering and glancing over her shoulder to see if she was being chased, she felt the ice shift under her boots, and in the next instant a deafening shot rang out.

She didn't understand that she had been hit until she slammed onto the ice and began skidding and gasping and praying that this wouldn't be the end of her life.

She slid to a stop, her cheek pressed to wet ice and eyes locked on the masked figure hidden in the distant shadows.

Beneath her the thin sheet of ice gave way and she plummeted into the freezing depths.

Her last thought was of her son and the secret she had died for.

CHAPTER ONE

HOLLY DANES STOOD under the portico and pounded on the front door. She should've worn gloves. A hat would've been a nice touch. The tips of her ears felt numb. Before making the drive, she had shoved her revolver—a Smith & Wesson J-Frame Center-fire, as snubbed-nosed as a bulldog—down the back of her jeans. No bigger than her palm, the compact metal bastard had absorbed the freezing temperature, and because of it an icy chill was radiating from where it rested against the small of her back, contributing to the misery of this ordeal.

Why the hell wasn't Rose coming to the door?

She glanced over her shoulder, scanning the dark driveway for Benjamin's car as if she could've possibly missed it when she had started up the walkway. If he had returned like Rose had mentioned when she cut their call short, it might explain why her sister wasn't answering the door. But his vehicle wasn't in the driveway, only Rose's sleek BMW cloaked in eight inches of fresh snow.

Her knuckles were chapped where they rapped again and again against the steel surface of the door, unsuspecting in its brick-red hue. By the looks of it, you would never guess the three-story house was a fortress, the sum total of each barrier—entrance door and rear fortified with state-of-the-art locks, the windows wired with alarms as well as the cellar's trap door round back—all masquerading as a stately Colonial home, so the opposite of her own that she had felt like a trespasser even when invited inside. Not that she had set foot in her sister's home recently. It had been two years to the day, in fact.

The fixture overhead dimly illuminated the window on the door, its tungsten glow causing a glare where frost had formed, but she could tell the living room lights were on. The foyer wasn't that deep.

Again she pounded on the door, this time with the heel of her hand to spare her frozen fingers, and called her sister's name. She was met with silence.

Shifting her weight, she eased back a step, mindful that the landing was slick with slush over thin patches of black ice, and studied the door as if a way to break in would jump out at her.

That's what would be required, right? What Rose's distressed tone had implied? The subtext of her staccato panic, the grand leap from desperately pleading for help to entirely abandoning the request had filled Holly with grim intuition.

Estrangement hadn't broken their connection.

Her twin was in trouble.

Center Harbor was a small town and last she had heard, Benjamin had just taken over the accounting at his parents' resort on Squam Lake. He had been sleeping there. Making excuses for his absence, he had explained the disarray of the Wythe Resort's bookkeeping, the importance of his new position, and the money it would afford Rose and the baby.

Standing under the portico, sensing Rose was near but unable to let Holly in, pitched the memory of their last encounter—the one that had ended their relationship—into the forefront of her mind.

Benjamin was nothing if not consistent.

He liked avoiding his family.

The last time she had been at this house, Holly had sat on the living room couch listening to her sister rage at her husband over the phone in the next room, his home office. Rose's footfall had indicated pacing—angry pattering punctuated with a stomp, turning on her heel to stampede in a new direction. She had probably had the receiver clamped between her cheek and shoulder, the telephone in her fist, the cord restricting her, maybe wrapping her legs, instigating her frustration, not that Holly had seen.

Her particular brand of outrage, the shrill tone and scattered arguments, which had ranged from reasonable to hysterical—*This family will fall apart if you're not here,* and *What if Tucker chokes on a grape? I don't know the Heimlich maneuver!*—had tipped Holly off.

It had taken her less than a minute to locate the evidence of her suspicion as to why Rose sounded like a jittering maniac. Hunting for the television remote controls, finding an old one in the coffee table drawer, and popping the battery compartment open—Rose's most treasured hiding spot—Holly had been confronted with the heart-sinking fact that her sister had started up again, as she stared at the 8-ball, plastic packed to the gills with cocaine. The discovery had stunned her, but the revelation that followed had been far worse.

Rose was still breast-feeding.

"Give me that," she had demanded, snatching the plastic bag, her eyes firing enraged, though the faintest hint of remorse shined through. Holly hadn't even heard her sneak back in.

"What about your son?" she had shot back.

Insisting, "This is old," Rose had tucked the 8-ball into her pocket and tried to stare her sister down, but to Holly she had only looked indignant.

Holly couldn't remember what she said next, only that she had begun screaming accusations and Rose hadn't held back either. When words had failed—her twin combating her every point—Holly lunged, fingernails clawing at her sister's jeans, desperate to take the drugs as if doing so would mean Rose wasn't a junkie, didn't have countless stashes hidden throughout the house, wouldn't slip into the same secretive darkness that Holly had already pulled her out of.

Rose had slapped her so hard across the face that it had rattled her brain, her tongue catching between her teeth. In an instant, her mouth had filled with blood, which trickled out the corner of her mouth as she stared in wide-eyed horror at the woman whose face she shared. In that moment, Rose had looked like a complete stranger, her eyes fixated on the 8-ball of cocaine resting on the floor between them.

Holly had told herself if Rose picked it up, she would walk out the door and never come back.

Rose hadn't just picked it up. She had seized it, examined the plastic for punctures, and exhaled with heavy relief to find it intact.

Wind whipped at her sideways, jarring her from the memory, as snow flurried down from the roof and settled under her collar. She couldn't wait under the portico forever, not when there was no indication of Rose inside.

Out of frustration, Holly aimed her revolver at the deadbolt, but then thought better of it. A gunshot would terrify Tucker if he was asleep in his bedroom, not to mention set off the security alarms, alerting the police. If her sister was passed out on the couch in a drug induced coma, which in Holly's mind would be the best case scenario, Rose would lose custody of her son the second the police put two and two together.

Descending the slick steps with caution and trekking through knee-deep snowdrifts with her revolver gripped firmly in her right hand, she started for the back of the house.

The snow became compact as she cut towards the porch and she noted tracks leading out to the lake, but thought nothing of it. The second she realized the sliding glass door leading into the living room was open, her stomach dropped. Her fears mounted tenfold in an instant at the distressed sound of Tucker shrieking from within the house.

As she walked swiftly, kicking up powdery snow and wincing at the sting of it creeping down her boots, Tucker's cry erupting into full-blown wailing, concern sprung in her chest.

Slush lay over the porch, a sign it had been salted. When she reached the sliding glass door, she made an honest effort to stomp the sopping mess off her boots, but the attempt only splashed ice water onto her jeans as well as the shiny wooden floor inside the house.

It crossed her mind to take her boots off so as not to warp the wooden floor with water stains. Back when she had visited often, Rose's every complaint had centered on Holly's inability to appreciate nice things—*Use a coaster,* and *Don't bang the piano keys,* and *Turn on the exhaust fan when you shower or else we'll have a mildew problem.*

Tucker's cries were lacerating her eardrums, a horrific sound that also hit her like a knife to her gut, her nephew screaming bloody murder and at times gurgling just to breathe.

She eased the sliding glass door closed behind her.

Rose wasn't passed out on the couch.

As she charged through the living room, which could've been featured in Better Homes & Gardens, it was so artfully decorated—oak furnishings, a plush pink sofa-set, abstract paintings on the walls that to Holly had always looked both childish and pretentious—her ears pricked up, attuned to Rose's domestic sound effects, but there weren't any. The house was quiet except for her nephew's anxiety.

But that didn't mean the house was safe. She cocked her revolver.

Though Tucker's bedroom was at the top of the stairs, she followed his cries to the end of the first floor hallway and found him in his crib, his little hands clutching the railing. His face was wet with tears, and snot was running from his nose.

Seeing him, her heart ached with regret for the months that had been wasted, the estrangement having prevented her from being in her nephew's life. As she searched blindly for the light switch panel, her vision blurry, tears misting her eyes, she smiled at Tucker in hopes it would calm him.

Discreetly, she tucked her revolver down the back of her jeans.

He quieted when the lights came on, his expression brightened with recognition, and soon a goofy grin spread across his face.

She couldn't believe how big he was. His strawberry-blonde hair was a mess of cowlicks just like hers and as she scooped him up, making a ledge of her forearm for him to sit and hugging him tightly for all the months she had missed—*God, I love you*—it dawned on her how strange it was for him to be in the playroom instead of upstairs.

For reasons that had seemed cruel, Rose had kept Tucker down here to Ferberize him during infancy, the grander plan of which was to move him upstairs into his big-boy bed when he was old enough. During the few phone calls Rose had placed to her sister over their months estranged, she had found ways to mention this amidst her frenzy as though the subject of Tucker helped her catch her breath between panicking over things Holly rarely understood.

But he was three now.

Tucker murmured and seemed suddenly at ease staring up at her as though he understood he was with family. But he hadn't seen her since he was one. He couldn't possibly remember her. She suddenly realized Tucker thought his mother had returned.

"You're okay," she cooed, her voice going high and breathy to soothe him. She swayed and he nuzzled into the crux of her neck, his wet face pressing against her skin. He felt like warm putty and smelled a bit poopy.

The crib, the diapers, was this coddling or negligence?

Tucker was getting too old for all of it.

"Let's get you changed, huh?"

She stepped carefully over scattered toys towards the dresser, but clipped her heel on a plastic train. When she glanced down, the smiling gray face of Thomas the Tank Engine was staring up at her. She kicked it aside and juggled the weight of her nephew as she pulled the top drawer open. It was filled with linens so she tried a few more and found a bag of diapers in the bottom drawer.

Holly felt uneasiness grow as she changed her nephew out of his soiled diaper and into a fresh one.

Rose had been outside when she had called. Holly had heard wind grazing the receiver, muffling her sister's disjointed assertions. Those tracks in the snow led straight to the lake and what little light the porch fixture had provided, she had been able to tell her sisters footprints veered out onto the ice.

As she got Tucker situated in his crib, his verbal skills returned and he protested, "No!" then called her *Mom* a number of times, clutching at her hair where locks spilled over her shoulder into his face.

"I'll be right back," she assured him, smoothing his hair down and giving him a nervous smile. She grabbed the plastic toy train off the carpet and offered it to him, but he chucked it at the wall yelling, *bang!*

It caught her off guard and because of it, she walked with a sense of urgency down the hallway. A harrowing intuition told her that she would find Rose out on the ice, but to cover her bases she first checked every room in the house.

The downstairs bathroom contained only the faintest scent of her sister's perfume. Benjamin's office was airless. There was no sign of Rose in any of the rooms upstairs, though her sister had left the master bedroom in complete disarray—dresser drawers open to varying degrees, the comforter a mountainous heap on the floor, the TV chattering from the corner of the room.

Leaving the warm house, Holly felt the icy wind knock the air right out of her lungs. She glanced towards the lake and noticed tracks in the snow. Following them and noting how the footprints became further and further apart, which confirmed her sister had broken out running towards the lake and onto the ice, she neared the icy shore and scanned the darkness across the lake.

She was nervous about wading out onto the ice. Not one winter had gone by without news reports of children or some drunken fool with grand delusions of fishing having fallen through the ice.

Passing the snowdrift onto the black sheet of ice, her heart fluttering so rapidly in her chest that she felt suddenly light-headed, she pressed onward. After letting out an uneasy breath, shifting her gaze from the ice beneath her boots to the darkness ahead, she sucked in a lung-full of air as if oxygen could loosen the knot that was twisting in her stomach.

Rose had thought Benjamin's car was pulling into the driveway. She had hung up on Holly. And whatever had followed, had compelled her to flee out onto the lake.

Her heart punched out of rhythm when she spotted a hole in the ice up ahead. She didn't blink as she eased farther out, fearing the worst as she began closing the five-yard gap, Tucker's high-pitched voice echoing through her head—*Bang*.

Though it was excruciatingly dim, she saw blood streaked across the ice at her feet. It was unmistakable, yet her mind kept offering alternatives—mud, oil, paint—pathetically hopeful that it wasn't what she thought. Kneeling, she touched it then examined her fingertips, but they were clean. The blood had frozen to the ice. Her gaze snapped up, locking on the hole in the ice that was now three yards ahead.

If the ice thinned where it neared the hole, she wouldn't get away with walking. She knew enough to spread her weight out as much as possible to limit the risk of falling through so she eased down onto her stomach, planting her elbows on the ice, and began pulling herself the rest of the way.

Soon the ice was wet, lake water having seeped up. She ignored her numbing thighs, the chill against her stomach where her coat failed to meet the waistband of her jeans, and came to the edge of the hole. The surface of the lake was as smooth as glass. Black. Her sister wasn't floating beneath.

Holly muscled backwards, pushing herself away from the hole to safety and wondering why she had sensed that her sister was out here. She wanted to scream and cry, but she had walled-off those emotions years ago. Instead she hung her head, letting her forehead rest on the ice, pinching her eyes shut, and hunting for ideas as to what she should do next, where she should look, who she should call if not the police. Could she call the cops? Or would she be met with the rigmarole of having to wait forty-eight hours before filing a missing persons report. Was Rose even missing?

When Holly opened her eyes, her sister's lifeless face was staring up at her through the ice.

She gasped, scrambling to her knees then shuffling backwards, straining to grasp that Rose was trapped under the ice.

Not trapped.

Dead.

She couldn't get back to the house fast enough.

Slipping with every third step, she ran towards the shore and picked up her pace when she reached the snowdrift where it had blown out onto the lake.

How could this be happening?

What had Rose gotten herself into that she had wound up dead beneath the ice while her son slept inside their home?

Why would her sister run away from the house instead of towards it where she could have easily locked herself in, called the police, and waited for help to arrive?

Holly had a good mind to do just that, but as soon as she locked the sliding glass door behind her, the disturbing reality of it all took hold.

She barely heard Tucker call out, "Mommy!"

"Give me a minute," she said, not liking the dismissing tone in her voice, as she pulled her emotions together enough to find the staircase.

Taking the treads two at a time, she reached the landing and hurried down the hallway into the master bedroom. After closing the door to shut out Tucker's incessant questions—*What time is it?* and *Can I have water?* and *Daddy?*—she unzipped her coat pocket and used the frozen claw of her hand to scoop out her cell phone then searched through her contacts for Benjamin Wythe's number.

The line opened up after one ring, but before his voice came through, Holly heard the melodic giggling of what sounded like a young woman in the background.

"I checked out the house," she asserted to steal his attention from whatever woman he was with this time. "You need to get over here."

Benjamin directed his smooth voice away from the receiver, getting his guest to be quiet, but his tone was gravely deep addressing Holly. "What's the problem?"

"Rose is dead."

He said nothing.

"Hello?"

"You shouldn't have called me."

"What?" she blurted out, astonished. "You asked me to come over here."

"You should call the police."

"I plan to," she shot back. His reaction wasn't what she had expected. Tense silence ensued. He didn't ask how his wife had died or where Holly had found her. He didn't seem alarmed or shocked. Benjamin had been absent from Rose's life to say the least, but she would've thought she would get more from him than this. "Benji, your wife is dead. It looks to me like she was killed. Get your ass home."

In the background, the woman whispered something breathy and Holly could almost see her cloying at the forty-year old man, maybe pouting for sex or at the very least eager to compete with the caller who had the audacity to take up any of her lover's time.

Benjamin rushed through a stunted goodbye, and Holly heard a click and the line went dead. She snorted a laugh, appalled he could hang up on her so easily.

Her hands were thawing out so she tucked her cell in her pocket and scanned the bedroom, but she was too overwhelmed for her eyes to work.

The police would comb every inch of this house as soon as they concluded Rose Wythe had been murdered and Holly would be damned if she let them get sidetracked from catching her sister's killer.

She hoped like hell Rose hadn't relapsed, but she systematically worked her way through every room in the house checking for hidden drug stashes anyway.

After twenty minutes, she had found a dime-bag taped to the underside of the toilet bowl lid and three 8-balls—one tucked in the toe of a Jimmy Choo, another wedged beneath a mini-fridge on Benjamin's side of the bed, the man liked his nightcaps but not enough to journey down to the kitchen, and the third stuffed inside one of Tucker's stuffed animals where the nape of its neck had sprouted cotton, whether her nephew or her sister had mangled the bear, Holly couldn't understand.

And that was on the second floor alone. The ground floor proved even more bountiful, a fact that deeply disturbed her.

All told, by the time she sat on the living room couch after setting her findings on the coffee table, Holly was looking at about a quarter-pound of cocaine; more than enough to kill her sister if Rose went on a bender.

But it wouldn't kill her.

Someone else already had.

And fathoming that was the force that compelled her to tear open one of the little baggies, tap out a heap of powder, chop it with the plastic edge of her debit card, scrape the drug into a long crisp line, and snort it with the only bill she could find in her wallet.

She had never felt closer to her twin.

CHAPTER TWO

THE LED LIGHT panels angled across the lake were bright enough to illuminate a football field. The Center Harbor PD had set up five of them, each on eight-foot stands, each weighing approximately 200 lbs. Three were on the shore, the last two strategically placed on the ice as close to the hole as possible without compromising the safety of the volunteer firefighters and medics that were working to retrieve the body of Rose Wythe.

Detective Lucas York had ordered one rookie to watch those lights and listen out for moaning, a sign the ice was about to crack. If it did, his team would have very little time to abandon retrieval and get to the shore.

The rookie, Officer Bobby Gibbs, who was barely out of diapers in Lucas's estimation and whose voice trilled whenever he got nervous, crouched equidistant between the two LEDs, his head snapping left and right, gaze shifting from one light to the other like a ball boy at a tennis match. He was taking his duty very seriously.

There were too many men on the ice; too much heavy equipment. Lucas had shouted at the team several times to keep their distance from one another, so that their body weight wouldn't strain the ice. He had been met with glares from the senior medics and wide-eyed confusion from the junior firefighters as if there would be no way to carry out the order.

Grouped tightly together as they were, the ice wouldn't hold.

Lucas kept his eye on the diver, as the man bobbed in the water, readying himself to have another go at submerging. His breath came out in white clouds. There was no way his wet-suit would ward off hypothermia if he didn't get out of the water soon. But the body had been drifting towards the shore.

Gibbs straightened up, drawing Lucas's attention, and shouted, "I think I heard the ice whine."

"Whine?" Lucas questioned.

The rookie nodded, terrified.

"Tell me when it *moans*."

Gibbs twisted his mouth to the side, furrowing his brow, but crouched down again, getting back on task.

Splashing and adjusting his mouthpiece, the diver slipped beneath the surface, while the firefighters yelled their encouragement to the tune of, *You got this, Carl!* and *Think warm thoughts!* and *Beers at Shenanigan's after,* because one of the guys had a cousin who owned the only bar in town that dared keep its doors open until four in the morning.

As the diver inched along beneath the ice, reaching the body and straining to hook his hands under the dead woman's armpits, Lucas stalked around the hole at a distance, coming to the far side of it, the team five yards ahead, the Wythe house glowing like a Thomas Kinkade postcard in the distance, the twin sister somewhere inside.

Lucas hadn't lived in Center Harbor long. Though this was his first case with the Center Harbor Police Department, he had worked his fair share of homicides in Plymouth, the most notable of which revolved around a prostitution ring where two under-aged girls had been brutally murdered. Closing the case had earned him accolades that in his mind he didn't have a prayer of living up to so he had decided to move from the small northern town. It had been more impulsive than reasoned, but Lucas had long since accepted that side of himself. In fact, he rarely questioned it or even thought twice when barreling headlong towards change.

The diver surged to the surface, hugging the body tightly. Without hesitation, three firefighters hoisted the dead woman onto the ice, lining her parallel to a stretcher on which they placed her.

Lucas had to bark to be heard over the teams cheering. "Don't cluster!"

"Moaning!" yelled Gibbs, who they also ignored. He shuttered, staring at the ice beneath his boots. "It's cracking!"

Just as the firefighters got to their feet, each lifting a corner of the stretcher, the body shifting precariously on top, Gibbs bolted for the shore and not a second later one of the LED lights plummeted through the ice, splashing into the lake.

As Lucas jogged away from the hole, someone shouted, "Reroute!" The firefighters veered left, avoiding the compromised ice but nearing the remaining LED and they soon realized their error.

The ice shifted beneath their feet. Hollering ensued as they maneuvered away, shuffling along a narrow strip of what everyone hoped was thick ice.

Carrying the stretcher, the men couldn't spread their weight, but Lucas could keep away from them and not be the straw to break the camel's back.

Calmly, he stilled, breathing deeply and steadily.

"York! Get off the ice!" It was Gibbs this time, screaming from the shore, his hands cupped around his mouth.

But Lucas couldn't risk the rescue team's safety. He waited, heart punching up his throat, the glare of the last LED in his eyes, and watched his men cross the threshold to the backyard where an ambulance was idling, its lights blazing red and white in manic alternation, its rear doors open, ready to transport Rose Wythe to the morgue.

Finally, he started for the shore, arching around the fractured ice and taking slow, prayer-filled steps.

"I radioed Cody McAlister," Gibbs told him, as he stepped onto an inclined snow bank along the shore.

"Great," he said dryly. He would prefer to examine the body without his partner. "Where's my medical examiner?"

"She was shot in the chest," said Gibbs, indicating he assumed a preliminary examination might wait until morning, as if he was even remotely high enough on the totem pole for the privilege of such an assumption...

Lucas tried not to berate the young cop, as he ushered him to the stretcher and pointed at the wound in Rose Wythe's chest. "She was shot between the shoulder blades. This is an exit wound.

I need a second opinion on the caliber. I need the medical examiner."

"I think he went off to Shenanigan's."

"Get him back here," he ordered.

"Second opinion? You can tell the caliber?"

Lucas glared at him, exercising his last shred of patience by adding, "Nice work with the LEDs."

If it hadn't been below freezing, Gibbs would've turned scarlet.

"Now, Officer."

"Right, on it." As he produced his cell phone, sent the call through, and pressed his phone to his ear, he asked, "What's your guess?"

Indulging him, he supplied, ".48," but didn't elaborate.

Gibbs wandered off, sounding apologetic in his effort to summon the medical examiner.

Lucas leaned in and studied Rose Wythe's face. Her lips were gray, her hair icicles. The skin on the tip of her nose as well as her chin were gone, those parts of her that had adhered to the under-wall of ice. He noticed a silver chain around her neck and felt blindly for the pendant that he figured had slipped around to her nape. When he set the silver heart on her chest, he resumed his examination. Her left cheek had minor lacerations, presumably where it had slid over the ice. But Lucas could see past the cuts and abrasions to the woman beneath. He could almost picture her alive, her cheeks rosy, her eyes bright. Maybe she had been the type to smile at the drop of a hat. Maybe she had gotten more beautiful when angered. The necklace was of interest to him, though he couldn't pinpoint why. He found the clasp and unhinged it then pocketed the jewelry, acutely aware he was risking his job.

What kind of person would shoot a woman in the back as she ran away?

A tar heart.

It wasn't a real term. Lucas had invented it; the psychopathy of a killer, its toll on the human heart. Killers didn't emote, not like normal people. Their capacity for empathy was limited, if it existed at all. They often felt stuck, imprisoned in the obligation to be normal, pretending to be like everyone else. It weighed on them, oppressed them, heaviness black and sticky as tar. Or that's how Lucas thought of it.

Killing brought them to life. Thrilled, perhaps electrically when indulging in murder; the killer felt light and free. But it wouldn't last. It couldn't. Not if they were truly warped.

Rising from contemplation, having sensed he wasn't alone, he found his partner, Cody McAlister, rounding the gurney and angling over the body.

Like Lucas, Cody had received notoriety as the result of a previous case he had solved, but unlike Lucas, his partner had bounced around afterwards, moving from town to town, department to department in the months that followed the Kendra Cole case. Perhaps he had felt suffocated by his own success or maybe he had left the small town in search of the next newsworthy crime. Lucas didn't know for sure. Cody had never told him. They were still in the butting-heads phase of their new partnership.

"We swept for shell casings," Cody mentioned. "The killer must have taken them."

"How's the sister?"

Cody frowned stiffly. "You might take a crack at her."

He cocked his brow, curious.

Indicating the body, Cody suggested, "Let's get her to the morgue."

As soon as he said it, a medic appeared, creeping into view from the driver's side and waiting in hopeful expectation for the final word.

"Don't you want Roger to take a look?"

Dismissively, Cody shrugged, "Roger's two beers deep at the bar," as if he were at a loss for motivating small-town, underpaid, and overworked assistants. "Tomorrow will be soon enough."

In addition to being furious with the M.E., which he suppressed like a pro, Lucas had to admit he was impressed the man could knock 'em back so quickly. Roger had only just left ten minutes ago. Changing the subject, he asked, "Where's the husband?"

"That's what I would like to know."

Sheepishly, the medic inched closer. "Final word?"

Cody didn't glance at Lucas for confirmation, but obliged the young man. "Go ahead."

"Would you say that's a .48?" Lucas was pointing to the wound in Rose Wythe's chest, preventing the medic from collapsing the gurney legs as he motioned to shove the body into the ambulance.

"I'd say a .42. The report will tell us."

His words were friendly enough, but his tone had been adversarial.

Lucas gave him a curt nod to end the conversation and started for the house, but turned after Cody said, "Let me know what you think of the sister."

Holding his gaze for a beat before setting off towards the porch, Lucas's response came loud and fast but only in his mind.

His thoughts about Holly Danes were unrelenting.

Sliding the glass door aside, he entered the living room where police officers were obtrusively rummaging through drawers with little tact as though the killer would've possibly thought to stash the murder weapon within these four walls.

Lucas told his officers to sweep the upstairs rooms.

Seated on the couch with a mug of coffee in her hands was Holly, her right arm cradling a young boy. The kid looked conked out when Lucas flicked his eyes in their direction, waiting for his men to shuffle out and give him privacy with the woman.

He hadn't seen her in upwards of ten years.

When the living room was quiet except for the murmuring voices of officers in nearby rooms, Lucas finally took in the sight of her.

She looked exactly the same, though her fawn-brown eyes weren't only round but glassy, likely from balling her eyes out all night. Her pronounced features, the Grecian slope of her nose and truncated lips that reminded him of the Statue of Liberty, swept him into a time-warp—their chance encounter, the dive bar empty of customers though the bar-back had a definite presence, Lucas's unshakable interest, and her shy reluctance as she had fished a stray olive from her martini glass.

It hadn't been until the morning after, when he had woken alone in bed, that he realized their long, sex-filled night hadn't been the start of something exhilarating. It hadn't been the start of anything at all. He had driven out of Center Harbor after that three-day weekend meant to clear his head and found he had managed to do the opposite, thoughts of Holly Danes cloying at him from the back of his mind. When he had put in his transfer, he had deliberately chosen the one town he hoped she still lived in.

And there she was, staring at him with stunned recognition.

Under her breath she said, "Damn," and stiffened nervously, as he sat at the far end of the couch. Between them, the young boy jostled his feet in a fit of dreams, shuttering a rocky exhale, and then stilled. "I already spoke with the other guy."

"You're still making jewelry?"

She smiled, but the offering was mild.

"Can you tell me why you think Benjamin Wythe isn't here?"

Exhausted, she supplied, "He's probably sleeping."

"We would like to know where."

"A motel? I'm really not sure. We aren't close."

Lucas fell silent to give her the impression her answer had been satisfactory. Pressuring her too soon, too hard wouldn't be productive.

"I can take Tucker for the night," she went on as if that was what he had been getting at. "Look, this is all a shock to me. I haven't seen Rose in nearly a year."

"What made you think to swing by?"

Holly sniffled, wrinkling her nose, as she freed a hand to wipe it, but to Lucas it seemed like she was stalling. "I was on the ice for awhile," she mentioned, excusing the gesture. "Rose called me. She sounded... I thought I should go over to the house. Before she got off the phone, she said that she thought Benjamin had just pulled up the driveway. I already told that guy, McAlister, all of this."

What struck Lucas most was her complete lack of emotion. It didn't seem characteristic, but then again, he hadn't seen her in years and their night together had been just that—an unforgettable eight hours, not enough to trust that he could possibly know her.

It occurred to him that though her eyes were glassy, there was no sign of puffiness or smeared mascara. "Why hadn't you seen her in a year?" He asked, wondering the impetus of their estrangement.

"We just... were too busy," she said vacantly. "It has nothing to do with why she was killed."

If it had been anyone other than Holly sitting on the couch, he would've told them that he would be the judge of that.

"Was she wearing a necklace?" she asked, once again jumping topics.

"Not that I know of," he lied.

She narrowed her eyes skeptically in response, but the squint was barely perceptible. "I thought I saw a thin chain around her neck."

"I can call the morgue if you like," he offered, carefully gauging her expression. Color was coming into her cheeks, indicating her heart rate was quickening.

"Please do," she said in a far away voice. Her gaze softened as well and soon lowered to the boy in her arms, the mug of coffee she had been passing between her hands, its steam waning. Then her eyes brightened and she met his gaze. "I didn't tell the other cop about the security cameras. Benjamin had at least four installed around the perimeter of the house."

"There are four?" he asked, surprised.

"They're above the floodlights," she explained. "You wouldn't notice them, especially at night. You would just be blinded by the lights. The cameras record onto a server that's located in the basement."

"That's fairly high-tech," he commented. "What does Benjamin do for a living?"

"Hospitality," she said easily. "But he's been out of work."

From outside, Cody neared the sliding glass door, stomping snow off his boots, then eased it open, letting himself in. An icy gust of wind came with him, but he quickly slid the door closed.

"Excuse me," he told Holly and joined his partner at the door.

"There are cameras hooked up-"

"Where are the evidence logs?" Cody barked, cutting him off. "You told me you would leave them on the passenger seat. The guys can't find them."

Taken aback, Lucas kept a poker face, wracking his brain. He couldn't recall being asked. "I was half asleep when Tammy called."

"You were awake when I talked to you," he pointed out, not at all concealing how annoyed he was.

"Sorry, Cody, I must've forgotten." He shouldn't have spoken so casually using his partner's first name instead of his last, but at least he had held his tongue from saying what he really wanted to. Center Harbor was supposed to have more money than his former precinct and it was ridiculous that cops were expected to supply their own forms and evidence bags and latex gloves during after-hours investigations. Hire a damned night-clerk to make runs, was Lucas's feeling.

The way Cody was glaring at him made him wonder if the man even cared about the evidence logs. Typically, the officers would file them next-day. Maybe his partner was itching to get on Lucas's case for anything no matter how insignificant.

Without thinking, he snuck a glimpse at Holly, which Cody didn't seem to appreciate. He was gaping at him, but Lucas ignored him.

A thin trickle of blood was dripping from Holly's right nostril.

Nearing her and fishing under the necklace that was also in his pocket for a tissue, he said, "You might need to get checked out. I think we have a medic floating around somewhere."

Confusedly, she glanced up at him just as blood hit her lip. She dabbed it with her finger, realizing the nosebleed. "I'll be fine," she said, accepting the tissue.

"Tip your head back," he suggested.

"Really, I'm fine," she said, declining. "Happens all the time when it's cold out."

He didn't trust the statement. They had met during winter. The bar had been chilly. They had drunk whiskey to ward off the draft. Outside they had taken a long stroll, drinking beers from paper bags and yelping when the wind kicked a flurry of snow in their faces. The motel they had stumbled upon had been no better, its heater clanging and unreliable. Not once had Holly gotten a nosebleed. There hadn't been any bloody tissues in the bathroom trash receptacle when he had riffled through it in hopes of finding evidence he had remembered to use a condom, the night having been a blur in that department.

Holly wadded up the tissue he had given her and tucked it into her pocket. The nosebleed had been quick and uncharacteristic of your common, run-of-the-mill winter dehydration, which afflicted children more often than adults.

"You've been helpful, Holly," he told her. "We won't keep you here any later. Thanks a lot for your time."

She pulled the boy against her chest, rising to her feet.

"Need help getting him to your car?"

"I'm fine," she said quickly. "You'll let me know about the necklace?"

Quirking his mouth into a somber smile, he told her that he would and walked her to the entrance door and opened it for her.

She stepped outside, but turned, looking up at him, while the child murmured in her arms. "Will there be an autopsy on Rose?"

She seemed apprehensive.

"I don't see the need for it. Her cause of death is cut and dry."

Letting out a carefully measured breath and nodding to herself, she started for the steps. Lucas watched her from the doorway, as she made her way through a snowdrift illuminated by stark floodlights, and got Tucker situated on the passenger seat. After she rounded the front of her vehicle, making brief, nervous eye contact, and climbed in behind the steering wheel, Lucas eased the door closed and leaned against it.

Cody wouldn't appreciate Lucas making an unauthorized move, but after the punitive lecture on evidence logs he couldn't care less. Pulling his cell phone from his jeans, the image of Holly nude on top of him burning into the forefront of his mind where it competed with his take on her shady behavior, he found Roger's number.

When the line opened up to one very inebriated medical examiner, Lucas told him to run a full autopsy on Rose Wythe.

CHAPTER THREE

THE ROAD WAS SLICK and unfolded under the shock of her Saab's headlights. Holly had been meaning to buy new tires. The tread on her current ones were nearly bald. She could feel them skipping and spinning every so often when the rubber met with black-ice. Shifting her foot between the accelerator and the brake, she scanned the snow dunes along the shoulder where they spilled into her lane, slowing and veering around them whenever necessary.

On the passenger seat Tucker was jimmying his legs, watching flurries slip over the windshield, a show he seemed to enjoy. She should've asked Lucas to get the child's car seat from Rose's BMW and help her install it, but she hadn't wanted to drag out her exit, spend even one minute longer with him than she had to.

But avoiding him had its consequences. When she had buckled Tucker in, the nylon strap, which should have spanned his chest, had lain awkwardly across his face, Tucker being much too small for it.

He had whined in protest until she tucked the restraint behind him. The only device protecting him should the vehicle careen off the road was the lap belt, but it hung loosely across his stomach, the nylon having been stretched to the limit years ago.

Holly gripped the steering wheel so tightly her knuckles were white. She felt jumpy, yet exhausted as though the cocaine in her bloodstream was dissipating, but wouldn't go down without a fight.

She shouldn't have snorted those lines. The first had brought her to her senses, frying off the mind-bending sight of her sister beneath the ice and bringing her fully into her surroundings—sharpening her vision, heightening her hearing, she had been able to smell the air more clearly. It had softened the surrealism of her heartache, stilled her panicking thoughts, and magnified a delusional sliver of hope that maybe she would find a way to get through this.

But one line hadn't been enough. She had done a second and a third until her skin was buzzing like a hive and her rationality was reduced to a child's pragmatism—*Walk outside, hide the drugs in the glove compartment, set the revolver under the driver seat, return to the living room, call the police, check on Tucker, wait.*

Now that she was high, after years of wondering what it would be like, she realized her error. She felt like a jumpy, jittery, paranoid mess and she couldn't wait for the coke to leave her system.

Why had she done this to herself?

She was only asking herself rhetorically.

She knew exactly why.

Over the years she had come to the realization that she had been too hard on Rose, that the estrangement was her fault—a self-righteous act that wasn't good for either of them. Rose hadn't come back into her life as a result of Holly's ultimatum, she hadn't cleaned up, hadn't changed for the sake of her health or the safety of her son.

And when Holly's miscalculation had finally dawned on her, when she had experienced the stark blowback of having walked out on Rose that night—Holly the one alone and miserable, regretting every word she had spoken and choice she had made—she had begun wondering...

Thinking about it, fantasizing even, exploring the idea that sharing the habit, the addiction with her twin—her urge rising only when the hole in her life where her sister had been felt too dark to bear—might be the only thing that would bring them together.

It had taken seeing her sister dead beneath the ice to make the leap.

Sitting on the couch and staring at Rose's stash earlier that night, Holly had been confronted with her last chance to truly know her sister. She had told herself it would work, perhaps it would cloak her sadness in a warm blanket, that it might even be wonderful, that if nothing else it would bring her and Rose together even though her twin was dead.

Holly pumped the brakes, coming to a rocky stop at an intersection, and waited for the traffic light to turn green. Gazing out the driver side window at a sparse row of naked Birch trees, she saw the lake, its frozen surface, the scattered patches of thawed ice reflecting the glow of lights coming from the Wythe Resort, her destination.

At this hour the resort looked like a mansion from The Great Gatsby era—twinkling and proud, boasting class and intimidating those not affluent, welcoming the elite few who could afford such accommodations. But Holly had been inside. In the light of day she had touched the walls and tasted the whiskey. It was all smoke and mirrors like the set of a television show, impressive only when seen through the lens of make-believe.

The traffic light wasn't turning so she eased her foot on the gas, rolling left through the intersection.

Not everything Holly had told the detectives was a lie. Benjamin had worked in hospitality and he had been unemployed... until recently. After years of rebelling against his parents, grueling years spent managing any hotel in town that didn't belong to Warren and Sarah Wythe, Benjamin had inadvertently run the Lakes Tavern into the ground and had no choice but to keep his family afloat by accepting a position at his parents' resort. Last month, he had been christened Assistant Chief Financial Officer, a title that sounded important, but meant very little. His father, Warren Wythe, wasn't quite ready to pass the crown. As far as Holly could tell from her bird's eye view of the dynamic, Warren never would be.

Driving through the resort parking lot was a challenge. Mountainous snow banks lining the narrow perimeter had collapsed onto the asphalt. She cut the wheel left then right, weaving her way through. The west side of the resort was under construction for an extension and because of it, the far end of the parking lot was being used to store materials under massive blue tarps, as well as two parked bulldozers and other machinery that Holly couldn't identify in the dim light.

She pulled up next to one of the bulldozers, which had been collecting snowfall, killed the engine, and flipped off the headlights so she wouldn't wake the guests sleeping beyond the row of windows that her Saab was facing. Tucker murmured as if lifting from a dream, but settled into heavy breathing. A draft seeped through the vents on the dash, alerting her to what little time she had before the car would be cold.

Quickly, she leaned over and opened the glove compartment. The drug baggies spilled out, tumbling across the compartment door. A few fell to the floor mat, but she strained, plucking them up. She made fast work of stuffing the plastic bags into her coat pockets. But two bags wouldn't fit. She stared at them in her palm—one contained roughly an ounce of cocaine wrapped in wrinkled plastic, the other was a plump, square inch Ziploc. She studied it. She was familiar with the bag. Her jewelry studio had millions. Bags this size were meant to hold beads and chains and gems, not drugs.

She felt eyes on her and glanced up to find Tucker interested. He reached to take a bag, asking, "What's that?"

Damn, her heart was racing. She closed her fist around the bags, stammering to answer, and finally settled on, "Adult stuff. Ready to see Daddy?"

He brightened, straightening up in the seat and looking out at the resort and the parking lot, trying to place his surroundings, where Daddy might be.

Holly couldn't bring herself to tuck the last two bags of cocaine into her pocket. She felt the weight of them in her tight fist and cursed at herself; her irrational need to feel close to her twin waging war against all reason. She already felt ill. Did she really want to hang on to these?

She shoved them into the glove compartment and, flipping the door closed, let out a long sigh, her breath a thin white cloud.

Climbing out of her Saab, her boot hit a sheet of black-ice and she nearly lost her balance, but caught the armrest just in time. After quietly closing the driver side door, she rounded the front of the car, opened the passenger door, and freed Tucker from his seatbelt. Scooping him into her arms and shifting him onto her hip, it dawned on her that she hadn't brought any diapers, clothes, toys, all the items that Tucker required on a moment to moment basis. But she nudged the door closed with her hip and began trekking through the snow that lined the walkway leading to the resort entrance.

As soon as she stepped inside with Tucker wide-awake on her hip and asking more questions than she could process—*Daddy's here?* and *Can we make a snowman?* and *What's that, what's that, what's that?*—she felt enveloped in warmth.

However, no one was manning the front desk. The lobby was quiet, the lounge beyond, vacant by the looks of it. She bypassed the desk, turning the corner down the hallway that led into the east wing. It smelled like cedar, no doubt the Wythe's had kept a Christmas tree in the lounge, milking the holidays as far into January as they could get away with.

She checked the room numbers as she went and paused when she reached 112, the room Benjamin had disclosed to her back when he had first moved into the resort—*Don't breathe a word of this to Rose*, he had told her. Holly couldn't have. She hadn't really been speaking to her sister, only answering the random, midnight phone calls that woke her every four months.

Tucker boomed out, "Can I have raisins?" and she hushed him in favor of listening through the door. When she had approached the room, she thought she had detected the flittering voice of a woman, the one she had heard in the background when speaking with Benjamin on the phone earlier that night. But as she leaned in, pressing her ear to the door, the only sounds on the other side were of footfall and then the quiet click of a door.

She knocked and stepped back, in case Benjamin needed to spy her through the peephole.

Giving the door another knock, she said, "Benji? It's Holly," and the door popped open, drawing inward and revealing Benjamin, who was wearing a pair of navy boxer-briefs, a white dress shirt off-kilter and unbuttoned down the front as though he had just thrown it on, and a very annoyed look on his face.

"Can I come in?" He was just staring at her, his chestnut eyes sharply holding her gaze, so she offered him his son, maneuvering the squirrely boy against Benjamin's chest, but he backed away. "Take your son."

Pulling her inside by her arm, Benjamin scanned the hallway and shut the door. That's when she realized he didn't look annoyed. He looked paranoid and rattled.

Tucker began fussing in her arms and trying to wriggle free. The queen-sized bed was a disaster, its comforter bunched at the foot of the bed, the pillows laid haphazardly—one in the center of the bed, another on the floor. Holly set her nephew on the edge of the bed anyway and plowed her fingers through his cowlick-hair, glancing at his father.

"Cops are at the house," she told him.

"Rose's body is still there?"

Holly covered Tucker's ears. He was old enough to know his mother's name. "At the morgue."

Benjamin's gaze drifted to the floor and he began eating his lower lip, his eyes shifting worrisomely.

Something clattered on the other side of the bathroom door and when Holly glanced over, she half expected the door to pop open, but heard muffled scrambling instead.

Nearing Benjamin, she unzipped her coat pockets. He was standing near a dresser, the top drawer of which was already open so she began depositing the drugs inside, resting each bag on a stack of folded shirts.

"Is this why she died? Did it have something to do with this?"

His response sounded dubious and uneasy. "I have no idea, I haven't been around."

When she looked at Benjamin, she couldn't fathom what Rose had seen in him. To Holly, he was a bottom-feeder, a coward, magnetized only to those who built him up and overlooked his many flaws—the spoiled sense of entitlement, the stubbornness, the indignation that the world owed him something it hadn't yet delivered. He was attractive, but it hadn't gotten him as far as he would've liked. He wasn't that charming or that deep.

And yet despite the friction that often plagued their interactions, Holly and Benjamin had grown close, gradually connecting through the years thanks to her sister's unrelenting addiction.

When Holly had walked out on Rose, she had walked into Benjamin's life. They had developed a relationship based solely on surviving Rose's secrets, the majority of which neither had gotten to the bottom of. Benjamin was the closest living thing to her sister and Holly had welcomed him into her life because of it. She had a love-hate relationship with him, one that had been born out of necessity rather than interest. And ordinarily, she would give him the benefit of the doubt, but the way he was burying his head in the sand—over the phone and now in this hotel room—astonished her.

"I need you to start talking," she asserted, keeping her tone low and firm.

"Someone killed her? I don't know anything." His shaky voice contradicted his statement.

"The police are crawling over every inch of your house."

Benjamin smiled strangely and said, "I hope they catch the son of a bitch."

"How are they going to do that? I've known Rose my whole life and when it came down to it, when they asked me, I realized I know nothing about her at all." She paused to reel in her emotions. "You know her. You used to have an idea about where she would disappear to," she pointed out, referencing a time when Benjamin had cared about his wife's whereabouts long before these recent stunts of shacking up with random women. "We only had a guess as to what she was doing when she was gone and that was last year. So how are the police supposed to figure out what you and I never could?"

Holly let that hang for a beat, but the effect didn't register the way she had hoped. Benjamin met her with a defeatist attitude, his eyelids heavy, his mouth taut with an apathetic frown.

"What are you going to tell the cops when they come knocking?" she challenged.

"Did you tell them I was here?"

"You think they won't find you? Your name is on the sign out front. There aren't that many Wythes in Center Harbor." She ran her hand down her face. "If you don't help the police, they're going to think you killed her. Why the fu-" she stopped herself from swearing. Tucker was building the comforter into a mountain at the foot of the bed. When she returned her gaze to Benjamin, she let out a carefully measured breath. "Why didn't you come to the house when I called? So what you're..." Again she had to stop herself from blurting out the F word. "Screwing around. That doesn't make you guilty of murder. And you didn't kill her, right, Benji?"

A moment passed and he said nothing. Her stomach lurched.

Finally, he breathed the word, "No," but she didn't find it reassuring. "But I haven't been at the house for a reason."

Her brow furrowed, her eyes widening, taking in the sight of him. He didn't seem concerned that someone had killed his wife.

"Did you see this coming?"

"Let the police do their job," he concluded. "Stay out of it."

"Why? Because you think they won't find anything and this will all go away?" Finally, after so many hours she broke down. Tears stung her eyes at the thought of the person closest to Rose abandoning her when it mattered most. She pinched the bridge of her nose between her thumb and index finger then rubbed her eyes, sobering up from emotions that felt too strong to navigate. "I couldn't bring any of Tucker's things. He needs diapers and clothes. Go back to the house or buy them. I'm done with you."

Before she reached the door, he said, "Wait."

As she turned slowly to face him, she felt apprehensive to meet his gaze. But then his expression changed entirely. His dark eyes grew round, and he suddenly looked worried.

"I can't take him. Not tonight," he said.

Holly glimpsed the bathroom door and snorted a laugh.

"You can take a quarter-pound of cocaine, but not your son?"

"Can you watch him for a few days?" he begged.

Decisively, she crossed the room and grabbed Tucker, pulling him onto her hip. When she reached the door, she asked, "What do you know that I don't?"

He held his breath, whatever explanation she was angling for was caught in his throat and though his mouth hung open, prodding the words to come out, none did. It wasn't until she opened the door that he said, "You carry, right? That pistol?"

"Most days."

He seemed to be weighing the fact against whatever threats he thought were out there. "Good."

"Don't treat me like a stranger. Not now."

The bathroom door clicked, drawing open and a pair of screaming eyes glared out. The face they belonged to—high cheekbones that could cut glass, a straight mouth and angular jaw, all framed with sandy-blonde hair, shoulder length and greasy at the roots—wasn't a woman at all.

Benjamin had a teenage girl in his hotel room and the red dress she wore was as loose as it was senseless this time of year.

In a melodic tone, light as a feather, the girl asked, "Join me in the shower?"

Snapping at Benjamin, Holly said, "You've got to be kidding me."

He directed his answer at the girl, but kept his eyes on Holly, "In a minute."

The bathroom door closed but for a crack and Holly could feel the girl's eyes on her. It was enough to drive her from the hotel room.

She walked briskly down the hallway, Tucker jostling on her hip. He felt suddenly heavy or maybe that was her own exhaustion, a cocaine crash following the high; or perhaps it was the result of dealing with the police, those incessant questions, answering to a man she had used in her youth—basking in the rare luxury of forgetting who she was for one night.

Lucas York.

She pushed him from her mind in tandem with opening the entrance door. Icy wind slapped at her sideways as she trekked with Tucker in her arms, following the tracks she had made on the way in, though they were dusted over with fresh snow.

After getting her nephew situated on the passenger seat and climbing in behind the steering wheel, she attempted to visualize where Benjamin's room was located in terms of the parking lot. Had his window faced the lake or the lot? She hadn't even noticed the color of the walls, much less what was beyond the windows. Still, she had the urge to spy, suss out just what in the hell he was doing with a teenage girl. Where did her parents think she was right now? What child could get away with spending a night away from home with a forty-year old man, and what disease was Benjamin suffering that he craved that kind of company?

Worst of all, she wondered if she was enabling him. Babysitting Tucker for a few days would only give Benjamin the opportunity to revel in whatever reckless abandon he was choosing over dealing with his wife's murder.

Her gut told her that Benjamin had known Rose was in danger, and had seen her murder coming in a sense, but had done nothing to protect Rose.

The feeling was unshakable.

Holly muscled the gear-shifter into reverse and backed her Saab out of the snowy parking spot. When she put her car in gear, easing onto the gas, her eyes were locked on the many rooms of the Wythe Resort, but each was dark.

It wasn't until she reached the end of the parking lot and spied a lone window, brightly lit from within, that she set the car in neutral, pulled the emergency brake up, and grabbed her revolver from the floor beneath her seat.

If Benjamin thought he could keep something from her, he was dead wrong.

CHAPTER FOUR

THE JEWELRY STUDIO looked nothing like an oasis, but to Holly that's what it was. Her refuge, her sanctuary, where life's cruelties couldn't touch her.

However, she couldn't concentrate on the necklace she was supposed to repair. Her chair felt hard under her ass. The lights seemed too dim. She had slept badly, the long night haunting her.

When she glanced up, Tucker was watching her from the floor, the blue of his eyes appearing black in the low light, stripped of childlike innocence, suspicion in its place. Or maybe she was just paranoid.

His mouth puckered then opened into the shape of a heart, as he began examining his hands, which were tarnished gray, having toyed with the spool of chain she had offered to keep him entertained. He was seated next to an industrial space heater that looked powerful enough to launch a 747 into the air. It whirled and clanged noisily. The thing was on its last leg and the constant sound effects were grating on her nerves.

She was still jumpy from last night, but not because of the lines she had snorted or because she had seen her sister's frozen face beneath the ice, though each continued to disturb her. She was on edge because of Benjamin, what he had said, what she had done.

She shouldn't have gone to the resort.

Edging towards Tucker, she took quick stock of the studio for his benefit. Baby-proofing it had been daunting, and ultimately she had given up.

Storage organizers sat behind him, each metal compartment was closed, but there had been no way to lock them. Set against the opposite wall were a row of workbenches topped with a strewn mess of jeweler's tools—pliers and hammers—which she would've hung on the pegboard along the wall, there were enough nails in it, but they protruded at awkward angles and her tools kept falling off. She had reasoned he wouldn't climb onto the table without her noticing so she could easily intervene if it came to that.

Her worktable was likely the worst offender. Plastic bottles of abrasives and tubes of adhesives were scattered about. God forbid he got his mouth around one of them, but Christ, would a three-year-old do something like that? Or was that type of behavior reserved for infants?

Satisfied he wasn't in immediate danger on the cement floor, she crossed the room to a shelving unit that homed dozens of spools of chain. Perusing the shelves in search of a snake chain, trailing her finger past all the options—wheat chain and hesche, rolo chain and ball, herringbone and popcorn and figure-8, each style in silver and brass and gold—she realized the studio was filthy. Every inch of it was covered in a thin film of dust that made the room look gray and hazy.

Or maybe that was the coke in her veins. She had done a bump before they left the house, the only thing she could think to motivate her after the long, sleepless night she had suffered—*Rose could get through this.*

She found a spool of snake chain in silver and plucked it off the shelf. Returning to the worktable, she slapped it down harder than she had meant to, but was already turning for the middle workbench where a Crock Pot, filled to the brim with diluted Sparex, sat on a hot plate. She cranked the burner to its highest setting and tried not to panic that her heart had just punched out of rhythm.

A giant window partitioned her studio workspace from the actual store. Bunched at the left side of the glass was a black curtain, which she neared. So that she wouldn't be tempted to stare into the store that so reminded her of her twin, she began slowly drawing the curtain closed, but couldn't stop herself from eyeing the area, her heart sinking with loss.

Her store was lined with display counters—glass tops and red satin shelves on which necklaces and rings, bracelets and pendants rested. Velvet pedestals stood artfully positioned throughout the store, intuitive to the meandering flow of her customers, of which there were none at the moment.

She hadn't yet flipped the Open sign hanging on the entryway door. Neither had she ventured to that side of the window.

She had come in through the rear entrance, unwilling to set foot in the polished half of her property, which didn't at all represent who she was, but rather Rose.

It had been her sister, not Holly, who had decorated the store, chosen the particular shade of satin under the glass countertops, and placed each pedestal. She had even hung the paintings, having found them at various flea markets around town many summers ago. Rose had used a curator's eye, deciding which piece should go where. *Shopping isn't a chore, shopping is an experience*, Rose had explained, twirling on her heels and shooting a knowing smile at Holly, who had been sulking in the corner with her arms folded, not quite getting on board with how fancy the place was turning out. *It's called Shackles for a reason; it's for the everyman not the elite*, Holly had insisted. Her sister had sashayed towards the final painting in need of a home, an abstract cluster of tulips, and countered, *you want money and the elite of this town have it.*

The statement had summed up Rose and the difference between them—when Rose looked at a person, she calculated their value; when Holly did, she got lost in the story behind their eyes. When Rose encountered a customer in a tailored dress, she quickly ushered her towards the diamond-encrusted items. Holly didn't even notice what her customers were wearing. She tried to match her jewelry with the person's vibe. Both sisters had made a hefty amount of sales in the few months Rose had worked at Shackles before meeting Benjamin, hoarding drugs, having Tucker, and getting herself killed. But during that period only Holly had seen Rose's strategy for what it was—hungry.

Agitated, Holly finally closed the curtain and rounded her worktable, but clipped her toe on one of the legs, hissing, "Damn." It hadn't hurt, she was just annoyed with herself for being clumsy even though she knew the cause. She wasn't built for drugs.

No sooner than she sat, a clatter came faintly from the front of the store.

She pulled the black curtain aside when she reached it, peering out at the store. Beyond the glass entrance door was Lucas York, cupping his hands against the pane and straining to see through the glare.

Breathing the word, "Crap," she let go of the curtain, her mind racing for how she might get away with pretending she wasn't here. She had parked out back, but he could easily stalk around the corner, cut through the alley, and discover her vehicle. Again she peered through the curtain and spied him planting his fists on his hips and examining the awning overhead. He checked his wristwatch, yanking his thick winter coat up his forearm, and then gave the glass door another firm pound.

"Go away," she said under her breath.

Behind her the Crock Pot began bubbling over and she rushed to it, lowered the burner and fanned the rising steam.

When she had seen Lucas York stepping into her sister's living room last night, Holly hadn't believed her eyes. Her heart had begun galloping, which had kicked up the drug in her veins. The unexpected surge had made her vision acute, locking on the man from her past, while the room had distorted, shifting all around him, around her with unnerving surrealism. She had clenched her teeth in hopes he wouldn't recognize her. The shock that her long-ago one night stand would be investigating her sister's murder had pitched her into a state of white-hot dread.

The closeness they had shared, the intimacy—not just of their nude bodies merging in a dingy motel room, but also their undeniable connection, the way in which they had related to one another—had felt like destiny.

She had spent years trying to forget him.

But as soon as Holly had met his gaze in her sister's house, she saw the faintest ripple of recognition behind his blue eyes. Not only had he remembered. The glint in his eyes told her that he had never forgotten.

As Lucas had slept the morning after their tryst, she had snuck out and doing so—having been given his deepest, darkest secret—had been akin to theft. She had known it then and it had been confirmed in the house last night. She had taken something from him and he wanted it back.

Pinching her eyes shut and gritting her teeth in preparation, she drew the curtain aside for the third time and said a silent prayer that this dance wouldn't continue.

He wasn't there.

She let out a shuddering breath of relief and started for the Crock Pot, but startled at the sound of someone pounding on the back door.

Tucker called out, "Hello?" and Holly shushed him, while Lucas shouted his response.

"This is Detective York. *Lucas.*" He knocked, gently this time, knuckles softly rapping. "Holly, are you in there?"

Quickly, she scooped Tucker off the ground. The effort came with a groan, but she helped him to straddle her hip. If she could play the burdened aunt, the mourning sister, the fledgling jeweler wallowing at rock bottom, maybe she wouldn't have to answer any of his questions.

"Hang on," she shouted, not that she needed much time. She shuffled to the door and made slow work of turning the deadbolt.

When she yanked the door inward, a sharp flurry of snow fluttered over him, accumulation from the storm gutter no doubt. He let out a breathy laugh, scraped the woolen hat off his head, and slapped it free of snow.

"Do you have a few minutes?"

She frowned, debating, and then indicated she might. Hovering in the doorway, she was unsure where to look, though she was certain that staring at him wouldn't be her best move.

When she didn't invite him inside, he added, "I don't want the little guy catching a cold."

Holly noticed his eyes flaring at the sight of Tucker's dust-stained fingers.

"I've got him for a few days," she said, finally widening the door for him.

"Nice of you," he said casually as he had a look around the studio, gradually edging around the worktable. "Benjamin hasn't returned our calls." His eyes sprung from the spool of chain on the table and locked with hers. "But you talked to him?"

"What?"

"You said you've got Tucker for a few days, so Benjamin told you to take him?"

"No," she said quickly. "A few days is what I figure. I haven't talked to him. Is that what you wanted to ask me about?"

He frowned and resumed his survey of the studio, "Reminds me of my uncle's garage." Lucas worked his woolen hat into his coat pocket, but it didn't want to fit. "He's a car guy, cars and motorcycles."

She wasn't sure what she was supposed to say so she smiled with an intentionally awkward air in hopes it would hurry him along.

He sniffed the air and sniffed again. "Smells like pickles."

"That's the pickler," she supplied, indicating the simmering Crock Pot. When he narrowed his eyes at the burner, confusedly, she explained, "After I solder metal, the surface is usually marred with firescale." She was deliberately using terms he wouldn't understand so that he would learn his lesson. "I like Sparex, but any alum will do."

"Ah," he said, keen to her ploy. "Just like making pickles."

"Hence the name..." She shot him an unfriendly smile.

Weathering the chill that was rolling off of her, he said, "You must have been pretty surprised to see me at the house."

"I was."

Tucker was getting heavy so she used the excuse to break eye contact, setting him down, taking his little hand, and walking him over to the space heater where he instinctively plopped on his butt and began wrestling his shoes off.

"I was shocked to see you," he said, his tone arching honestly. "I knew you lived here and everything. I only started at the police department a month back and you crossed my mind." He let that hang then stuffed in a qualifier. "I didn't know a soul in Center Harbor, which is why-"

"Right."

"Anyway, I didn't expect to see you, certainly not under these circumstances."

It occurred to her that he might not have come to her studio because of the investigation and she wasn't sure if that made her feel less uneasy or more.

"Considering I'm working this case," he went on, trying to sound reasonable, which alerted her to the possibility that what he was about to say might not be. "I thought, maybe, well, that I ought to come down here and assure you that I won't let the past cloud my judgment."

She furrowed her brow. "How could it?"

"I just wanted to set your mind at ease."

Holding his gaze, she couldn't keep up a standoffish act. He seemed like a genuine guy who was staving off a bout of guilt over their long-ago night together and she didn't want him suffering on her account.

"I wasn't worried about it," she told him with an affirmative nod.

"I'm glad."

He took a moment to fish around the front pocket of his slacks and when she saw a thin, silver chain coming out, she immediately recognized the necklace. She rushed to him and he offered it with a smile. She hadn't seen it in years—the cable link chain, the silver heart pendant, the jagged opal at its center. She turned it over in her hands, and it wasn't until she pinched the clasp open and fastened it behind her neck, causing the chain to spill over her shoulders and the pendant to tap against her collarbone, that she realized how close they were standing.

Taking a few steps back, she thanked him and Tucker piped up about being hungry.

"Can I have a pickle?" he asked when he had her attention.

"There are no pickles here, Tuck."

He screwed his face up, her statement clashing so badly with the scent in the air that he couldn't accept it.

"We'll get lunch in a bit," she told him.

His response was a groan.

"I wanted to ask you about something," said Lucas, stealing her focus from Tucker. "We ran a ten panel on Rose."

She froze and her breathing turned shallow, knowing exactly which drugs a ten panel screened.

"We're just looking for leads at this point," he explained. "Anything that might start us off in the right direction would help."

"I thought you said you weren't going to do an autopsy?"

"An autopsy is different. Rose got arrested some years back-"

"Eight," she said, sharply correcting him. "It was eight years back, a lifetime ago."

"And it was drug related," he pointed out.

"It was a spec of cocaine in her purse. It was nothing. She was twenty-five, a kid. It was a mistake."

"I get that you feel the need to defend her, but the ten panel tested positive for benzos."

Holly kept her mouth shut.

"Now," he went on. "We're still working on tracking down Benjamin and I know you haven't seen much of your sister in the past year, but if you could tell me anything at all about her dealer or the people she might have-"

"I don't know about any of that."

"She had a cocaine..." Holly could tell that he was hunting for a word other than *problem*. "She was arrested for cocaine, as you said. And we found cocaine in her system."

"Okay," she said quietly.

"Look, I'll level with you. Nine times out of ten, the husband did it. Benjamin didn't come home last night; we haven't been able to get in touch with him. He's looking pretty good for this. But I want to come at this from every angle, in case he didn't do it. So I'm not waiting." He paused for her to respond. "Anything you want to tell me?"

It amazed her how easily he could flip from the softy who had brought her Rose's necklace to a hard-boiled cop with an almost inhuman ability to pressure her, but she honestly didn't know the finer details of Rose's drug addiction. And that's what she told him, folding her arms, twisting her mouth to the side, and biting the inside of her cheek.

He stared at her. The space heater whirred on the floor. The Crock Pot bubbled on the workbench. Tucker was rattling a tail of chain across the cement. She felt a sharp burst of tinnitus flare in her right ear and she knew it would ease off if only he would stop studying her.

Lucas extracted his wallet from the back pocket of his jeans and found his business card, which he set on the worktable. "If you think of anything; my cell is on there as well." When she didn't acknowledge his suggestion other than scrape her teeth over her lower lip, he walked to the door, mentioning, "It looks like Benjamin's at the Wythe Resort, go figure." After yanking the door open and stepping out into the chilly afternoon, he added,

"You didn't think to mention his parents own a hotel?"

"I don't know Benjamin at all. We really aren't close and last I heard he wasn't speaking with them." She hated that she sounded like she was pleading. "I didn't think he would go there."

He scrutinized her for a beat.

"They're not very nice people," she went on as if for his benefit and not to prevent him from setting foot into Room 112. "I doubt he's there. You would only be wasting your time."

"Is that so?"

She shrugged and replied, "Or not."

His tone softened as he said, "Nice seeing you." He strode off through the slush.

When she closed the door, the image of Benjamin swarmed her mind—his flexing face as he had screamed, the vein in his neck throbbing, the rage and anguish competing behind his eyes—she had never seen him like that. She had never stood over another human being, angling down, turning wild; barreling head first into something she knew she would regret.

But she didn't regret it.

All she needed was to forget.

She was going to need a hell of a lot more cocaine.

CHAPTER FIVE

SETTLING BEHIND THE steering wheel of his Ford Focus, Lucas angled the rearview mirror so that Shackles reflected on the glass. As he studied the storefront, straining to see past the glare of sunlight bouncing off the windows for the woman inside, he blindly fit the key into the ignition and turned the engine. A harsh blast of icy air poured through the vents and the muffler began rattling. Slapping the grates closed and adjusting the dial in the interim that it would take his car to warm—idling for five-minutes was standard—Lucas considered Holly's responses, the restraint she had used, her tight-lipped demeanor, the way her eyes had shifted uncomfortably before each answer. She had seemed more invested in guarding the truth than helping him find it.

She had also been high.

The maroon awning above the entrance rustled in the wind.

He was familiar with the signs—the dilated pupils, the fidgeting she probably hadn't realized she was doing, her barbed temperament, all painting a distinct portrait he was familiar with thanks to years on the job. He had to hand it to her, though. She had curbed the impulse to ramble aimlessly and had navigated his questions with an impressive degree of self-control, not once swerving into a frenzy of deflecting explanations.

Exhaust seeped into the car, stinging his brain and nudging him to get going. He wedged his fingers between the vent sliders, checking for heat, and cranked the temperature dial to High. After a lingering glance at Shackles in the rearview, he repositioned the mirror, put his car in gear, and eased into the street where traffic was flowing at a steady pace.

As he drove, he pondered Holly's motive for attempting to convince him not to bother with the Wythe Resort.

He had assumed giving her the necklace would earn him full disclosure or at the very least an indication from her that she was picking up what he was putting down—that he had bent a little rule for her, that to him following police procedure wasn't as interesting as sneaking a favor, that if she wanted he could position her above the law. His gesture had screamed, *I can make this right if you tell me everything*, but it hadn't even reached her ears. Obviously, he had handed the necklace over too soon.

Between her cocaine high—whether a habit or an innocent experimentation, he had yet to figure out—her muted responses, and her sense of urgency that he not waste his time at the hotel, Lucas couldn't brush over the possibility she might have been covering up Rose's murder, though he would like to think it was for no greater reason than protecting Benjamin Wythe. Either way, she was clearly hiding something.

Pine Road was marred with frost heaves where it hooked east around Dog Cove, the resort in the distance across the lake. His Ford Focus bounced over juts and dips, scraping the undercarriage. He squeezed the brakes, hoping that the muffler wouldn't jostle loose.

When he reached the intersection of Pine and Keewaydin Roads, he hung a left, rounding the cove onto asphalt that was both smooth and thoroughly plowed. He supposed the Wythes had paid private contractors to keep this stretch of Keewaydin pristine, perhaps unwilling to allow their guests to suffer the indignity of an unpleasant drive to and from the hotel. The town certainly hadn't paid for it. The Department of Transportation tended to allocate the majority of its funds to fill in potholes along Main Street and other well-traveled roads at the expense of the rural ones or so he had gleaned in the four weeks he had lived here, not that their policies were unique.

Lucas downshifted, pulling into the parking lot in front of the resort where cars sat under a good foot of snow. With the recent snowstorms, two to be exact, which had granted only four days of clear skies in-between, he imagined the guests hadn't had cause to venture out, all their needs having been promptly met by the hotel staff.

At the far end of the lot, a handful of construction workers were shouting at one another about how best to remove snow from their equipment, while the rest of them carried support beams in teams of two towards the west side of the resort.

Lucas couldn't help but smile. The Wythes must love the eyesore their west wing had been reduced to.

He had never met them, but their reputation was no secret. They owned this town. And they went to great lengths to make that fact known.

After squeezing his clunker between a silver Lexus and a late-model Cadillac, both under heaps of snow but only one at risk of being dented if he wasn't careful opening his door, Lucas kept his car idling in Park and fished his cell out of his coat pocket.

He owed his partner a phone call, but wasn't exactly eager for the reprimand that would surely come if and when Cody heard about the autopsy Lucas had ordered. His evidence logs blunder the other night shouldn't have earned him such a severe reaction from Cody, but Lucas couldn't deny it hadn't been his first oversight.

Inside of four weeks with the Center Harbor PD, he had made several errors, mostly administrative, and Cody had caught every single one of them—not submitting receipts with his expense reports, forgetting to print his name after his signature on a Criminal History Request form, and thinking he had emailed a victims advocate with an update when he hadn't. What was eating Lucas was that harmless slip-ups, or slip-ups of any variety for that matter, weren't characteristic of his track record with his previous precinct. Worse was the fact that when questioned about it, he had little recollection of having completed the order in the first place, the monotony of menial tasks far too mundane to hold his attention.

Aiming to spare his ego from blows, which would only shake his resolve, he determined that he would call Cody after speaking with the Wythes and not before, and elbowed the door open.

It struck the Lexus and a miniature avalanche of snow plummeted into his car.

He grumbled, "Christ," and scanned the parking lot for witnesses as he climbed out.

The only other car not buried under snow was a rusted-out Audi idling near the entrance. He hadn't noticed anyone driving in. A cloud of exhaust was streaming out of the tailpipe, obscuring his sightline of the passenger who sat in silhouette. Whoever they were, they didn't appear to have seen him clip the Lexus.

He started for the entrance, walking through slush puddles. Ice water seeped through the seams in his boots, dampening his socks. The sunlight was blinding the way it reflected off the snow-cloaked vehicles, but as he neared the hotel, he stepped into the shadows made by the portico blocking the sun.

When he lifted his gaze, a young woman threw open the entrance door on her way out, her angular eyes locking with his. She lingered for his benefit, leaning against the glass to hold the door for him, as she wrapped her long coat closed.

Quirking her straight mouth into a secretive smirk, the sharp lines of her cheekbones as well as her jaw softening in a way that unnerved him, she looked as if she might say something.

He grabbed the edge of the door and hesitated, not wanting to brush against her while passing through. She didn't move despite his gentlemanly patience, but rather made slow work of freeing her sandy-blonde hair from beneath her coat-collar while gazing up at him.

"I've got the door," he pointed out, feeling strangely invaded by her not-so-subtle interest.

She played with the trim of her coat, a faux-fur material that was a poor excuse for sable. It was also matted, and the skirt she wore—black and tight and dangerously high on the thigh—had a tattered quality, revealing she likely didn't belong at the Wythe Resort, if not for her economic standing then her age. She was pretending to be much older than she was.

Finally she sauntered out, but after a few steps twirled airily on her heel, following him with her eyes.

He let out a breathy laugh at her confidence, shaking off the idea of her and motioning inside.

But he didn't get far.

When she asked, "What's so funny, *Killer*?" it shocked him so badly that he paused. "What's so funny?" she repeated.

Slowly glancing over his shoulder, pivoting towards her, as she rocked back on her heels, he asked, "What did you call me?"

Through a coy grin, she whispered, "You heard me," swaying like a little girl, and then strode off.

It was his childhood nickname, one he hated, but not more so than the people who had branded him with it; *Killer*. They had meant to mock him whenever they had called him that, patronizing his desperate yet feeble attempts to fight them off, to defend himself, to escape, sprinting to the muddy alcove where a boulder met with the foot of the hill behind his house, his only hiding spot.

No one had called him Killer since he had run away from home when he was seventeen.

How did she know his nickname?

Following her, he stepped out onto the walkway, turned the corner, snowdrift spilling into his boots, and saw her rounding the Audi that had been idling. She yanked the driver side door open, unaware she was being watched, and slipped into the vehicle so he quickened his pace through the snow. But she had gotten too much of a head start. She reversed out of the parking spot and just as he was about to shout for her to wait a minute, he saw the passenger. No longer a silhouette, he recognized the girl.

It was Mary Cole.

He had only met the sixteen-year old once and the encounter had been uncomfortable. After transferring to the Center Harbor PD, his new partner had invited him to dinner. Cody had a house on the lake, which he shared with his girlfriend, Hannah and her much younger half-sister, Mary. Other than her choice of dress—short-shorts in the dead of winter with a crop-top that left little to the imagination—Mary had seemed innocent enough, taking charge of cooking dinner and fetching beers for Lucas and Cody while they got acquainted in the living room. It hadn't been until Lucas had ventured down the hallway in search of the bathroom that Mary's peculiarity blossomed. She had followed him, stepping soundlessly then slinking into the doorway so he couldn't pass. She had said nothing. Her breath had reeked of Listerine as she suggestively pursed her lips, grasping hold of his belt-buckle, an overture so jarring it had baffled him into momentary paralysis. When he had reacted, he was slow and sloppy, urging her back; indecisive about whether he should proceed into the bathroom or run for cover. He went with the latter, rushing up the hallway and returning to the dinner table, his bladder aching for relief as he slid into his chair, his face plastered with a disturbed smile, trying to make sense of what the hell had just happened.

Mary was pure trouble, and it seemed she had met her equal.

He watched the Audi putter off along Keewaydin and disappear behind the tree line, cedars and balsam firs weighed down with snow.

When he started for the entrance, his cell phone vibrated in his slacks. He groaned seeing Cody McAlister's name and number flashing across the LCD screen, but he made himself answer.

"Yeah?" he said, passing into the warm lobby, the decorum of which—exposed wooden beams along the ceiling and rustic furnishings—reminded him of a high-class ski lodge. It was surprisingly dim, the light fixtures overhead giving off an amber glow that barely reached the carpet, or maybe his eyes hadn't adjusted, having been shrunken by the blinding light outside.

"Our IT guy got into the server in the Wythes' basement and pulled the footage from all four cameras," he stated. "But there's a problem."

Lucas stepped aside so an elderly couple who looked like they belonged in an AARP commercial—dignified, thriving, refusing to be bogged down by arthritis or the fine-print in their insurance policies—could pass by. Then he continued on to the front desk where the lively young clerk behind the counter already seemed inconvenienced that she hadn't helped him yet. "I'm listening."

"An hour of the feed is missing."

"From every camera?"

"That's right. The footage rolls through 1:18 am then jump-cuts to a timestamp of 2:24 am," he explained.

Lucas turned his shoulder to the clerk, who had been staring expectantly at him. He wandered towards the window where a pair of sofa chairs were angled around a marble table, and spoke quietly. "So the killer stopped the feed beforehand."

"If they really knew the house and the equipment it could've been an afterthought," he countered.

Lucas didn't agree, but the implication remained. "Benjamin's looking good for this."

"Unless the guy who installed their security system doubled-back four years later to carry out a long-standing grudge, yeah I think this case is as straightforward as they come. I don't see anyone else with access. Are you at the resort?"

"Yeah, are you coming over?"

"The roads are a mess. If Benjamin is there, bring him to the station."

"Hey," he cut in before Cody could let him go. Thumbing the fronds of a ficus he had assumed was real, he worked his jaw, debating whether or not to tell his partner what he had just seen. "I should tell you..."

"Make it quick."

Easing into the issue, he asked, "Mary should be in school, right? Two o'clock on a Tuesday?"

A groaning sigh came through the receiver as though Cody not only knew where this was going, but had seen the outcome so many times it had aged him. "Where did you see her?"

"Here at the resort. She drove off with some girl, who by the looks of it didn't seem like the best influence."

"Thanks for letting me know," he said curtly then grumbled sarcastically about needing to deal with this right now. "Let me know if you locate Wythe."

Lucas cut in with, "Who's the girl, Mary's friend?"

"Why? You think you know her?" He shot back.

"No." Lucas stared out at the snowy field beyond the window, the girl's melodic voice laced with cruelty echoing through his mind, *Killer*. "She acted kind of familiar."

"Familiar?"

Beyond ready to abandon his inquiry in favor of ending this suddenly pointless phone call, he told him, "Never mind."

But Cody offered the girl's name, saying, "Roberta. Roberta King. Know her?"

Lucas paused, wracking his brain, but all he got was the faintest intuition. "Nope."

"Then you must have heard of her," he concluded. "Big case last summer in Laconia, the King cult." He reminded Lucas to let him know if he got a read on Benjamin then hung up.

As he approached the front desk, the clerk, whose name plate read *Ashley*, perked up, ready to be of service.

"Is Benjamin Wythe staying here?"

She immediately said, "No," and strained to keep her smile lifted.

He cocked his head at that, flicking his gaze to the monitor beside her. "Don't you have to check?"

"I've been on double-duty since a few employees got snowed in," she complained, rolling her eyes as if she didn't buy her coworkers excuses. "I would know if Mr. Wythe was here."

"Humor me."

She stiffened, broadening her shoulders and letting out a little snort as though insulted that he didn't believe her. Typing angrily, her fingertips scurrying over the keyboard, her eyes quickly scanned the monitor. She shook her head, glad to be correct. "No, he isn't here."

Lucas found the notepad he kept in his inner coat pocket and flipped a few pages to refresh his memory. "Are Warren and Sarah available?"

"I don't know what to tell you. Benjamin isn't here."

"That's okay," he said easily, trying to get her back on track. "What about Warren and Sarah?"

"Those are the owners."

"They're also Benjamin Wythe's parents," he pointed out, amazed at how committed she was to her duty as gatekeeper.

"What is this about? I'm sure I can help you," she offered, desperate not to involve the owners.

He was gentle with her when he countered with, "I'm sure you can't."

She shrunk in response then, putting on a brave face, she pressed the desk phone to her ear and dialed. "Who should I say is here to speak with them?"

"Detective Lucas York."

Her brows snapped up to her hairline and her face flushed, but she was already turning her back and whispering into the receiver. When she faced him again, returning the phone to its cradle, she told Lucas to have a seat in the lounge. The Wythes would be with him momentarily.

He found the lounge across from the front desk. Guests of the hotel occupied the majority of sofa-chairs, which were arranged identical to those in the lobby, replete with artificial ficus plants and tables that probably weren't marble. The far wall as well as the one perpendicular had floor-to-ceiling windows where sunlight shafted through, bathing the spacious lounge, though the amber fixtures overhead were strong contenders.

The nook where the two walls met, hugging a lone sofa-chair as stiff as it was red, was vacant so he took up there, sitting on the edge of the chair and checking his wristwatch for no other reason than he didn't want to stare at the lobby like an obedient dog.

More time passed than he would've liked before a regal-looking woman in her early sixties breezed in through a door marked *Private*, which was situated in the opposite direction of where he had told himself not to look.

She took a moment to smooth her hands over her ash-brown hair, giving the bottom curls a little lift with her palm, as she scanned the guests scattered throughout the lounge. There was something off about her expression—bewildered eyes, a sense of not quite grasping her surroundings. When she spotted Lucas, she feigned a smile, but it seemed loose and lost, and made her way towards him.

He stood, and meeting her half way, extended his hand, which she shook limply, as she nervously blotted her lips together.

"Detective York," she said in a deeper tone than he would've expected given her dainty facial features and the tailored, lavender dress-suit she wore—the voice of a washed-up drama coach trapped inside Anna Wintour.

"Sarah," he said. "Thanks for taking the time."

Retracting her hand as if he was tainted, she said, "Please, call me Mrs. Wythe."

He was tempted to ask her if she was feeling alright but went with, "I apologize to have dropped in unannounced" instead.

The light behind her eyes shifted, an indication she was straining to focus or concerned, he couldn't decide which one.

"Is there somewhere private we can speak?" he asked, glancing quickly at the door she had emerged from and mentally formulating how he might tell her that her daughter-in-law had been killed.

"Certainly."

Sarah led him through the lounge the way he had come, and after they rounded the front desk, they started down a hallway that he gleaned was the east wing. The rooms were numbered, but they didn't stop at any of them. Instead, they came into a library where Sarah began reciting the history of the Wythe Resort, noting its architect whom Lucas had never heard of and the story behind a few pieces of art, as if she was giving a tour. Had she forgotten about taking him to a private room to talk? Or had she confused him for a guest in the two minutes it had taken to traverse the hallway?

As she elaborated in extreme detail about the particular sculpting tools required to carve the curled lips of the marble angel she was fondling, he got the distinct impression that she wasn't all there mentally and blurted out, "Is your son around?"

"Benjamin?"

He smiled, relieved she was still on planet Earth.

But her gaze slipped past him and she waved. "Warren, this is...?"

She looked confused so Lucas supplied, "Detective York."

The older man approaching didn't seem pleased that his wife was on the loose or maybe his surly expression was meant for Lucas. After weathering formal introductions and shaking hands—steel grip, affirmative frown, eyes that penetrated Lucas as badly as every judge who had ever been annoyed with his sarcasm when cross-examined—Warren barked, "What's this about, Detective?"

"He's here to see Benjamin," Sarah offered excitedly as if suddenly remembering. She took Lucas by the arm and, smiling vacantly, laughed, "I should probably lie down."

Addressing Lucas, Warren said, "May I ask why you want to see Benji?"

"Is there somewhere private we can talk?" He asked, coming round the same bend.

Releasing Lucas, Sarah neared her husband and tucked a tuft of white hair behind his ear, and in response he affectionately captured her hand and kissed it.

"This way," he told Lucas, inviting him to follow as he guided Sarah towards the back of the library where a door stood ajar.

"A lot of rooms in this place," Lucas commented, stepping into what appeared to be a private study. The older man smiled in acknowledgement. When the Wythes invited him to sit on a leather couch, he obliged and waited for Warren to settle his wife on a sofa-chair. "About Benjamin..." He paused while Warren sat on the chair beside his wife. "If he's here, I'll need to talk to him."

"Slow down," said Warren. "Benji is resting."

"So he is here?"

Sarah chimed in with, "I haven't seen him today."

Directing his point to Lucas, the older man explained, "He had a late night."

"Really?" Leaning forward, he asked, "What was he up to?"

Sarah turned to her husband and chuckled as if in the throes of an inside joke, which Warren didn't exactly participate in. He hushed his wife, taking her hand and tapping it. When she sobered up, he said, "I'm not my son's keeper. What he chooses to do between those four walls is none of my concern."

It was starting to sound like the Wythes were under the impression their son hadn't left the resort all evening so he questioned them.

"By the sounds of it," said Warren, "the music and the talking, I don't imagine Benji went anywhere last night."

"The roads are terrible," Sarah added, flexing her face into a frown and widening her smoky-eyes as if telling the scary part of a children's story.

"Do you know who he was talking to?" Lucas was poised, pen-tip to notepad, eager for a name, but Warren only opened his hands, at a loss.

"His business is his business," he shrugged.

Frustrated, Lucas held his breath and when he let it out, he delivered the news that no in-laws ever wanted to hear, "Rose is dead."

Warren narrowed his eyes at Lucas and his mouth formed words that wouldn't come, while beside him Sarah furrowed her brow confusedly at her husband as if waiting for the translation.

After a long moment, Lucas said, "I'm sorry" to break the silence.

"How did she die?" Warren asked.

Relieved that the hard part was behind him—disclosing the ins and outs of a crime didn't unnerve him quite like delivering the initial blow of the news itself—he told them Rose had been shot, her body retrieved from Squam Lake, and that it was possible the shooter had intimate knowledge of the house, all the while Sarah began trembling and Warren pressed his mouth into a hard line as though he might get sick, though he had his wits about him enough to grip his wife's hand.

Another stunned silence ensued. The first person to speak was Warren. "You think my son did this?"

Sarah's mouth drifted open, catching up to her husband's point. "That's why you need to speak to Benji?"

"I need to speak with Benjamin because he was married to Rose and I'm looking for leads. Now if you wouldn't mind waking him up, I would appreciate it very much."

He hadn't meant to take a tone and would've felt badly if it had registered, but the Wythes seemed to be drifting off into another dimension.

"If you could please tell me his room number," he pressed, rising to his feet and tucking his notepad into his pocket.

Sarah's voice was wind over reeds as she said, "One-twelve."

"The key?"

"Can't you knock?" she asked him, appalled.

Warren met his gaze. "The front desk. Tell Ashley she's fired if she asks questions."

Lucas walked with a sense of urgency, retracing the maze Sarah had led him through. When he reached the lobby, arching around the front desk, he was winded. He slapped his palm on the counter and Ashley rushed over to tend to him.

"Key for one-twelve, now please." She cocked her head questioningly so he added, "Police investigation," preferring to throw his own weight around as opposed to Warren's.

After she fetched it, he snatched the key out of her hand, thanking her, and took off. But after three steps he realized he had no idea where he was going.

Ashley must have had a genuine knack for working in the service industry, because as soon as he doubled back, she offered, "Down the hall the way you came, sixth door on the right."

He thanked her again, this time with a curt nod, and started off.

Finding the room easily, Lucas knocked on the door then listened hard, but heard nothing. He knocked again, stating, "Mr. Wythe? This is the Center Harbor Police, open the door!" But again he was met with silence and suddenly realized that the bad feeling worming its way through his gut wasn't from agitation his killer could slip away, but that something was wrong.

Refusing to waste another second, he fit the key into the lock and let himself in.

The smell hit him first. The unmistakable tang of drying blood, sharp and metallic, stung his nostrils. The room was shadowy, its lights off, the curtains drawn where the headboard of the bed sat flush beneath the window, but Lucas could still make out the shape of the bed, the comforter bunched over the footboard.

He found the light switch near the doorframe and flipped on the overheads. A soft glow filled the room, but the body wasn't apparent. Edging deeper into the room, he neared the foot of the bed and a dark stain on the carpet in front of the bathroom came into view. Quickly, he sidestepped and saw the body—face down, naked but for boxer-briefs, one arm resting by his hip, the other stretched above his head or what was left of it. He had been shot in the back of the head where the nape met his hairline.

Lucas crouched, examining the entry wound.

A cell phone on the nightstand flashed, catching his eye. He angled over the body and grabbed the cell. There was a missed call from a 603 number. Eyeing the screen, he noted the call was time stamped just after four in the morning and there was a corresponding voicemail message.

Knowing the message would require a passcode to play, he swiped his thumb over the LCD screen and selected the number instead. He hit Send, initiating a call to the 'missed call' number, and hesitantly lifted the phone to his ear as he backed away from the body.

A female voice came through, her tone youthful yet bristling with suspicion. "I thought you were dead."

CHAPTER SIX

MARY COLE KEPT her head down and watched snow melt off her boots and form a glassy puddle on the buffed floor. She wasn't so much standing as she was hiding beside a ceramic pizza chef—its thick eyebrow cocked jauntily, mustache arching with its smile, the pepperoni pie on its palm looking stale and faded from the corner of her right eye. The American flag on her left was doing a decent job of concealing her from the customers that were scattered throughout the pizzeria, but she still felt anxiety buzzing through her bones as badly as the neon sign over the counter—*PENIS!*

She stared at the word and realized the majority of the sign's lightbulb-letters had burned out. It was supposed to read, *PIES IN THE SKIES.*

Her name should've been called by now. She needed to not get caught, though it was unlikely one of her teachers or a school administrator would wander into Tony's during fifth period. Still, she couldn't afford to get in trouble again, not for ditching. Hannah and Cody could only dole out the same lecture so many times before they would be forced to leap to extreme measures, ground her completely, or worse... If they found out about the real stuff she was up to...

She crept towards the counter, shaking her platinum hair into her face like a clumsy crook too conspicuous to go unnoticed, and cleared her throat, not that doing so got the trucker's-delight behind the cash register to lift her eyes. She was too busy popping her gum and making the sauce stain on her uniform worse by rubbing at it.

"Yeah," she said without looking up from her pointy chest.

"How long for my pizza? It was a small olive for 'Cole'."

Turning over her shoulder, the girl barked, "Cole?" and Mary flinched along with the rest of the customers. "It'll be right out."

Behind the girl, a cook in the back slid a wooden peel into the industrial oven, wedging it under an olive pizza that looked like Mary's. When he drew it out, he shot her a wink and she scowled through her stringy, blonde locks, hoping she hadn't slept with the guy.

Soon the box was on the counter. Mary snatched it and quickly padded through the restaurant, glaring through her eyebrows and holding her breath, praying that she wouldn't have the bad luck of being caught skipping school by Mrs. Keller or the Phys. Ed. coach, who often stopped into the pizza parlour for a spontaneous slice.

The Audi was idling with its bumper pitched over the concrete parking-stop since her best friend had hit the brakes too late, adding yet another chink to the dimpled eyesore that was her car. Behind the steering wheel sat Roberta, one hand cupping her cell to her ear, the other draped over the top of her head, which was tilted towards the window. Mary guessed her friend didn't appreciate what she was hearing, but the smug curl at the corner of Roberta's mouth, the distinct arch of her eyebrow, begged to differ. She was intrigued.

Clamping the pizza box between her hand and hip, Mary popped the passenger's side door open, having gingerly squeezed the handle in order to open the door without the thing falling off—the quirks of this car were never-ending.

As Mary lowered in, keeping the pizza box level so the cheese wouldn't shift over the crust, Roberta ripped her phone from her ear, hung up, and dropped her cellphone into the cup holder on the dash then began jiggling the stick shift in Neutral.

"You got off that call fast," she commented, resting the box on her thighs and fastening her seatbelt.

"Don't I always?"

"Who was that?" Mary flicked her eyes at the cell phone as if clarifying.

Instead of answering, Roberta reversed out of the parking spot, swinging around and actively checking each and every mirror. Despite her effort, the rear bumper clipped the grill of a truck, jolting the girls on impact.

"Damn thing came out of nowhere," said Roberta, throwing the Audi in First and punching the gas, as Mary looked on, a wry grin spreading across her face. She couldn't wait to get her license. "It was no one," she added as a footnote after darting into traffic. When she hung a confident left, veering between a truck and a station wagon, the latter of which skidded to a stop, someone leaned on their horn.

"Christ, Roberta; who taught you how to drive?"

Her friend shot her a sideways glance that landed like an inside joke. "Was it busy in there?"

"Not too bad," she said, watching the road open up, the town center vanishing behind them, snow-kissed trees—naked yet adorned with icicles—thickening just beyond the shoulder. "I hate going in during school hours."

"I couldn't go," she said, innocently shrugging. "I already called in sick for my night shift."

"That sign says *penis*, you know."

Roberta threw her head back, letting out a cackle that both startled and thrilled Mary.

Most of the time, she had a good read on Roberta and this was one of those times. "You blew out those lights?"

"It took me like, I'm not kidding, two hours," she confessed.

"Damn."

"What?" she sang, leaning forward and wiping her sleeve across the condensation as it formed on the windshield. "They left me alone for two hours. Mopping tomato sauce off the floor got boring."

"No one noticed?"

"It has only been a few days," said Roberta.

"Still."

Sly as a fox, she settled her angular eyes on Mary. "Ain't no one looking up around here but you and me."

Mary eased at the thought and found Roberta's hand, and laced their fingers together.

The pizza box was scalding her thighs so she wedged her free hand under it. Roberta stepped on the gas, accelerating and merging onto the Daniel Webster Highway, which would take them south along Squam Lake. Eventually, the highway would hook around Meredith Bay and down to Lake Winnipesaukee where Roberta had promised Mary a special gift—their secret.

Roberta was beautiful—voluptuous and emaciated in the same breath, porcelain skin, and angular features, cat-like in her ferocity, fearless and dangerous because of it. Nothing could touch her, she liked to say. The worst already had. Strange logic that rang true for Mary as well since she had survived a similar past—endless nights spent shaving her mind down to a sliver, walling off, detaching from her body so she wouldn't have to feel what was being done to her, the harrowing fallout to recover, days filled with sucking on beer cans in hopes the shadows swallowing her heart wouldn't get the rest of her as well.

Soul-murdering, that's how it had felt.

It had made her hollow and nothing had filled her—not her father getting locked up, not the year of therapy she had struggled through sitting on a couch beside her mother and trying to wrap her head around the woman's epic blindness that so many horrors had unfolded in their house without her so-called knowledge—nothing on God's green Earth had filled Mary until the day she had met Roberta King.

The day that Mary had met Roberta, Mary had been lurking in the alley behind Tony's Pizzeria, the flickering streetlight overhead causing her nerves to ratchet up. She had just moved to Center Harbor from Wolfeboro, before that it had been Holderness from Gilford, so many boxes, always on the move, picking up right after settling down, precinct to precinct as though Cody had some kind of aversion to putting his roots down—always on the hunt for the next Kendra Cole case. The thing of it was, New Hampshire didn't have that many brutal crimes.

She had only wanted a six-pack, just a few beers to tide the night over. It wasn't simply a craving. Cravings she could ride out cooking dinner or trimming Hannah's hair, styling those brown locks around her half-sister's face that looked nothing like her own except for the eyes—blue and screaming. That night she had felt like she was being skinned alive, raw and furious, despairing and desperate, sinking so low she feared there was no bottom, only an endless abyss she would never be able to crawl out of.

She hadn't been able to stop thinking about Candice.

She had needed a little help—alcohol.

Having gotten a lead on a senior who checked out, Mary had shown up behind Tony's right on time. She had waited eagerly at first, ready to make the trade. As the minutes ticked on, she began kicking a rock, her heart plummeting all the while. Soon it was clear the kid wasn't coming and she dropped to her knees, curling into a ball and praying for death to take her in the form of a car peeling down the alley.

Instead, Roberta had stormed out the back door of Tony's.

And Mary hadn't died that night. She had been brought back to life.

Roberta had driven her to a liquor store where she said the clerk never checked IDs. After getting two cases of beer, they had sat on the hood of her car, talking and drinking and gazing up at the stars. When Mary got plastered with alcohol and began crying, Roberta hadn't recoiled or called the night off, but wrapped her arms around her, holding her tightly and saying, *I know.*

Mary snuck a glance at Roberta, as her friend squeezed the brakes, yanking the steering wheel one-handed and pulling down a snowy driveway. Roberta was so much like her that Mary just plain didn't know where she ended and her friend began. The thought made her smile.

Slowing to a stop in front of a Colonial house that hadn't been lived in for upwards of six months—its For Sale sign, warped and spray painted with red graffiti, pitched crookedly in the deep snow—Roberta said, "I seriously hope the car doesn't get stuck."

"Wicked hope the car doesn't get stuck," Mary chimed in, flattening the vowels with a thick New Hampshire accent.

Roberta laughed then told her that she sounded terrible as she climbed out into the deep snow, her purse hanging over her shoulder.

They started through the drift, veering away from the empty house, the owners of which had moved down to Manchester so they could easily visit their son who had been incarcerated for manslaughter—a sad story that Roberta only talked about when drunk. Small State as it was, Quinton Avery had been locked up in the same facility as Mary's younger sister, Candice, but Mary didn't let herself go there, as she stalked towards the shed.

It was their place, the secret they shared, though the more time Mary spent with Roberta, and the longer they knew each other, the clearer it became that Roberta had her own secrets.

Considering what they had been involved in, she feared to imagine.

"It's unbelievably freezing in here," said Mary, following her friend into the shed. She latched the shed door, set the pizza box down, and huddled on a milk crate, figuring she would soon get the shivers, her teeth chattering and fingers turning numb.

"This'll warm you up," she stated, yanking a space heater from the corner, plugging it in, and getting it whirring. Then, dumping her purse upside down, she added, "And so will this."

Dozens of cocaine-filled baggies began falling, plopping and shifting where they collided with one another on the floor.

Mary beamed a big smile at her friend. "This is my surprise?"

"Happy birthday."

Roberta crouched, scraping a second milk crate across the floor until it sat flush against Mary's. When she sat, she wasted no time fishing a square mirror out of her bohemian coat.

Mary pinched one of the bags off the floor and eyed it closely, working the powder between her fingers and feeling the fine grains through the plastic.

"Where did you get it?"

"You know where I got it," said Roberta, brushing the question off in favor of tapping a heap of powder onto the mirror now resting on her lap.

Mary watched her for a beat, as Roberta used her index finger to stroke the powder into a thick line. "I don't like him."

"You don't have to like him," her friend countered airily as if she wasn't being confronted.

"I don't like you going there."

"There's no reason to go there anymore." Roberta met her gaze and offered her the mirror, but she didn't take it.

Instead, Mary studied her, but couldn't make sense of Roberta's easy expression. "So... what? You're not going to sneak off to the resort anymore?"

Roberta gave her a mild frown, her brows drifting upwards, relaxed about shaking her head, and seemed so reserved in her watery agreement that Mary was entirely thrown.

"What aren't you telling me?" she pressed.

"Benjamin's out of the picture and that's all you need to know." Again, she offered the mirror to Mary. "This cocaine isn't going to blow itself."

Apprehensive, Mary stared at the thick line of white powder, catching her own reflection in the glass. When her friend nudged it closer, she relented, taking the mirror and watching her blue eyes shift unsteadily on either side of the white line.

"You're not going to freak out this time," Roberta said encouragingly. "We'll just do a little and sell the rest."

That wouldn't be how this would go, but Mary pretended she didn't know that. She took the rolled dollar bill that her friend was handing her, and snorted the line.

She heard squealing and realized it was her, as she pinched the bridge of her nose, stomping her foot, completely forgetting the mirror on her lap. It clattered to the floor, kicking up cocaine like a miniature blizzard. Roberta was rubbing her shoulder, brushing her hair behind her ear—*breathe, just breathe, you're good*—and gradually Mary opened her eyes, brain zinging and senses surging, acutely aware of everything except for how cold it was in the shed.

As Roberta took her turn, forming a line of coke across the mirror and placing her rolled bill to her nostril, Mary felt the rush gradually washing away, and a gentle warmth swept through her in its place. Her thoughts softened. Memories she had kept walled off peeked at her, no longer menacing, but light and easy, digestible.

It was moments like this she could let herself think about Candice, the disturbed mind of her younger sister who looked like an angel. Kendra was no longer dangerous territory, though it wasn't lost on her that Mary was traveling a similar road, stealing away to do drugs so the constant pain wouldn't eat her alive.

When Roberta was finished taking her bump, she licked the mirror and tossed it on their pile of drugs, freeing her hands. She wrapped an arm around Mary, closing the gap between them, and draped her hand over Mary's thigh, her friend's face so near hers that she could feel the heat rolling off Roberta's cheek.

Her friend shifted, angling the cool tip of her nose against Mary's temple, and whispered, "Do you love me?"

Mary nodded, breathing the word, "Yes."

Being held in Roberta's arms, sensing her friend's craving, knowing what she needed, what she was angling for, caused a terrible conflict to worm through Mary's chest.

Slowly, Roberta grazed her nose across Mary's cheek in lazy, wanton circles and soon her lips were brushing the broad canvas of Mary's porcelain skin—the curve of her cheekbone, the valley beneath her lower lip—until finally she eased her mouth against Mary's, not a kiss, but the softest human touch.

THUD.

The girls were startled. Their eyes locked on the door. The noise had sounded like a car door slamming shut.

Suddenly, Roberta dropped to her knees and began frantically grabbing and throwing the baggies into her purse.

Outside, boots stomped through the snow.

"Awe, hell," Roberta hissed, quickly hiding the drugs. "Jake must have seen my car outside."

Panicking yet hoping it might not look as bad as she thought. Mary scanned the shed trying to see it with fresh eyes—random drug bags peppered across the wooden floor, Roberta scrambling around on her hands and knees, baggies spilling out of her purse almost as quickly as she shoved them in. The mirror was dusted, cloudy with cocaine where it lay on the ground. And yet, as bad as it clearly seemed, it wasn't worse than the fact that Mary was standing there.

Jake Livingston did not like her.

He pounded on the door. "Roberta?"

Again, Roberta hissed, "Damn," snapping her eyes at Mary.

Dashing around the room, Mary collected the uncooperative baggies, plucked up the mirror, and stuffed them into her pockets, as her friend swallowed hard and shouted, "I'll be right out!"

"What the hell are you doing over here?"

She feigned an answer that to Mary didn't sound quite right. Roberta was too jittery to play this off. But just as Mary walked towards the door, ready to fall on her sword for both of them, her friend grabbed her shoulders and began shoving her towards the window.

"Just go," she whispered, hoisting the rusted window pane up. A sharp gust of wind blew in. If it was cold, Mary couldn't feel it.

"What about you?" she asked, swinging her leg over the ledge.

Roberta pushed her out and she fell with a plop into the snow.

The last thing Mary saw was her friend's hand waving her off. Then snow fluttered from the roof on impact of the window closing.

She was quiet about getting to her feet and dusting snow off her jacket. She stayed crouched down low, as she made her way around the back of the shed, ducking under frozen sapling branches so they wouldn't whip her face and lifting cedar fronds so the sharp needles wouldn't slap her.

When she came to the road, she kept to the shoulder as unpleasant as it was to trek through the dirty snow.

She was a long way from Center Harbor.

Dusk was settling over Messer Street, casting the snow-lain scenery in an eerie light. She wondered what would become of her night, where she would go and what she would do, now that Roberta was...

She winced for her friend and prayed for Jake to be merciful once more. If Mary was on thin ice with Cody, the ice had long since cracked beneath Roberta's feet as far as Jake was concerned. It gave her hope, however, that Gertrude remained oblivious.

Pulling her cell phone from her pocket, she debated calling Hannah. She had already fed her sister a line about babysitting until eleven-thirty and it wasn't until hours of groveling had passed that Hannah had finally agreed, not thrilled about her working so late on a school night.

Mary wished that Rose was still alive. The woman enthralled her and wouldn't hesitate to bail her out.

Her heart was fluttering—thin, tacky trembles that didn't feel strong enough to keep her alive. A sudden rush of dizziness reeled through her head and she stumbled, tripping then righting her balance. She stilled, her knees bending softly, her hands stretched out as though the ground were moving beneath her feet.

Was this the coke or was she under a siege of grief and mourning and fury that the woman she had come to admire and respect and maybe even love—those red fingernails that turned magically nude in the light of day, the devious glint in her eye that came with her every smile, the way she painted lipstick over her mouth, sitting at the vanity mirror while draped in silk, lingerie peeking out where her robe had slipped from her shoulder...

How the hell could Rose be dead?

A car horn bleated behind her and when she glanced over her shoulder, trees whirling all around her, she saw Roberta's Audi rolling to a stop.

"Get in," she called out through the open passenger side window. Leaning over, she popped the door, as Mary, dumbfounded, stared at her. Roberta's smile seemed effortless. "Cocaine is a tool to get us in the right frame of mind so we can do what we have to." She lifted her eyebrows in agreement then ordered. "Get in. They're waiting."

CHAPTER SEVEN

TUCKER FELT LIKE a sandbag on her hip—heavy and malleable, his head resting on her shoulder, his legs dangling freely, slush dripping from his boots onto the laminate flooring that was pretending to be oak as badly as the precinct counter she was nearing. The receptionist behind it didn't pivot in her chair or lift her gaze, but kept her phone braced between her ear and shoulder, her mouth pulling down at the corners as though the person on the other end had just ruined her morning.

Holly jutted her hip, jostling Tucker back into position before he could slip down her leg. His little fist was entwined around the thin, silver chain she was wearing—Rose's necklace—which caused the metal to cut into the side of her neck.

She felt anxious just being here, and sensed her luck might quickly run out when it came to dodging the police's questions. She might not get away with supplying minimal answers this time. She was antsy to get this over with and walk out of here unscathed.

Getting to the precinct had been enough of an ordeal.

Her nephew had thrown two fits before she had managed to get him out of the house. The first had involved his socks or rather his refusal to wear them. When he had reached a certain decibel, shrieking his protest at a frequency that rattled her brain, she had caved and he immediately quieted. The contrast had been so stark that she had stared at him in astonishment. The next outburst had revolved around his breakfast, which she soon learned should've been Cheerios. The scrambled eggs and buttered toast she had prepared were so offensive, Tucker responded by shoving his plate off the table. The toast had tumbled, leaving a trail of crumbs after bouncing against the floor and the eggs had landed in a globular heap, both of which he found amusing enough to give up his tantrum in exchange for wild laughter. By the time she had deposited him on the passenger seat he was conked out, exhausted, and Holly hadn't been too far behind. Spilling onto the driver seat, her hand had gripped to the steering wheel for balance, as the morning paper—the article she had read, as engrossing as it had been alarming, the phone call that had followed resonating the news—weighed on her mind like an albatross.

Tucker whined in her ear and began squirming so she lowered him to the ground, sensing he might flare up again if he didn't get his way instantly. He rubbed his eyes groggily then smiled and the sight of him brought her a rush of calm.

But it was short lived.

The receptionist slapped her phone into its cradle, the gesture filled with good riddance, as she shook off the long-winded, one-sided conversation she had just survived, and rose, meeting Holly at the counter.

"Can I help you?"

"Yeah, I got a call from Detective McAlister. He asked me to come in."

The phone was back to her ear, her fingers hovering over the keypad. "Your name?"

"Holly Danes."

The receptionist, who looked more suited to work in a nail salon than a police station, seemed to glimpse Holly with fresh eyes and a hint of pity shined through—no doubt viewing her in the context of her murdered twin—but she began punching in an extension and soon angled her shoulder, directing her words softly into the receiver. After nodding and adding a "Yes, Sir" into the exchange, the receptionist returned the phone, gently this time, and asked Holly to have a seat without any indication of how long it might be.

Tucker had been comparing his height to the counter, lifting and lowering his hand between the top of his head and the wooden lip, not so much measuring as sensing how he stacked up. When Holly took his hand, encouraging him towards a bench across from the front desk, he boisterously demanded, "How high?" and didn't blink until the receptionist cocked her brow.

"Do you like hot chocolate?" she asked in a singsong tone that told Holly the woman had experience with children. "I can get you a cup."

It was a beat of furtive staring before Tucker decided he didn't mind she had avoided his question. He nodded emphatically then buried his face under the hem of his aunt's winter coat.

Holly thanked the woman and watched her tromp through the bullpen, swaying her hips as though she was the much-needed feminine touch around here, not that Holly saw any evidence it was appreciated.

When the receptionist rounded the corner beyond her view, Holly helped her nephew onto the bench and sat beside him, thumbing the hem of her coat where it met with the back of her jeans to be certain the bulge from her revolver was concealed.

She scanned the room, nervous all over again for how this might go. The bullpen was spacious, flanked with desks paired nose-to-nose—detectives facing their partners, cracking jokes and jabbing shoulders as if paperwork didn't require their full attention, or so she imagined. Overall, the precinct seemed to have a folksy quality, both in terms of decorum and staff. But realizing this only contributed to the tension tightening around her chest and her throat, she didn't want to lose her edge or lower her guard.

She couldn't afford to soften, not after reading the Livingston article that had detailed, in gross accuracy, the manner in which Benjamin had been found dead:

After yanking up the emergency brake and cranking the temperature dials on the dash so Tucker wouldn't catch cold, Holly had torn through the resort with such intensity that barreling into the lobby, rounding the front desk, and stalking up the hallway had been an absolute blur.

When she had barged into his hotel room—the gun cocked in her hand, her finger on the trigger, vaguely surprised he hadn't locked the door—Benjamin had bolted upright in bed, urgent about getting the young woman's mouth off his erection. Hustling her into the bathroom, as the girl used shallow, unperturbed steps, glaring at Holly over her shoulder like a posturing cat, irritated and in no way threatened by the intrusion, Benjamin hadn't said a word.

As soon as he had shut the bathroom door, he lifted his hands, his gaze trained on the gun, and began spewing apologies.

It had only made her more furious. His complete abandonment of Rose, the way he had turned his back on her during their marriage, his avoidance of the house, of her sister's body, the detectives, had given her no reason not to pull the trigger. And his apology, as frantic and pleading as it had been, had explained nothing.

She had ordered him to shut up and though he obeyed, he had begun creeping towards her, easing one foot in front of the other so imperceptibly that when he lunged at her, darting his hands around hers, yanking the weapon upwards and twisting it out of her grasp, she hadn't even sensed it coming.

The gun hadn't gone off.

Confidently, he had demonstrated what little power she had, knocking the chamber loose and spinning the cylinder, holding her back with one hand braced around her throat and watching the bullets spill out, Holly taking swings at him all the while. She had failed to deliver one good punch, but tripped him, freeing her throat well enough to scream. She had angled over Benjamin where he had hit the floor. She had seen fear in his eyes, but it hadn't been for his life. Rather, it was a look of sadness as though he knew a chasm stood between them and he had no way of mending it. Nothing would ever be the same.

Drained, Holly had given up. When she had reached for her revolver, he didn't hesitate, setting it in her palm. She felt hollow collecting the stray bullets.

Walking out to her idling Saab, she had hoped he would die.

But she hadn't killed him.

The receptionist was approaching, her high-heels clicking over laminate. She offered Holly a Styrofoam cup, steaming with hot chocolate. "I can keep an eye on the little guy."

"McAlister's ready for me?" She asked, a sudden cramp in her stomach threatening her composure, though she kept her eyes on the steaming cup as she watched Tucker wrap his hands around it, careful not to let go until she was sure her nephew had a firm grip.

"He is," she confirmed in a chipper tone. Whatever had transpired around the corner had lifted the receptionist into an entirely different mood. "Just go on back into Interview One," she instructed. "Ask along the way if you're unsure."

Apprehensively, Holly got to her feet and wondered why the woman wouldn't escort her. It wasn't like she had asked directions to the bathroom at a truck-stop diner.

She made her way, crossing through the paired workstations where detectives seemed to have settled into their day, hunching over their desk phones and pouring over reports. Straight ahead was the Sergeant's office according to the placard on the door. The window lining his wall was striped with aluminum blinds, though they were open, giving her an obscured view of his quarters, which appeared disheveled.

Hanging a right, she found a hallway. The first door on the left was open and as she neared it, she confirmed she had the right room, reading *Interview Room One*.

In an instant she felt claustrophobic. The windowless room couldn't have been larger than twenty-five square feet. There was a narrow table in the center of the room, a single chair on one side and two on the other. Overhead, the fluorescent lights were buzzing, but it didn't compare with the punch of her pulse throbbing in her ears.

She pulled out the chair opposite the others, assuming Cody and Lucas would sit across from her, and tucked herself onto it, unnerved that the door was now behind her.

Cody breezed in, rounding the table and eyeing the manila-filing folder in his hands, the contents of which she feared to imagine. "Sorry to keep you waiting," he told her, closing the file.

"Don't worry about it." Her voice sounded frayed so she cleared her throat. "I don't mind. I'm shocked over that article, and the timing of it all." At the sound of footfall behind her, she glanced over her shoulder and found Lucas stepping into the room. He offered her a grim smile and she breathed, "Hello," her voice once again sounding frail.

Cody seemed to linger beside his chair until Lucas had a seat after which he followed suit. Before either delved into questioning her, a silent conversation ensued where it appeared Cody was nudging his partner to initiate the interview, yet the exchange seemed tense as though Lucas might prefer to hang back and observe.

Despite this, he was the first to speak. "Clearly, we're as thrown as you are. Since Benjamin was unreachable last night after his wife was found dead and it was an effort to locate him, we had a strong hunch he might have been responsible for Rose's murder." Lucas opened his palms and shrugged. "Now it would seem whoever killed your sister went after Benjamin, perhaps after Rose had been shot, or possibly before."

Holly let out a shuddering breath, her gaze drifting to the table, the folder, and Lucas's hands, which were now clasped together.

Using a gentle tone, Cody asked, "Do you have any idea who might have done this?"

"I really don't," she said, meeting his gaze. "If he was at the resort, then couldn't you talk to Warren or Sarah? They had to have closely interacted with him. Maybe they know something."

"We are," said Cody.

"When was the last time you saw Benjamin?" Lucas wasn't just looking at her. He was watching her, scrutinizing her demeanor, expression, and her every reaction, though it was subtle.

"Um," she mumbled to fill the silence as she wracked her brain. She had to say something, be decisive, and answer confidently, but she couldn't lift out of the rising panic that was petrifying her, her mind going blank. "Not since Rose," she said finally and added, "Two years or so?" She couldn't tell if they were disappointed or suspicious. Cody's expression was a stiff wince and Lucas's eyes narrowed. "Were you able to watch the security footage?"

Flicking his eyes at his partner before returning his gaze to her, Cody said, "I don't think we're dealing with a crime of passion here or anything in the ballpark of impulsiveness."

She felt the gravity of his statement, but hadn't a clue as to what it meant and her expression must have alluded as much, because Lucas explained, "There's about an hour missing from all the footage."

There came a knock and Cody apologized, jumping up and cracking the door. He spoke softly behind her, while Lucas kept his eyes on her. Restlessly, she began picking at a hangnail, but felt his gaze lower to the pendant hanging just beneath her clavicle.

Quietly, he asked, "How's Tucker taking all of this?"

Dumbfounded that he would care and also stunned at herself—it hadn't even occurred to her to explain to Tucker what had happened to his mother—Holly realized she had stopped breathing. She also realized that Rose and Benjamin had appointed her legal guardian of her nephew should both of them ever die, a fact Benjamin had brushed over less than a week ago during one of their argumentative phone calls.

"Holly?"

"Yeah? Sorry, I..."

Behind her, Cody slipped through the doorway and into the hall, drawing Lucas's attention, and she used the opportunity to pull herself together.

"I'm not sure he's old enough to understand any of this," she told him in a controlled tone. "Legally, I'm Tucker's guardian now so I probably have a ton of paperwork I should get to."

Leaning forward, Lucas locked eyes with her then diverted his gaze only when fishing his hand into the inside pocket of his jacket. As he pulled his hand out again, Holly saw a bullet between his thumb and index finger and once again the wind was knocked right out of her. "Do you recognize this?"

She swallowed, making certain her throat would be clear. "It's a bullet."

Scrambling, but only in her mind, she tried to recall how many bullets she had collected off the floor of Benjamin's hotel room. She hadn't counted, but must have left one behind.

"It's a .32 caliber," he stated, rolling the short bullet between his fingers. "I found it in Room 112 at the resort."

"Oh?" she offered after he had set his eyes on her.

"It wasn't the caliber that killed Benjamin. He was shot in the head with a .48, the same caliber bullet that killed your sister."

Bravely, she managed to ask, "Why are you telling me this?"

He tucked the bullet into his inner pocket, glancing past her to intuit whether they were about to be interrupted. "It's a highly unusual caliber."

"I don't know anything about calibers, or about bullets, and I don't know why you're telling me any of this."

"You don't?" he challenged, lacing his fingers as he leaned in even further.

He was trying to rattle her and it was working, though she prayed it didn't show.

"You own a gun, several, I thought." Since she said nothing, focusing on her breathing and willing the air to do more than flow thinly up and down her throat, he then mentioned, "The list is pretty long and it includes a revolver of the same caliber as that bullet." After a beat, he asked, "When were you there?"

Inside, Holly was screaming at herself to tell him about the teenager who had been in Benji's hotel room, the girl who Benjamin was having an affair with, the last person who had seen him alive. But there would be no way to convince him that the young woman was a worthy suspect without also placing herself in Benjamin's hotel room that night. And she refused to admit as much.

"Holly," he said quietly. "Were you there that night?"

Whispering, because it was all the strength she had, she said, "You can't possibly think I was there."

He held her gaze, saying, "I do think you were there, which is why Cody doesn't know about the bullet."

His disclosure blindsided her. It was almost too much to process. Lucas thought she had killed her brother-in-law and because of it he was withholding evidence from his partner, from his precinct?

Words wouldn't come, not for a long moment, and when they did, she didn't recognize the sound of her own voice. "I didn't kill Benjamin and I definitely didn't kill my sister."

"Then tell me what happened," he prodded.

"I can't. I don't know what happened." She suddenly felt like her eyes weren't working. She squinted, but her gaze wouldn't settle. Rubbing her forehead, she begged herself to keep it together just long enough to get out of this room, but she knew she was coming undone. "Why would you cover that up?" she whispered.

"Same reason I brought you the necklace. The history between us, or something like that."

"Damn."

"Benjamin wasn't killed with a .32," he repeated.

"But you think I did it?"

"I think you need help. I think you were high the night Rose was killed and I think you were hovering at the same altitude when I stopped by your studio the other day."

She groaned, though softly, and couldn't meet his gaze.

"I think you're neck deep in something you're not going to be able to handle, not while caring for a three-year-old."

She tried to get mad, but it wouldn't come. He wasn't threatening her with all this. He was looking out for her, yet she couldn't wrap her head around his reason.

"I can't help you if I don't know everything you know."

Ordering herself to maintain her lie that she hadn't been in Benjamin's room that night, she drew in a deep breath, but just as she was about to assert as much, Cody returned, whipping the door open and closing it fast and firm before getting situated beside his partner.

"Again, sorry about that," he offered easily, as Lucas cocked his head interested to know what had transpired out in the hallway. In response, Cody brushed over it, saying, "Paperwork," then opened the manila folder to a form and pressed his pen against the first blank field. "I'm going to apologize in advance for these questions. I hope they don't rub you the wrong way."

Like your partner? she thought, feigning a smile of agreement that felt strained.

"The night Rose died," he began, avoiding the words *killed* and *murdered*, which she had already gotten used to, "when did she call you?"

"Around one," she stated.

"Do you happen to have the time stamp on your cell phone?" He asked as if he had just thought of it.

Holly riffled through her coat pocket for her phone and after unlocking the screen, opened the call log and showed him. "Right there," she said, pointing to Rose's name and number.

Cody mumbled, "One twelve," as he jotted down the time on his form.

Glancing at her cell, she offered, "It was a four minute call."

"Thank you," he said, noting the duration. "And where were you when she called?"

The lie flew out of her mouth faster than she could stop it, answering, "McCoy's."

"Great bar," Cody commented, his mouth curling with a crooked smile as though a fond memory was taking hold.

Why had she lied? So she could place herself in a public setting, have an ironclad alibi? They could easily check into it and surely would. She felt her eyes widening at her error so she made herself blink, thankful only that both of them were looking at the form as Cody filled in her answer.

"When did you get to McCoy's?" he asked, trilling his pen between his fingers.

She was loath to elaborate, but decided on a time when McCoy's would've been crowded. "Eleven. It was supposed to be a nightcap."

"No judgment," he said, shooting her an understanding smile.

Lucas on the other hand was probing her with his eyes.

"And when you left your sister's after we spoke with you, where did you go?"

Though she didn't look at him, she sensed Lucas was stiffening on his chair. "Ah, well, I had Tucker so I went home."

As Cody made his note, Tucker surged to the forefront of her mind. The receptionist was watching him. What if she asked him about last night? Would Tucker remember it? Would he tell her about the drive to the resort, how Holly had brought him into Benjamin's room? About the fact that Holly had left him in the car afterwards?

She tried not to panic, but it was dawning on her what these questions amounted to and the realization brought on terrible paranoia. Had they mastered the least recognizable good cop - bad cop routine? Lucas had attempted to level with her as though he were on her side and would get her out of this and now Cody was asking for her timeline and whereabouts last night, which couldn't possibly be in the ballpark of anything a detective would angle to know if they believed they were speaking with an innocent person. And yet there was something off about Lucas. She sensed it. His interest in helping her seemed to run deep and personal. And Cody's good-natured remarks about McCoy's and his thoroughly apologetic attitude was just that—harmless, or seemingly so.

"Okay," said Cody, flipping the folder shut and concluding the interview with a smile. "We're good."

She got to her feet only after they did.

Cody held the door open for her, but instead of passing through, she asked, "Are you guys still at my sister's house?" Before they could answer, she explained, "I have Tucker now and I would rather not uproot him."

Lucas clarified for Cody's benefit. "Holly has custody."

"For the next week or so at least I was thinking it would be easier to move my stuff into the house rather than take Tucker out of his home."

"We did everything we could there," said Cody, encouragingly. "So by all means; we'll give you a ring if we need to get back in."

She smiled nervously and stepped into the hallway, the detectives trailing after her. As she rounded into the bullpen, Cody sidled her.

"So you've got the little guy now."

"I do," she said, feeling the pressure of the interview dissipate now that she was walking towards the exit.

"If you ever need a night off or just some help around the house with him, my girlfriend's younger sister is quite the babysitter. I could give you her number."

It was the best news she had heard all morning. She accepted eagerly and when he jotted a cell number on the back of his business card and handed it to her, the smile on her face was one of genuine relief.

"Her name is Mary," he added, though he had clearly printed it above the number. "And she's a hell of a cook."

CHAPTER EIGHT

IT WAS ONE IN the afternoon by the time Holly thrust her shoulder against the front door of her sister's house, having scraped the key into the lock. Her hand felt like a frozen claw. Her fingers were numb. Flexing her cheeks to help thaw her face and holding Tucker's hand, she helped him into the foyer where he plopped on his butt and began wrestling his boots off in a wobbly effort to free his feet.

She eased the door closed behind her so the heat wouldn't escape and blew on her hands. Her ring and pinky fingers on her left hand were sallow, but the rest were flushed and tingling, circulation having failed her in both directions.

Reasoning not to get too comfortable, she still had to load in her duffel bag and the case of jewelry supplies she had grabbed quickly from the studio—abandoning her deadlines would be bad for business and she had already been struggling to make rent—she wriggled Tucker's boot off, placed it with the other under the entryway table, and wasted no time parking her nephew in front of the TV.

The remote control was resting on the coffee table, but it wasn't until she pressed the power button that she remembered the hollow compartment where Rose had often swapped batteries for drugs. Tossing the useless device onto the couch where of course it bounced and landed on the rug, interesting Tucker, she grumbled then pressed the power button on the entertainment set and began manually flipping through the channels until Dora the Explorer filled the screen.

"You like this show?"

Tucker lifted his eyes from the remote's rewind button, which he had been scratching and became instantly mesmerized by the plucky cartoon girl and her frenetic monkey sidekick as they investigated a lone flower sprouting up in a desert.

Holly adjusted the volume and crouched beside him, unzipping his coat, which she hung in the foyer closet as soon as she padded back.

Rose's winter hat on the shelf caught her eye. The wool cloche, gray and bell-shaped with a plume of feathers springing from its bow, was situated between two stacks of shoeboxes. Taking it down and glimpsing her own coat, Rose's singsong criticism filled her thoughts—*You can't wear a cloche with a parka, silly.*

Holly fit the hat squarely on her head and began rummaging through a few boxes, the scent of potpourri sweetening the air as she opened each one. She found a pair of slim, leather gloves and slipped them on only after returning the boxes.

Outside, she squinted through the glare—sunlight bouncing off the snowy driveway, blindingly bright—as she stomped over a drift to reach her Saab.

A sheet of ice slid off the rear windshield when she lifted the hatchback. She slung her duffel bag over her shoulder and grabbed her jewelry case by the handle.

She didn't bother locking her car after slamming the trunk, but simply started for the house, vaguely unnerved.

As she rounded through the foyer, heading towards the stairs, she glimpsed Tucker rocking on the floor—his fists balling the knees of his corduroys, legs jutting in a fight for balance, his bare feet touching the carpet before he pitched himself backwards, seeing how fast he could get his head to tap down, all the while engrossed in the plot of his show.

Perhaps feeling eyes on him, he glanced at Holly and grinned as if impressed with his game. "Mom, can you do this?"

"Not as well as you, I'm sure," she said with a smile.

Did she really look *exactly* like her twin sister?

The answer came when she reached the top of the stairs, stepping onto the landing where a silver-framed mirror reflected her face—fawn-brown eyes arching at the outer corners and rimmed with translucent lashes, the Grecian nose, broad at the bridge yet pulling downward into a dainty snub, lips as narrow as they were full. The face of Lady Liberty they had decided as little girls, combing through their father's encyclopedia, determined to see their future in its pages.

Wearing Rose's hat only accentuated their likeness and though her sister had dyed her rosy-blonde hair auburn to mask the strawberry hue, it hadn't distracted from the similarities—the light smattering of freckles across their noses and the glint of kept secrets behind their eyes.

How's Tucker taking all of this?

He didn't even know his mother was gone.

Holly pulled off her sister's hat and felt her hair spark, levitating with static. She smoothed her palm over her head, grounding the charge, as she trekked down the hallway and into the master bedroom.

It was the same mess it had been before the police had arrived, which meant they hadn't turned the place upside down and searched as intrusively as she would've thought.

Avoiding the bunched comforter that was spilling over the edge of the bed at the disheveled end, she set down her duffle bag and the jewelry case next to it, tossed the hat, and pulled her revolver from where it was tucked at the small of her back. The drawer on the nightstand would do, but before she deposited the gun there, she slapped the cylinder free and confirmed all six rounds were present as they had been that morning when she had loaded the weapon, then clicked it into place, her eyes widening at the thought she had left a bullet behind.

She couldn't believe what Lucas had done, risked his standing to cover up the possibility that she had been there. His reason for doing so was as disturbing as it was flattering, and both made her skin prick with dread.

Why had she lied and said she had been at McCoy's?

Shrugging out of her winter coat and sitting on the edge of the bed as she unzipped the breast pocket, Holly tried not to think about Rose. But when she extracted a plastic bag of cocaine from her coat, it seemed there was nothing else in the world on her mind. She stared at it in her gloved hand.

What was this life she was suddenly living?

She threw the baggie in the drawer with her gun, pushed it closed, and hoped Tucker wasn't inquisitive enough to discover either.

Next she found her cell phone and the business card Cody had given her, and began dialing Mary Cole's number. While pulling her gloves off with her teeth, her cell phone clamped in the crook of her shoulder, she realized the girl was probably in school at this hour, but figured it wouldn't hurt to leave a message.

"Hello?" she asked when the line opened up to hushed whispering in the background.

The girl's voice was feathery. "Who is this?"

"Hi, your step-dad gave me your-"

"Cody? Yeah, he's not my step-dad. Is this Holly Danes?"

It sounded like she was slapping at a friend to be quiet, yet Holly didn't hear the tell-tale sound effects of kids in a hallway between classes. She detected lazy jazz playing on the other end.

"It is," she said quickly. "I heard you're a qualified babysitter? I'm looking for someone to watch my nephew."

"Now?" She sounded alarmed.

"No, in general."

"What's the pay?"

Holly hadn't even thought about it. "Ah, well, he's three. What would you charge?"

"Maybe something like..." she trailed off and Holly imagined the girl calculating the highest possible figure she could get away with. "Maybe ten an hour?"

"Sounds fair," she said, surprised that Mary hadn't gouged her.

"But if you flake and don't get home when you say you will, then it'll cost you another two an hour."

"Okay."

"And if you *cancel* then..."

Holly waited impatiently while the girl cooked up another fee.

"Hang on," she grumbled. Somewhere in the background another girl told her to *hurry the hell up*, but Mary didn't respond. "Okay, you have to cancel three hours in advance, and if you don't, then you pay me half of whatever it would've been to watch... What's his name?"

"Tucker," she said dryly, envisioning no scenario where she would cancel.

"Cool. Just text me whenever. I don't drive, but Cody or my sister can bring me over."

Holly heard the other girl chime in—*or me.*

Concluding the conversation, Mary added, "I know the Heimlich maneuver."

But Holly cut in with, "How much lead time will you need?"

"Huh? No, just text me whenever and I'll come over," she told her, making the cancellation clause of their negotiation entirely moot.

"Sounds good. Talk soon." As Holly set her cell phone on the nightstand, it dawned on her that Mary's wide-open schedule—*text me whenever*—implied she might not work for any other families, but Holly decided that would be to her benefit and made her way through the hallway and down the stairs, where she joined Tucker in the living room.

A commercial for Toys 'R Us was playing softly so she muted the TV and scooped Tucker up, giving him a few bounces before settling him on her hip, as she stepped towards the couch.

The idea of explaining to him that his parents had died was daunting. She studied his face, his round eyes were as blue as a summer sky and shifting over the TV screen, the particular brand of intrigue in his expression endearing her. Were there terms simple enough for him to understand that his parents were gone and never coming back?

Finally, she sat with him on the couch, helping his spindly leg to straddle her lap. She laced her fingers through his.

"Tucker," she said softly, stealing his attention from the next cartoon that had begun, "about your parents..." Her mouth went dry, her throat felt raw and scratchy, so she swallowed, but when she tried to come out with the terrible truth—that she wasn't his mother, that his mother had passed away, that she was his aunt—she couldn't get the words out no matter how plainly they formed in her thoughts. "How can we entertain you while I get some work done?"

In response to the question or perhaps avoiding it, Tucker freed his hands from hers and clutched the silver chain around her neck, eyeing the heart-shaped pendant.

She unfastened the clasp. The chain spilled loosely from her neck then dangled from his hands as he examined the pendant. She maneuvered him off her lap, setting him on the couch and when she reached the TV set, she unmuted the sound so he could watch the next animated show about a gap-toothed dish sponge living under the sea.

As she rounded into Benjamin's home office, angling to dig up the Joint Will that Benjamin had told her about, Lucas's bizarre pretense leapt to the forefront of her mind. *I think you need help,* he had told her in the police station, justifying how he had acted on her behalf, hiding the stray bullet and never mentioning it to his partner, entirely assuming she had contributed in some way to Benjamin's murder. And in the wake of remembering came a flash of their long-ago night a decade prior.

I can help you, he had said, lying on his side between the sheets, searching her eyes as if hoping to find a part of himself inside her. She hadn't needed help, not other than what his body could provide—taking the sting out of life and giving her an escape if only for a few hours in a dingy motel room.

Lucas had been the one in need of help, but he couldn't see it, didn't recognize that his urge to rescue was a misdirected instinct to save himself. Holly had easily pegged him. It had been the look in his eye, his hunger thrusting into her, the delicacy and desperation to implant his very essence in her so he could find himself in another human being, so he wouldn't be alone, so he would no longer be the only one of his kind.

Lying there beside him, as he had elaborated, detailing her qualities, which both rang true and revealed his own, Holly had sensed his tremendous sorrow.

What happened to you? he had asked her, tucking her hair behind her ear and making her wonder about the degree to which his past had destroyed him.

Growing up? she had whispered, at a loss for being able to mirror the sad story of his life.

While he had curled her against his body—her head resting on his shoulder, her leg draped over his nude waist, her hand grazing his chest—he had begun opening up, using vague terms and at times dropping in mind-splitting admissions. Holly had puzzled over why she was messed up in the distinct way that she was. Nothing truly awful had ever happened to her, nothing that even remotely compared to the beatings, the starvation, and cruelty that Lucas had been describing.

I shouldn't be telling you this, he had said grimly. *I've never told anyone. It isn't something women want to hear.*

It's okay, she had breathed, strangely content to be the keeper of his secret.

The recollection washed away and Holly muscled open the filing drawer of Benjamin's desk and began thumbing through the hanging-folders, scanning each tab for the word Will, as she tried not to analyze how Lucas's dark past might have informed his decision to bend the law in her favor.

She couldn't find the Will.

Annoyed, she glanced around the office, her gaze darting from Benjamin's framed Dartmouth diploma on the wall to Benjamin's books on business and finance lining the shelves to Benjamin's mini-bar in the corner of the room, stocked only with his favorite liquors and not her sister's. It certainly was his office, alright. There wasn't a hint of Rose anywhere or their son in this room.

Holly pushed away from the desk, as it occurred to her that Rose might have stashed the document upstairs.

Tucker yelled "I'm hungry!" when she passed through the living room.

Without slowing her step, she suggested, "How about grilled cheese?" and he beamed a big grin at her. "Two minutes."

After padding up the stairs, diverting her gaze from the mirror as she rounded the landing, and making her way into her sister's walk-in closet, which was set back just shy of the master bedroom, she spied a trunk poking out from the veil of her sister's hanging dresses.

It looked officey enough so she yanked it clear of the garments and popped the latches, hoping to find the Will inside.

As soon as she pitched the lid of the trunk vertical, she saw an envelope resting on top of a folded blanket.

The envelope looked thick and when she peeked inside, she discovered a stack of cash. One hundred dollar bills. She was suddenly bogged in mind-bending confusion.

There had to be at least six thousand dollars here, she estimated, as she thumbed through the bills. She placed the cash on the blanket inside the trunk and turned the envelope over in her hands.

A stationary card dropped out.

Printed in a masculine hand, the card read—*You're dead to me. Don't come back.*

CHAPTER NINE

"MEET YOU out front?" Cody asked.

Without looking at his partner, Lucas said, "Ah, you want to head over together?" while engaging the safety on his GLOCK before fitting it into his holster, a classic shoulder system he hadn't broken in. The leather dug through his shirt where it spanned his ribs, chafing his side.

"Makes sense to carpool until the roads clear up."

It wasn't the roads or Lucas's unreliable Ford that Cody was worried about, but Lucas in general. Ever since Cody had returned to the interview room where Lucas and Holly had spoken privately, he had been keeping tighter tabs on him, shadowing Lucas's every move, calling his cell whenever he was out of sight regardless if Lucas had only stepped into the men's room. It had been less than twenty-four hours of this and he wasn't sure how much more he could take.

Keeping things light, Lucas teased, "You just like showing off that Dodge of yours," and slammed his locker shut, which reminded him of the high school football team he had never made. He was fairly certain the precinct had the exact same lockers.

Cody grinned with an air of modesty, folding his arms and glancing at Lucas's winter coat where it rested on the bench beside them. "That goes without saying," he allowed. "It'll also give us some time to talk."

Lucas didn't like the sound of that.

Pulling his coat on after his partner had handed it to him, he snuck a glimpse at Cody whose waning smile looked brittle enough to crack.

As they left the locker room, Lucas felt slightly unnerved that he had consistently forgotten to buy a combination lock. The notion that anyone could pop his locker open and spy the dregs of his disheveled life was an unsettling thought.

The bullpen was filling up, detectives walking briskly to their desks and phones blaring from every corner of the room. Cody sidestepped for Tammy to cut in-between them. The receptionist slowed, making a point to shift her flirtatious eyes between them before she swayed on through.

Angling to get inside his partner's head, Lucas asked, "What was your take on Holly Danes?"

"What do you mean?" he said, brushing over the subtext.

"Grilling her for her whereabouts?"

Cody paused once they reached the entryway and zipped up his ski jacket, but the hesitation gave Lucas the impression that he was buying time to formulate a response.

"I wouldn't say I *grilled* her."

He was evading and it made Lucas's stomach lurch as he followed Cody outside into a flurry of wind-driven snow that marked the onset of another storm.

Using short steps to cross a sheet of black-ice, his partner added, "We've got zilch on the surveillance footage, it'll be weeks before ballistics gets us names on the .48 calibers, and when they do, we can expect it'll be a long list. Christ, half this county owns a forty-eight. Holly Danes is all we've got to go on."

"But you don't think she did it," Lucas said, his tone towing the line between a question and a statement, as he waited, his shoulders hunching against the wind, for Cody to unlock his truck.

"I think we have a double homicide and no viable leads," he pointed out, implying Holly was of interest to him if for no other reason than pouring over her whereabouts would give him something to do. He pressed the key-fob and his truck bleated, but before he rounded the hood for the driver side, his eyes flared, catching the light. "I've been waiting for a case like this. I'm going to nail this guy to the wall and the only way to do that is to look into every single detail and confirm every last word I hear."

Though Cody was his partner, he hadn't exactly built Lucas into his vision of success.

Climbing onto the passenger seat and shutting the door, he weighed his options in terms of drawing Cody's interest away from Holly. Lucas couldn't be certain of her involvement in the murders, only that she had undoubtedly been there, both in the hotel room and at the Wythes' house, and eventually his partner would find out.

If and when he did, Cody wouldn't just be fired up. He would be tenacious and could frame her motivation any number of ways—the estrangement from Rose could've driven Holly to kill, perhaps her revolver had jammed and thinking fast, she drew a .48 on Benjamin, maybe this was about securing custody or some need to move into the estate, or perhaps she had gone on a murdering rampage after Rose had caught her stealing drugs.

Lucas felt in his gut that no matter how circumstantial or outlandish the reason, his partner would eventually present a case against Holly Danes to the Sergeant that would be a bitch for Lucas to dismantle.

The most damning piece of evidence, second only to the .32 caliber bullet he had pocketed, was the Joint Will he had come across in the Wythes' home office. It had been amended a week prior, leaving all assets to Holly. When he had glanced at it, his back to the officers, his thumb and forefinger widening the hanging folder enough to scan the document as he mentally scrambled for a way to clear the cops from the room, Benjamin's signature had jumped out at him. It hadn't looked right, didn't resemble the one that Lucas had seen in the checkbook register. After instructing the officers out of the room by spinning a thin excuse around the importance of searching the master bedroom, Lucas had hidden the document in his inner coat pocket, fighting the surge of adrenaline that was rushing through his veins all the while.

He hadn't fought the impulse to cover for the woman who at the time had just driven off—evidently towards the Wythe resort—but he had questioned it.

An identical brand of compulsion had come over him in the hotel room when his gaze had landed on the bullet.

He felt responsible for Holly, yet didn't know why.

As they drove—Cody leaning into the steering wheel, straining to see through the flurries that slipped over the windshield, its wipers thwacking back and forth, short sips of visibility, Lucas watching the shops along Kelsea Avenue, the foggy storefront windows and shopkeepers shaking salt from tin cans onto the sidewalk—Cody glimpsed Lucas from the corner of his eye and asked, "You ever work a case this big up in Plymouth?"

He frowned, pretending to give it some thought since his partner obviously wanted to hear that he hadn't. "We had crimes of passion, a wife killing her husband because he smacked her one too many times. Accidental shootings, kids and guns where you file reckless endangerment forms, put a parent in jail to appease the town. Nothing major," he lied.

"You'll get a feel for it."

The encouragement didn't land except condescendingly, which Lucas hardly appreciated, and because of it he couldn't keep from demonstrating his aptitude for this kind of crime.

"He doesn't have access to a full range of emotions."

"The killer?" Cody stiffened behind the wheel as he turned up Main Street.

"Sadness, joy, nervousness," he began listing, "most importantly empathy, aren't in his repertoire of emotions. He's numb, but easily insulted."

"You think he killed two people because they insulted him?" he challenged, staring at Lucas for a beat before returning his eyes to the road.

"I think he's provoked by insults. I think the emotion is one of the few gravitational forces that he responds to. I don't think this is about your usual motives—money, betrayal, or insurance. I think it goes much deeper than that. Our killer has been festering for a very long time, plotting and refining his attack and plotting more carefully, perhaps months in the making."

"Where is this coming from?" Cody rolled to a stop for a red light and shifted on his seat, giving Lucas his full attention. "I'm not disagreeing, just interested in getting inside your head."

The woman who had been on the other end of Benjamin's cell phone came to mind—*I thought you were dead*—but Lucas wasn't ready to lay that card on the table. "I have a hunch." The look on Cody's face told him that he wouldn't get away with as little. "The light's green."

Cody eased on the gas, tires crunching over icy snow, as they drove through the intersection. "Sounds like you're describing a serial killer."

"I don't think he's killed before," he clarified, feeling suddenly too warm. He angled his vent towards the window. "But I don't think we've seen the worst of what he's planning on doing."

"Who's left to kill? Holly?"

Suppressing a smile, Lucas said *Bingo* but only in his mind. Luring Cody away from suspecting Holly would be a delicate procedure, one he would have to craft off the cuff and hope like hell it panned out.

"You think she's scared?" he pressed when Lucas hadn't responded. "Intimidated or just paranoid and that's why she was tight-lipped at the station?"

His partner seemed to consider the possibility that Lucas had introduced, falling silent, his eyebrows knitting together, evaluating as if the contradictions would dance into alignment on their own, as he pulled the truck along the curb in front of McCoy's and killed the engine.

Interrupting his partner's reverie, Lucas commented, "Looks like a real drinkers' bar," and stepped out of the truck.

McCoy's was a one-story slab of weathered bricks. Its aluminum awning was bowed under a heap of snow and the sign above it—painted letters, fading yet boasting *liquor, beer, karaoke*—gave Lucas the impression this was where alcoholics came to die. And the boarded up windows weren't helping, neither was the fact that its doors were open in the afternoon, though he reasoned that with darkness closing in at half past four all winter, welcoming customers at 3 pm wasn't entirely uncalled for.

If it looked dismal from the outside, McCoy's was damned miserable within.

The odor hit him first, as he edged over creaking floorboards that were damp with melted snow. It smelled like bleach and stale urine, which drew his eye to a bearded man who was shuffling drunkenly out of the bathroom that was in unfortunate proximity to a pool table. The bathroom door slammed against the edge of the table and the man stumbled.

Cody barreled ahead for the bar, but Lucas took his time, passing booths made of cracked vinyl where drinkers were hunched over their pints, their elbows planted on sticky tables, the profound lack of conversation thickening the air, as Jimmy Buffett twanged quietly from the jukebox.

Lucas couldn't picture Holly stopping in this dump for a nightcap under any circumstance and the revelation gave him a terrible feeling.

Joining Cody at the counter where the bartender—a burly man in his forties whose greasy hair was tied in a low rattail—was running a stained rag over one of the stools, Lucas debated telling his partner about the woman who had called Benjamin's cell phone. He decided if things went south in terms of Holly not having been at McCoy's, he would.

Their phone exchange had been brief if not intriguing. After hearing her comment how she had thought Benjamin was dead, Lucas had to force himself to breathe, a flush of urgency rocketing his heart rate through the roof. *Who is this?* he had demanded, pressing the cell phone to his ear in a white-knuckle grip. Her response had come swiftly, *Your wife stopped by last night?* It wasn't until she had hung up and Lucas discovered the bullet gleaming from the carpet just shy of the dust ruffle lining the bed that he knew unequivocally Holly Danes had been in that room. Holly looked exactly like Benjamin's *wife*.

He had traced the number before deleting it from the call-log, but learned it was a prepaid cell, bought with cash, no known information.

If he had a viable suspect, it was the woman on the other end of that call, but he couldn't bring himself to loop Cody in. Call it the habit of working alone or a penchant for secrecy, he had no intention of being a team player, not with Holly's innocence on the line, not until he knew for sure who he had spoken with on that call, and interviewed her.

Casually, his partner thumbed through his cell phone, as the bartender returned behind the counter. "I'm Detective McAlister and this is York."

"What can I do for you?" asked the man, as he dried his hands on the rag and threw it over his shoulder.

Cody glanced quickly at his cell, the photo of Holly—a muggy driver's license shot—before stating his question. "Were you working on the 12th?"

"Probably," he grumbled. "I'm here almost every night."

"Was it busy?" asked Cody, nearly setting his cell on the sticky bar then thinking better of it.

"Not too bad. You boys want a drink?"

Declining, Cody held up his cell phone for the man. "Did you see this woman?"

The bartender leaned in, studying the photo of Holly Danes. In the photo, Holly's head was tipped down, a glint of amusement filled her eyes. She looked like a confident fugitive, everything about her facial expression screamed, *You got nothing on me.*

Cody waited for the bartender to show some sign of recognition.

After a long moment of looking at the photo, the bartender frowned, saying, "She wasn't here."

Lucas pulled Cody away from the bar and began making excuses. "Holly is single. She lives alone. Her nerves probably got the best of her at the thought of admitting she was all by herself."

His partner didn't look convinced as he thanked the bartender and collected his cell phone. Tucking his phone in his jacket, he neared Lucas. "Holly lied to us. Not smart of her."

"You would've done differently?"

"I think you're seeing what you want to see," he stated, delivering a hard look with his point. Lucas felt himself shrinking so he straightened his spine. "Don't tell me you have a thing for her?"

Laughing it off landed badly so Lucas swallowed. "No," he said, not liking the edge in his tone. "I don't want to get caught up chasing a red herring."

Cody started for the door, giving the bartender a wave. When they stepped onto the snow-lain sidewalk, he explained, "The Wythes had a Will. Holly's the primary beneficiary, but that wasn't always the case."

Lucas cut in with, "When did you find this out?"

"Earlier today," he relented, his eyes softening apologetically. "I put in a call to their attorney and when I went through the evidence bags that our guys collected at the house, there wasn't a hard copy. I don't know that Holly took the Will that night, but it's possible. Look, I know you have all these ideas about the psychology of who's behind this, and you don't want to believe it boils down to money, but it might." Before Lucas could object, he added. "Bottom line, Holly told us she was at this bar and she wasn't. Which means we have to find out if she was at the resort that night."

"I already spoke with the Wythes. Warren and Sarah didn't mention her-"

"Warren and Sarah aren't exactly night owls. They probably turn in at eight o'clock. Did you talk to the desk staff? The maids? Anyone who may have floated through that hallway?"

"I can double-back," he offered, but again Cody had his own ideas.

"I've got it covered," he said easily, as he cleared a nasty puddle of slush, rounding the hood of his truck.

Lucas waited for the bleat to indicate the vehicle was unlocked then climbed onto the passenger seat. The second Cody got situated behind the steering wheel, Lucas offered, "Want me to swing by Shackles?"

"Christ," he said with a laugh, turning the engine before putting the truck in gear. "Hell of a name for a store. No, I'll talk to her."

"Don't put me on the bench, coach," he warned without a shred of humor.

If Cody was one to lighten the mood, especially in the face of rising tension, and he was, this time he made no attempt, but eased the truck into the street with perfect form—blinker clicking, checking his mirrors, and merging into slow flowing traffic.

When they reached the precinct, Cody rolled to a stop right in front of the door and told him, "The resort has a number of security cameras-"

"You think I messed up?" he blurted out, staring at his partner.

Cody's smile was a wince and he paired it with an affable shrug. "You didn't ask the Wythes about it. You're not thinking on your feet and I get that you're still adjusting to the department."

"I'm adjusted," he objected.

"You've been struggling with your admin. You're forgetting to do things and forgetting things that you've done. I think this is because you're stressed." Cody let that hang, as he studied Lucas's reaction. "Why don't you take the rest of the day to get caught up on your paperwork, maybe go home early, relax, and clear your head?"

Feeling Cody's eyes on him, he stepped out of the truck and didn't glance back as he slammed the door and trekked over the icy sidewalk towards the entrance.

Fuming, he barreled through the bullpen, avoiding Tammy's singsong greeting, which set his teeth on edge. By the same measure, he averted his Sergeant's furtive glance, though it caused him to clip shoulders with Gibbs—*Rough day?*

As he rounded straight through to the locker room, he wasn't aware the rookie cop was trailing after him until he turned for his locker.

"Heading out early?" Gibbs asked, his eyes brightening with interest, but Lucas barely heard him. "We could grab a beer."

"What?" Peeling his coat off, he realized a beer sounded good, but the idea of keeping Bobby Gibbs's company was enough to sour the deal. "I can't, sorry."

Edging towards him, his shoulder scraping over the thin slits of the lockers, Gibbs said, "Cody's not easy. He's a perfectionist and doesn't love having a partner."

"Yeah, well, he's not the only one." He could feel Gibbs's penetrating stare, which wasn't what he needed right now. "If you'll excuse me?"

"Yeah," he said, backing off and nearing the door. "If you ever feel like blowing off some steam..." He pointed two thumbs at his chest.

Lucas smiled and promised he would think of Gibbs if he ever *did* feel like blowing off steam, just to get the guy out of the locker room.

He almost didn't know what to do with himself, he felt so riled up. It wasn't the fact that Cody had called him out on his absentmindedness. It was that he knew his partner was right.

Why had Lucas been slipping?

It wasn't as simple as blanking out when boredom set in. More and more he had been functioning in an autopilot haze of deep thought, zones he couldn't lift himself out of, not easily. Often he wasn't even aware he was bogged in such a state. It was crippling and yet so familiar that it didn't concern him, not as much as it unnerved him that people had begun to notice.

Lucas balled his coat and flung it angrily into his locker, which caused an avalanche of items to tumble out. Grumbling, he kneeled and began collecting the mess—a bent tube of toothpaste and toothbrush, its bristles frayed, an old sweatshirt, and several deodorant sticks.

He was about to shove the heap into the locker when he noticed a business card resting on the metal floorboard. Scraping it off the locker floor, a strange mix of confusion and familiarity washed over him.

Diamonds.

The black card featured the silhouette of a voluptuous woman arching her back, breasts swelling, hair flowing freely, the feminine point of her knee aligning perfectly with the white, cursive stroke of the *D*.

He wanted to laugh. The guys must have slipped the business card through the locker slats, their not-so-subtle way of suggesting he should take a load off. If he weren't the only cop in the locker room, he would've complimented the officers on their collective practical joke.

But Lucas couldn't shake the feeling that funny wasn't what this was.

CHAPTER TEN

HOLLY COULDN'T FOCUS. She had two necklaces and one anklet to repair. Her customers had been waiting, but when she sat at the kitchen table with her jewelry case, her thoughts kept darting from one ugly scenario to the next.

Tucker was situated beside her at the table with the sandwich she had made for him, a grilled cheese which he was pulling apart to see how far he could stretch the cheddar,

All she had to do was fit pliers through a gapped ring and pinch to secure the broken pendant and move on to the next piece of jewelry that needed to be fixed, but the envelope she had found consumed her.

You're dead to me.

It was exactly $6,500 in cash.

Don't come back.

Rose had been paid off, warned to stay away, but from who, and why?

Tucker wasn't making progress with his lunch so she wrapped cellophane around the broken bits of his sandwich, tucked the leftovers into the refrigerator, and rinsed his plate.

A drive or maybe a walk might help clear her head, but both options seemed complicated considering she couldn't leave her nephew alone. She decided on a bath, as she wiped ketchup off Tucker's face and planted him on her hip.

When she reached the upstairs bathroom, it occurred to her that Tucker's big boy room was directly across the hallway. After getting him situated on the carpet with a Thomas the Tank Engine toy train and a few children's books, she then noticed a music box on top of the dresser.

She wound the brass key and it began playing, tinny chimes to the tune of You Are My Sunshine, as the carousel of wooden animals turned slowly.

She left his door wide open, likewise the bathroom, and began drawing a bath, adjusting the temperature dials until steam billowed up from the rising water.

Shielding herself from her nephew's view with the bathroom door, she began undressing, folding each garment and setting it on the toilet lid. When she wriggled out of her jeans, the card stock note in her back pocket inched out.

She read it over, standing nude and listening to the music box play faintly across the hallway. The upper edge of the card was embossed with the silhouette of a temptress, as alluring as she was inviting, in the throes of widening her legs. Holly ran her fingertip over the bubbling image then set the card on the edge of the sink, wrapped a towel around her in case her nephew was watching the bathroom, and turned the tub faucet off.

As she eased into the hot water, dropping her towel on the tiles at the last possible second, she considered who might have written the note and how Rose could have possibly known them. There was no name on the card and no contact information. She couldn't be sure whether the stationary belonged to a business or individual, but knowing Rose, she could've gotten into hot water with either.

The image on the card was highly suggestive.

Bathing didn't so much clear her head as amplify her bone-quaking anxiety.

How deep had her sister's addiction gone? Had Rose tangled with the wrong man or woman? Had she disobeyed the card's warning and gone back? What could she have possibly done to earn thousands of dollars in exchange for never setting foot in... Where...? A home, a business, someone's life?

Don't come back.

Had Benjamin known or found out? Or had he been completely in the dark like Holly?

What if the note had nothing to do with cocaine? Could Rose have been harboring another addiction?

Holly rubbed her eyes, her hot wet knuckles smearing her mascara, and when she lowered her hands into the pool, palms flush to porcelain, she challenged herself to mentally center, still her racing mind, and really see the bathroom around her and not the image of Rose trapped beneath ice. An image so like Holly's own face that it felt like a premonition.

Trills of steam wafting from the water, the white tiles lining the wall, her nephew smashing a plastic truck against one of the books she had picked out for him—she barely saw any of it.

Slinking out of the bath, water cascading off her every curve, she drew the towel around her and stepped out. She was careful to dry her hands before taking the card from the sink.

After checking in on Tucker, crouching and smoothing down the fine wisps of his strawberry-blonde hair and giving him a kiss, she made her way into the master bedroom.

The air was chilly and as soon as she let her towel drop, her skin prickled with gooseflesh. Standing over her duffel bag, which she had set on the carpet at the foot of the bed, she rummaged for a fresh pair of underwear, but her belongings were a nest of knotted garments.

Aggravated, she stood, grabbing her towel to cover herself, and doubled-back down the hallway to Rose's walk-in closet where the clothes were organized by garment—dresses with dresses, jeans with jeans, every section color-coded like a boutique. She put the unsettling card on Rose's vanity, having never parted with it, and decided on a pair of black, stretch jeans and a purple, cashmere sweater, both of which she draped over the back of the vanity chair.

When she pulled open the first dresser drawer, she found a wealth of bras and panties, but the styles didn't at all capture her sister. Exotic prints, flashy colors, and cheap materials seemed to be the theme. She began hunting through the options for something sensible, but the deeper she riffled, the racier the lingerie became.

It was bizarre. Rose would never have worn spandex, gaudy push-up bras, leopard print panties accented with rhinestones, or any of the other lingerie in this drawer. Across the board, she had dressed in designer wear and only the latest fashions. If a garment wasn't featured in Vogue magazine, then Rose hadn't worn it, period.

The card came to mind, its silhouette, the woman's suggestive pose.

Dressing quickly, she stepped into a pair of red, lacy panties, and pulling them over her hip bones, adjusted the thong. Next, she strapped on a cheetah print bra, which to her revulsion clasped in the front, and tried not to cringe when she glimpsed her reflection in the vanity mirror. As she slipped into her dead sister's jeans and sweater, she noticed they fit her well. She polished the ensemble off with a pair of high-heeled boots and a spritz of her sister's favorite perfume—Burberry Black. When she gave herself the once over in the mirror, she was relieved that the bra's print didn't show through the sweater's cashmere threads.

She looked exactly like Rose.

After fitting the card into her back pocket and grabbing her cell phone from the nightstand in the master bedroom, she brought Tucker down to the living room where her laptop computer was resting on the coffee table.

It was almost time for Dora the Explorer to start, so she flipped through the stations and adjusted the volume as soon as she had found the network.

Waking her laptop, she glanced at Tucker who was in the process of getting comfortable, lying on his stomach and shifting his little waist side to side.

When he seemed content, she opened Google on her laptop and placed her fingertips over the keyboard, racking her brain for what to plug into the search engine. The falling snow beyond her window instilled in her a crude sense of urgency.

She should text Mary Cole to see if she was available to come babysit, before the roads got really bad.

Decisively, she typed *Center Harbor, New Hampshire* into the search field, but couldn't come up with a differentiator. The woman's silhouette on the card conjured images of strip clubs and escort services in her mind, but neither were prevalent in this sleepy town. Then again, she wouldn't have thought designer drugs like cocaine were circulating either. They obviously were and they weren't terribly difficult to obtain.

So she tried her luck with both, typing *strip club* as well as *escort services* into the field. A list of articles filled the screen, but she ignored them, clicking on the Images tab, and began scrolling down the page, hunting for the voluptuous silhouette.

Suddenly, its likeness jumped out at her from the bottom of the screen. Black and rimmed with an edge of silver, the woman's form was identical in shape to that on the card which she had found with all that cash.

As she clicked the image, her skin bristled with a disturbing mix of longing and excitement, instantly intrigued she was one step closer to a world her sister might have embraced.

A website opened, purple filling the screen, black letters along the toolbar—*Diamonds*—the woman's silhouette softly lay behind it.

Perusing the home page, she gleaned Diamonds was an escort service located northwest on the border of Center Harbor and Plymouth where the

Daniel Webster Highway hooked around Squam Lake.

Had Rose been working there?

As Holly leaned back, staring out the window, Dora the Explorer arguing with her monkey, Boots, on the television, her nephew giggling uproariously in response, the revelation stunned her.

The cash, the garish lingerie, the distress in Rose's voice during that panicked phone call the night she had been murdered...

Her sister had been an *escort*?

But had it gotten her killed?

Had a domino effect crashed down on Benjamin afterwards that involved a perpetrator tying up loose ends?

Did it connect to the young woman who Holly had encountered—the last person to see Benjamin alive; and if so, how?

As Tucker plopped onto the couch beside her, she smacked the laptop closed and wriggled her cell phone out of her jeans.

Brushing Tucker's wispy hair, which possibly soothed her more than him—his head resting on her lap, the boy drifting off to sleep—she found Mary Cole's number in the call log and hit Send.

When the line opened up, she heard Mary ordering someone to quiet and the background laughter petered out.

Apprehensively, she asked, "Hi, Mary?"

"Yeah, texting is always better," she mentioned.

Holly glanced at the clock on the television set. "Did I catch you at a bad time?" It had been ages since she was in grade school and she wasn't sure if 2:45 pm meant the end of the day or the middle of last period.

"Don't worry about it, I just got out of class," she said off-handedly. "Do you need a sitter?"

"For a few hours. I know the roads are getting worse-"

"Hang on," she quipped, but Holly couldn't tell if the girl was speaking to her or to a friend. When she heard Mary's muted voice, hushed and urgent, she decided that the girl wasn't speaking to her. "I can come now. Text me the address."

As Holly assured her she would, she heard the girl in the background whispering questions—*How many hours?* and *Where's the house?* and *Do they have food?*—followed by the faint sounds of Mary slapping her off.

"See you soon," she said into the mouthpiece, then the phone went quiet and Holly realized the girl had hung up.

She was quick to text the address then, leaning back while cradling Tucker, she gently slipped her cell phone into her pocket.

Her nephew was conked out, but she managed to scoop him into her arms without waking him. After carrying him to his bed in the downstairs playroom and gently laying him on the blankets, she watched him for a beat and wondered if he would make it through his nap without having an accident. She had been avoiding diapers, training him to let her know when he needed the toilet, overseeing the task and helping him wipe thoroughly, offering him elaborate praise for being a big boy. But he might not have control over his bowels while asleep and the thought of him waking up soiled pained her so she made quick work of stripping him out of his pants, and fitting him under the blankets.

Wearing Rose's clothes, bathed in her sister's perfume, living in the house that had been her sister's home, tending to Rose's son in a manner she imagined was identical to her twin compelled Holly to rush from Tucker's room—high-heels tapping across carpet then clicking over hardwood floors as she rounded the living room and padded up the stairs.

When she reached the master bedroom, the eerie notion that she had slipped into Rose's life as easily as pulling on a robe was too strong to shake. Not only was she mirroring her dead twin, but she was also daring to investigate her sister's secret life, which could reveal aspects of Rose's personality she might not be able to handle.

Whether out of a need to embody another layer of her twin's psyche or to escape it, Holly grabbed a plastic bag of cocaine from the nightstand drawer, pinched out a bit of powder, and, placing her fingertips to her nostrils, sharply inhaled.

The hit stung her brain, awakening her senses, but not enough, so she took a bill from the cash envelope beside her revolver in the drawer, rolled it, and used her debit card to scrape the powder into a line after tapping a heap onto the table.

Leaning over the nightstand and angling the bill to her nostril, she snorted the line clean off the marble surface and when she straightened up, rubbing her nose and widening her eyes, she felt like she was buzzing, amped-up to barrel into Diamonds and demand answers.

The doorbell chimed, startling her.

How long had she been seated on the edge of the bed, envisioning her assault on the unknown man who had stolen Rose's life?

Bolting to her feet, she tucked her revolver down the back of her jeans, slapped the nightstand drawer shut, and walked briskly through the hallway and down the stairs, spilling into the foyer where the bell was chiming lazily again and again.

When she drew the door open, she was faced with a scraggly girl—bleached hair, stringy and falling at bedraggled angles onto her shoulders, sharp blue eyes intensely holding her gaze, eyebrows plucked into a pair of surprised arcs, reserved eagerness in her expression.

After inviting her in—Mary marveling her way through the foyer as if it were a museum—Holly noted the rusted-out Audi that had dropped her babysitter off, as it reversed in a careless arch before popping into First gear. Sunlight bounced off the windshield and the vehicle was puttering away before Holly had gotten any sense of the driver.

In the living room, Mary seemed to be appraising the furniture when Holly joined her. But she straightened up and began itemizing, "Emergency numbers, snacks, toys, rules, and special instructions," as though they were pressed for time.

"Well, you have my cell number," she said kindly, though the girl's militant approach slightly unnerved her. "If there really is an emergency, please call 911 first, of course. Kitchen's through there. And everything you'll need for Tucker is in here."

She led Mary into her nephew's playroom and tried not to feel embarrassed when the girl furrowed her brow at the crib.

"He's three?" she questioned, though quietly, respectful that the child was sleeping.

"He is," she said softly. "But he's a bit behind, developmentally speaking." She neared the girl as if confiding. "He still wears diapers when he naps."

She expected Mary to snort in judgment or at the very least cock her eyebrow, but the girl's gaze softened with understanding, as she nodded.

"I can do diapers," she said easily. "Where are the wet-wipes?"

Holly walked her through the supplies and their various hiding places, and soon Mary followed her into the foyer where Holly searched the closet and selected one of Rose's winter coats—a gray woolen walker with mink trim—all the while reiterating that she didn't expect to be gone for more than a few hours.

"I would prefer it if you kept downstairs," she added. "And please, no guests."

Mary looked her up and down, and an envious grin spread across her face. "You look like money."

The comment reminded Holly of her purse, which she had left on the kitchen table so she hurried through the house and snatched it, feeling strangely annoyed it wasn't her sister's.

Her wallet was tattered, she noticed, drawing it out of her cracked, faux-leather handbag as she returned. The bills inside looked fuzzy and faded, calling to mind how she had accidentally washed the thing a few weeks back, remembering her wallet only after the machine had run a full cycle.

Offering Mary a twenty, she said, "Keep him away from the lake. The ice isn't frozen over."

"This is more than a few hours-worth," she pointed out, tucking the bill into her jeans.

"We can work it out later. Thanks again," she said, stepping out and nearly slipping on the icy landing. These heels would be a trick to walk in.

When she reached her Saab, she didn't climb in behind the steering wheel, but rather stared at it, debating. Decisively, she stalked through the snow to her sister's BMW, fishing the car keys out of her purse, and climbed into the luxury vehicle.

At the end of the driveway, Holly pulled up the Diamonds website on her cell phone to memorize the address then took off.

The drive northwest seemed to happen without her, she was so deep in thought, though her trembling hands often anchored her back into reality.

Situated on the canal connecting Squam Lake to its twin, Little Squam, the three-story brick structure didn't look right, as she angled the BMW into an icy parking lot and rolled to a stop.

It was quite obviously an abandoned mill.

Holly counted twelve windows spanning the first floor, as snowfall quickly accumulated on the windshield. The glare from the sun made it impossible to tell whether or not any lights were on inside the building.

She would've driven off, chalking this excursion up to a lost cause, if there hadn't been a handful of vehicles scattered across the parking lot, their makes and models implying that those who came to the old mill had cash to burn. She spied a white Lexus and a black BMW that resembled the one she was driving except that its windows were darkly tinted. The other cars were parked too far away for Holly to guess their brands, but they boasted the same class.

The entrance was a set of double-doors, which she noticed were ajar. The door on the left was propped with a cement block.

Nervously and overcome with the craving that had been nagging at her the entire drive, Holly reasoned she would need a huge boost just to get out of her car and set foot in the building so she riffled through her purse for one of the drug baggies, tapped the white powder onto the crux of her hand, and aligned it with her nose, sniffing hard and wincing when the coke stung her brain.

A moment later, she stepped confidently out of her sister's BMW, though it wasn't lost on her this was insane. She should've given the envelope to Lucas, passed her theories on to him, and let the police handle this. But then again, she wasn't even sure of what exactly needed handling. Was her sister's killer inside? Or had the note, the cash, the embossed insignia of the escort service been nothing more than an unfortunate coincidence and not at all relevant to Rose and Benjamin's murders?

Her intuition extinguished all doubt and compelled her to place one heel in front of the other, as she gradually crossed the slick asphalt that was dusted with a thin layer of snow.

When she reached the propped door, drawing it open, she saw the first floor was an empty warehouse. Sunlight streamed in through the windows, but despite the glare, she noticed an alcove directly across from where she was standing.

Crossing towards it and keeping on the balls of her feet to soften the clicks of her heeled boots, she detected the faintest music, and when she reached the alcove where she noticed a set of stairs, she realized the music was coming from the floor above.

Jazz.

She ascended the stairs quickly, heels clicking against steel treads. As she rounded the landing, she came to a black door, the insignia of a woman's silhouette painted in purple across it.

Adrenaline flooded her veins and she couldn't stop her hands from shaking.

She took a few deep breaths that didn't help then nervously grasped her sister's necklace where it hung over her clavicle, feeling the cool, silver shape and grazing the pad of her index finger over the jagged opal. It didn't calm her, but was just the encouragement she needed to dig deep, push her anxiety down, and yank the door open.

The club was shabby. Roughly a dozen women dressed in lingerie as gaudy as the bras and panties that she had discovered in her sister's dresser, were lazing about, flaunting stiletto heels and holding cocktails.

The lounge was bathed in incandescent pink light that cast a rosy glow over the entire room—the white, leather booths and settees arranged haphazardly, white cubes positioned beside them, black wall-to-wall carpeting, and gauzy curtains draping from the lofty ceiling here and there to accent the decorum. None of it could distract from the overall dreary, stained quality.

The door slammed shut behind her and she flinched.

All eyes were suddenly on her.

Holly glanced from face to face, vaguely aware there was a bar at the side of the lounge, which she could easily escape to, flee from the laser glares of these women, whose expressions were shifting from disbelief to marked hostility—snorted laughs, raised brows, and pointed hatred.

One woman whose jet-black hair spilled over her lacey lingerie made a performance of setting her martini on the nearest white cube, sighing and standing as if she were about to speak for everyone. With an air of authority she advanced on Holly, swaying her hips and not at all shy about her virtual nudity. The thin strips of black lace over her chest and privates barely covered her.

"You've got some nerve," she hissed, grabbing Holly's arm so roughly that Holly wobbled, knocking back against the door.

"I'm not-"

"I thought we were clear on this," she cut in. "You got your money-"

"It was from you?" she asked confusedly, trying to free her arm. The woman wouldn't let go. "You wrote this note?"

Holly didn't get far scrambling for the note in her jeans. The other woman pulled her by the arm then shoved her towards a hallway that was past the bar.

As the woman prodded her onward, shoving and pulling her with brassy alternation, Holly realized they thought she was Rose, which meant the hooker who was now shoving her into an office believed her twin was alive and therefore couldn't have pulled the trigger.

But that didn't mean the man seated at the business side of the desk hadn't done it.

"Look who decided to show her pretty face," she barked, pushing Holly deeper into the office. "Ron, you guaranteed us that she wouldn't come back."

Releasing her, the hooker began pacing like a pent-in bull, as Ron placed his telephone in its cradle on the desk. Ron had the unremarkable quality of an automotive mechanic yet wasn't dressed for the part. Instead, he was wearing what looked like a mobster's suit, as though his life was a poorly planned Halloween party. He widened his deep-set eyes at Holly in such a way that told her that he also assumed she was her twin.

He looked shocked.

And he was doing a poor job of tempering his reaction. He straightened the knot of his emerald tie where it sat flush against his starched, black dress shirt. Pulling himself together, it seemed.

"Leave us," he ordered the other woman without a trace of the clunky New England accent that Holly had expected. The woman gaped in astonishment and threw her hands up, but Ron merely flicked his fingers and she buttoned up her objections and left the room, closing the door without another word.

Alone with him, Holly's heart started punching up her throat.

He pressed a button on his desk phone and spoke loudly in what sounded like Russian then leaned back in his chair with an air of amusement, grinning at her as if he had conquered his shock.

"What are you doing here?" He clasped his fingers together over his taut stomach and tilted his head as if waiting for a child to respond.

Confrontational, she stated, "You're dead to me," quoting the note to provoke him into taking responsibility.

He shot a friendly nod towards her, adding, "And don't come back. Yet here you are. Why?"

Though she sensed her tone would waver badly, she demanded, "What did I do that was so awful?"

His dark eyes flared.

Gradually, he stood, coming into his full height, which was alarmingly taller than she would've guessed. Then, as if a flip had switched, he charged at her, rounding the desk and advancing.

She couldn't back up fast enough. Her shoulder blades slammed against the door behind her. He grabbed her face with one meaty hand, seething and angling over her.

"What did *you* do?" he challenged, spitting each word through his teeth. Then, raging, he screamed, "Is this a joke? You want me to tell you what you did? You know what I'm talking about!"

With his hand squeezing her cheeks together she didn't have a prayer of explaining or pleading that she wasn't Rose. Why the hell did she think she could play this off, and waltz in as her sister?

Another spike of adrenaline rushed through her veins, but fight or flight didn't kick in. Her muscles felt like stone. She was petrified and the revolver tucked down her jeans might as well have been a million miles away.

Trading her face for her throat, his hand clamped tightly, cutting off her air supply, as he whipped a gun to her chin, metal pressing hard against her jaw.

Holly whimpered.

Terrified, she breathed, "I'm not who you think I am," but the look on his face—his brows rising and his mouth curling into an insulted snarl—told her that Ron assumed she was speaking metaphorically.

Before she could clarify to save her skin, he warned, "If you come here again, I won't make the same mistake."

He glanced down the length of her, squeezing her throat, then tossed her aside and tucked his weapon down his waistband, pacing away.

Jolting at the opportunity, she threw the door open, barreled down the hallway, a fresh surge of adrenaline flooding her veins so fiercely she thought she might faint before she reached her car.

After spilling through the lounge—hookers glaring and snorting good riddance—she careened into the black door and didn't breathe until she was in the stairwell. She let out a shuddering cry, keeling over, her eyes misting with tears in delayed reaction to having almost gotten herself killed.

She muffled her sobs, pushing on, running down the stairs then through the warehouse and tumbling out into the blinding afternoon.

How could Rose have gotten involved with a place like that, with a horrible man like that?

Her skin was crawling as she walked briskly through the blizzard-type snowfall to Rose's BMW, her thoughts turning towards her nephew. She could curl up beside him in his crib and sleep forever.

Or could she?

The thought of being in that house, wearing Rose's clothes, and continuing to live this life she had never asked for, sickened her. Bile stung the back of her throat, but she swallowed hard, climbing in behind the steering wheel.

Maybe she would pack up Tucker's things, gathering only the essentials, move him into her modest house on the lake, and leave the memory of her sister behind in that estate.

She resolved to call Lucas as soon as she got Tucker situated at her house, her real home. Then and only then would she explain to him Rose's involvement with Diamonds and the man named Ron who had likely killed her.

As she swung out of the parking lot, she immediately recognized the incoming vehicle—a beat-up Audi. It was the one that had dropped Mary Cole off at the house. She slammed on the brakes, eyeing the driver.

Piercing, cat-like eyes stared back at her, but the girl stepped on the gas, because the Audi lurched, tearing through the parking lot.

But Holly had gotten a good look at the young woman, who was unmistakably Benjamin's mistress, the one she had seen in his hotel room.

Bracing the headrest and angling her gaze through the rear windshield, Holly spied the young woman slamming her car door shut. Teetering on chunky heels, her legs long and bare, she made her careful way towards the entrance doors where she vanished inside.

Holly was reeling.

Mary Cole was friends with the girl.

The girl worked at the same escort service as Rose.

Had the girl known Rose?

Had Benjamin discovered his mistress and wife were moonlighting at the same seedy establishment?

Dizzying revelations complicated the finest thread of logic, which she had only just barely started to grasp, gripped Holly with mind-bending anxiety.

Resolving once again to contact Lucas was all she could do to stop herself from sinking further into mental quicksand.

She pressed the accelerator, easing onto the road.

Hovering around forty miles per hour along the Daniel Webster Highway, she drove over black-ice, snowdrifts, and pools of slush so broad that she hydroplaned twice—gripping the steering wheel tightly and latching onto thoughts of Tucker so her mind wouldn't split apart.

Dusk fell, as she veered off the highway, coming behind a salt truck that was crawling along Newman Road.

Four miles later, she turned up her sister's driveway and killed the engine after coming to a stop as close to the front door as possible, unable to contain how eager she was to hug Tucker.

Stalking through the snow, it took a moment to find her house key and as she fit it into the lock, having ascended the front steps, the door pushed inward on its own.

The door was ajar?

"I'm home," she called out, edging through the foyer and peering into the living room where the television was playing a Disney movie, though muted. "Mary?"

She shrugged her coat off and draped it over the couch, scanning the kitchen—marble countertops, closed cupboards, an organized dish rack, wind howling beyond the window, everything as it was.

But Mary wasn't there.

Tearing down the hallway, Tucker's playroom came into view—the dresser, toys scattered across the carpet, his crib...

He wasn't there.

Her chest broke out into a cold sweat, intuition taking hold and pitching her into dark unease. Her heart began punching against her ribs and she felt suddenly light-headed as she started back, not walking, but running to the stairs where she grasped the banister. She launched herself up the treads, taking them two at a time and caught a flash of her reflection in the mirror when she reached the landing—her eyes dark and fearful, cheeks gaunt, her face long and pale, aged by the epiphany she should've never left her nephew with a stranger.

She barreled down the hallway but halted when Mary stepped out of the master bedroom. Her stark blue eyes were white all round, her crescent brows flattened, her mouth a stunned oval, teeth parting as if in shock. She braced the wall as though she might collapse and when she finally met Holly's gaze, she began slowly shaking her head.

Dazed, her finger pointing unsteadily in no particular direction though it seemed to anchor the thought she was forming, she breathed, "We were downstairs..."

Nearing her, taking her by the shoulders, Holly insisted, "Where's Tucker?"

"I don't know," she said, her voice like wind over reeds. "I went to the bathroom and when I got out, he wasn't on the couch."

"What are you telling me?" she demanded.

"He's gone."

Holly paced away and plowed her fingers through her hair, her mind racing so fast she couldn't think straight. Again, she grabbed the girl's shoulders, forcing eye contact.

"When?" She shook her. "When did this happen?"

Remorseful, Mary admitted, "Maybe a half hour after you left."

"And you didn't call me?" she shrieked and the girl cowered, hanging her head.

"I thought he was hiding, playing a game or something," she pleaded. "You weren't gone that long."

"An hour," she asserted, planting her fists on her hips and pacing away again as if distancing herself from Mary would prevent her from killing the girl.

There was no use trying to compose herself. She was beyond panic, rising into full-blown horror.

"I didn't realize how long I was hunting around for him," she explained, scrambling through excuses. "It's a big house and I checked every room. I ran outside, scanned the perimeter. I looked everywhere and before I knew it you were back."

"Stop," Holly snapped, as she pulled her cell phone out of her pocket. She found the number for the precinct then thought better of it and dialed 911 instead. Her lips were trembling badly, but she relayed the emergency to the operator and recited the address, straining to keep her shaky voice steady. When she hung up, she couldn't look at Mary, but said, "The front door wasn't locked."

"I didn't even check it," she replied as if that made her innocent.

Holly couldn't deny that she shared the blame. She hadn't locked the door either or at least she couldn't recall doing so.

Her legs felt like rubber as she crossed the hallway and rounded the landing, vaguely aware that Mary was trailing sheepishly after her.

When she reached the bottom of the stairs, she let out a carefully measured breath and ran both hands down her face.

In the living room, she sat on the couch, her eyes glazing over, stupefied.

Mary edged into the room, wringing her hands. She dropped into the adjacent sofa-chair, and stared at Holly.

"You were in the bathroom?" she asked, trying to wrap her head around the unfathomable—how an intruder could have possibly darted into the house and snatched her nephew.

Air escaped between Mary's teeth and Holly realized it was a *Yes*.

"How long were you in there?"

"Five minutes-"

"And you didn't hear anything?" she demanded, glaring at the girl now that she could stomach looking at her.

Reluctantly, she confessed, "I was upstairs." As Holly absorbed the detail, Mary added, "I may have gotten sidetracked when I got out of the bathroom." She hesitated a beat, gauging Holly's reaction, and then quickly blurted out, "He wasn't alone for more than twenty minutes-"

"He shouldn't have been left alone at all," she stated, irate that the girl had the audacity to defend herself.

Shifting in the chair and squaring her shoulders at Holly, she argued, "You think I could've prevented this? Fought someone off? What if they shot me like they shot your sister or that guy?"

Holly remembered Ron's curt, Russian conversation, and connected dots that she couldn't be certain were there. But just as she was beginning to comprehend the detail the doorbell chimed followed by pounding on the front door.

Mary stood, but didn't rush off to answer it. Instead, she angled over Holly in an invasive manner, catching her off guard. "I know what you're keeping in the drawer of your bedside table."

Staring up at the girl with abject horror, she said, "You're threatening me?"

The girl straightened her back, her drawn-on eyebrows rising, as a police officer shouted, "Got a call, Holly, open up!"

"I'm not threatening you," she said easily. "Just making sure we're on the same page. You should hide your drugs better." As she crossed to the door, she told Holly over her shoulder, "I mean, you should hide your drugs better *right now*."

Mary crossed the foyer, opened the front door, and greeted the police officers, thanking them for coming.

Holly tended to the matter quickly, using urgent strides until she reached the second floor landing where she immediately tore down the hallway, grabbed the drug baggie out of the nightstand drawer, and rushed to the trunk in her sister's walk-in closet, all the while disturbed that Mary had not only discovered her burgeoning cocaine habit but seemed invested in keeping it secret.

After planting the baggie at the very bottom of the trunk and shoving it into place beneath the hanging dresses, she made her way down to the living room where two police officers, as well as Lucas, Cody, and a woman with dark, wavy hair were all angled around Mary.

As she neared them, her high-heeled boots clicked on the wooden floor, which drew their attention.

Approaching her, Lucas asked with grave concern, "Tucker's missing?"

On the brink of tears, she said, "What the hell is going on?" She realized she had grabbed his arm so she clasped her hands together.

"Let's start from the beginning," he calmly suggested. "Where were you?"

She realized he was assuming she had been here, so she shook her head. "Ask Mary."

Hearing her name, the girl flicked her piercing blue eyes at Holly and a trace of intimacy shined through as though she was hinting at their shared secret. It was unnerving.

But Mary quickly launched into the facts, giving her statement, while one of the officers scratched his pen over a report form, struggling to keep up with her account.

Holly watched them for a beat then discretely turned to Lucas. "I need to talk to you."

Interrupting their privacy, an officer approached Lucas and addressed him in a low tone. "I've got an Amber Alert out, but she should get a photo of Tucker for us to use."

In immediate response, Holly padded down the hallway, making a beeline for Tucker's playroom where she recalled seeing a number of framed photos resting on top of the dresser.

She chose one of Tucker beaming a toothy grin, his lips curled and eyes bright, sand blowing from his fists as he sat on the shore, then realized Lucas had followed her in.

Nearing her, he quietly asked, "What did you want to talk to me about?" He gently touched the small of her back where she kept her revolver.

Uncomfortably shifting, taking a step back so he wouldn't discover her weapon, she told him, "I'll tell you after everyone's gone."

His head tilted, brow furrowing, his curiosity piqued.

"I could tell everyone out there," she mentioned, offering him the framed photo as a means to urge him back, but he neither took it nor allowed her space. "But I would prefer to speak with you alone."

Agreeing, he whispered, "Okay," but began clenching his jaw as if waiting might kill him.

Without engaging him further, she hurried into the living room where Cody took the photo from her, glimpsed at it, and immediately passed it to one of the officers whose badge read *Gibbs*.

"We'll find him," Cody assured her, placing his hand on her shoulder and giving her a squeeze.

His kindness caused her to fall apart.

She choked down a sob, burying her face in her hands for a long moment, and when she lifted her head up, her vision was blurred with tears, but noticed the woman who had seemed familiar with Cody and Mary was offering her a sympathetic smile.

"Cody will find him," she said, affirming the detective's assurance. "He's the best when it comes to finding people."

Cody nodded affirmatively.

"I'm Hannah," she said, finally introducing herself. "Mary's sister."

Groaning, the girl corrected her from the sidelines. "Half-sister."

Addressing Hannah, Cody suggested, "Why don't you take her home while I finish up here?"

As Hannah hooked her arm around Mary's shoulder, shepherding the girl to the foyer, Holly asked, "Are you guys going to have to search through everything again? Should I go home, I mean to my real house?"

That prompted Cody to ask, "Is anything missing here?"

She shook her head, though she had no idea. She hadn't looked around.

Lucas was approaching from the hallway, but only to wave the officers over.

"I wouldn't recommend staying here at all," he said finally. "This house isn't safe if our perp is coming and going as he pleases. But we won't be too long. Just need to dust for prints, be thorough," he explained in a firm tone as if giving weight to the seriousness of the crime. Then his mood grew personal, his tone softening, and his eyebrows arching understandingly. "I'm so sorry this is happening to you." Holly began fidgeting with the hem of her sleeve, willing herself not to cry again. "I don't want you to beat yourself up for leaving him with Mary."

She let out a laugh, which caused her tears to spring. "I already am."

Lucas returned, as Cody guided her to the couch. She sat, her gaze locking on the snowfall outside where the bright flood lights lit up the porch, the backyard beyond it in darkness. The magnitude of Tucker's abduction was hitting her. She felt sick. She felt like a bad aunt and a terrible makeshift mother. A walking disaster.

She barely heard Lucas explaining to his partner that the officers were dusting the playroom for fingerprints. Their voices twisted into incoherent mumbling, though she caught Lucas offering to finish up here—*Go on home to Mary, she's going to need you, she's probably a wreck*. His response was a resounding, *No*.

Maybe she should tell both of them about Diamonds. Maybe she would have to. But she didn't trust Cody, not after his scheming display at the precinct, coaxing her into offering up her whereabouts, alibis that didn't exist. She wasn't sure she could trust Lucas either, but her reasons for that were entirely different.

Deciding that she would stick to the events of today and nothing further so as not to slip up with an accidental contradiction, she piped up, interrupting their hushed conversation. "I would like to tell you what I know now."

The detectives paused. She could feel their eyes burning into the back of her head and when she glanced over her shoulder at Lucas, the men quickly rounded either side of the couch.

She flipped her laptop open and refreshed the Diamonds homepage. "Please," she said, indicating they should have a seat. Mentally, she weighed the pros and cons of mentioning the envelope and decided doing so wouldn't be detrimental to maintaining her innocence, not like admitting she had been in Benjamin's hotel room would be.

Cody scanned the screen, reading out loud, "Diamonds."

"It's an escort service," she explained. "I found a note written to Rose that was embossed with this logo."

She pointed to the silhouette of the woman and Lucas stiffened beside her. Unless she was mistaken, she thought he had stopped breathing.

"I went there today, which is why I needed Mary to watch Tucker," she went on, producing the note from her jeans. Cody took it, and after studying it carefully, he passed it to his partner. "Everyone thought I was Rose."

"You're dead to me," Lucas read.

As a qualifier, Holly mentioned, "It was in an envelope full of cash. I think Rose was working there." She grimaced. Stating it outright left a bitter taste in her mouth. "A man named Ron seems to run the place," she continued, meeting Lucas's gaze. "He admitted he wrote the note and..." It was like she was back in that office again. Her pulse quickened. "I know you won't think it's evidence but when I stepped in that man's office, he went pale like he was seeing a ghost. I think he killed them."

"Okay," said Cody, absorbing the information. When she glanced at him, Holly could almost see his mind working—his eyes shifting over the screen, his jaw clenching.

"Before I left, he threatened me, thinking I was Rose. He also placed a very brief phone call—in Russian, I think." She locked eyes with Cody for emphasis. "I think he ordered the kidnapping. I think that's what that call was about."

"We'll talk to him," Cody assured her, determined. "This is good, Holly. This is solid."

Lucas was leaning towards the screen. He took command of the mouse pad, scrolling over the toolbar, and then clicked on the tab for *Girls*.

The screen filled with a grid of black squares, each with the Diamonds logo, each with an exotic sounding name written in cursive—Letitia, Gisele, Sonia, and the list went on.

Interested, Cody took over the mouse pad and clicked on the first name and the photo of a young woman filled the screen.

Wearing nothing but black lace, the girl in the photo looked like she was in complete command of her sexuality.

"Damn," said Cody. "They should call it Barely Legal."

Lucas said nothing and when she discretely angled her gaze to him, he seemed off, like he was deeply rattled. Sweat was beading across his forehead.

Cody clicked through a few more names and more photos filled the screen. He was searching for Rose's image to confirm Holly's statement.

A moment later, both of the detectives gasped.

Holly stared at the screen in disbelief.

Were her eyes playing tricks on her?

Or was the girl in the photo that had filled the screen none other than Mary Cole?

CHAPTER ELEVEN

MARY COULD HEAR them—muffled, overlapping voices, rising and falling in concerned waves downstairs. There was no way to make out what Hannah and Cody were saying, not with the ragged wind pinging sleet against the window.

Mary's bedroom looked how she felt—wasted.

The dresser was topped with an array of CDs, loose tissues and q-tips, old makeup containers leaving trails of pink and charcoal dust. The drawers were open and drooping, clothes billowing out as if trying to escape. Her gaze floated distractedly across the floor—textbooks and school binders lain awkwardly over crumpled jeans, USB and headphone cords tangled, the carpet beneath matted and stained though it had been brand new when she had first moved in.

Mary felt suddenly dizzy so she tucked her knees to her chin, shifting where she sat on her bed, and leaned her forehead against the cold windowpane.

It was too dark outside to get lost in the scenery, but she had it memorized—the naked maples, snow tracing every bent branch, the particular slope of the backyard, and cattails brown as death shooting up from the frozen shore. She could see it all despite her own reflection on the glass. And as she envisioned each detail, she willed herself to sober up.

Taking bump after bump of Holly's cocaine had been a mistake.

She hadn't been in the upstairs bathroom for ten minutes, but rather in the master bedroom, seated on the edge of the bed for far too long.

It had only been a guess. Rose had had dozens of hiding places and the nightstand drawer hadn't been one of them, but Mary had gotten lucky, or rather Roberta had. Her friend had called her and convinced her to hunt around upstairs. Mary had argued that they still had plenty—*Why look for drugs? We're set.* But when she saw the plump bag resting in the drawer, she was glad Roberta had coaxed her.

The last thing she felt now was glad.

What the hell happened to Tucker?

Downstairs, Cody raised his voice, something about grounding Mary that she didn't catch entirely, but Hannah's cutting response came high-pitched and clear as a bell—"You want to punish her?"

Cody stomped his way up the stairs and Hannah trailed after him with light, pattering footfall.

Expectantly, Mary stared at her bedroom door, its profound absence of a lock, the tattered Kanye West poster peeling off of it, corners curling where she hadn't taped them down.

Hoping like hell he would continue on down the hallway—she wouldn't survive a long-winded lecture—she glanced at her purse beside her. The faux-leather flap wasn't flush, but arching backwards against a pillow, leaving the pinch of blow she had stolen in plain view. Mary had scrambled for a tissue, tapped a pinch of Holly's cocaine into it, and had pocketed it madly in that bedroom. She made quick work of stuffing the purse under the comforter and covering the lump with a pillow just as Cody rapped his knuckles on the door.

"Mary?" he asked, sounding gentle and kind.

She didn't trust it.

"Studying," she called out, as she swiped her Algebra II textbook off the floor and returned to the bed with a hop.

It wasn't until the door cracked open that she realized the book was upside down in her lap.

Cody edged into the room, taking shallow steps and avoiding a pile of sweaters as well as her gaze. His brows were knit tightly together and the particular bend of his mouth was a look she hadn't seen on him before.

Angling in, Hannah folded her arms, her head tilting with a hint of sympathy, her blue eyes wide and discerning. "We would like to talk to you about what happened and make sure you're okay."

Cody's expression hardened as he finally looked at her, planting his fists on his hips. Whatever was weighing heavily on his mind, Mary got the feeling he hadn't clued Hannah in.

"I'm okay," she said, but realized she had sounded too relaxed. Her sister's eyebrows shot up as if no one in their right mind would be okay if in Mary's position, so she quickly revised her answer. "I didn't even know someone had gotten into the house. I didn't hear a thing."

"Can I have a word with her alone?" he asked Hannah.

"You guys can't ground me," she blurted out. "I didn't do anything wrong."

Though kindly, Hannah asserted, "For the time being it would be best for you to stay here at the house if you're not at school." Before Mary could object, she added, "Only until Cody catches whoever did this."

"So, I can't see my friends?" she complained, emphasizing the injustice.

"They can come here," she suggested, but Cody snapped his eyes to her as though it might not be so cut and dry. Meeting him halfway, Hannah said, "As long as one of us is home."

Mary didn't have it in her to argue. She felt sweat beading across her hairline. Her face felt hot. She hoped her cheeks weren't beet-red. "You shouldn't have asked me to babysit."

She was looking at the socks on her feet and Hannah had to fight to get her attention. When she had it, she said, "Mary, what happened wasn't your fault."

The look on Cody's face seemed to contradict that statement, but she nodded, demonstrating that she was willing to forgive herself.

Cody breathed, "May I?"

Hannah shot back, "She already spoke with the police. What other questions could you possibly have? I don't want her sitting here all night blaming herself after you treat her like a criminal."

"I wouldn't do that. Please." He was holding her arm, leaning into her ear, and as he spoke softly, Mary got the distinct impression his long-ago suspicion of her was re-emerging—messages scrawled in dirt, handwritten instructions, *Ask Mary* in connection with her mother's abduction, body parts surfacing, Mary turning a revolver against her own thigh and pulling the trigger, all evidence of her guilt.

She hadn't done it then, hadn't butchered her own mother in a twisted effort to bring God into the devil's house, and she hadn't taken Tucker.

But though Cody had come to understand her innocence concerning the Hermit Lake Tragedy, she sensed he wouldn't believe her now.

Hannah urged him back, her expression a patient mix of disappointment and confusion, but when he widened the door for her to excuse herself, she relented, offering Mary a brittle smile before stepping into the hallway.

As Cody closed the door, it felt like all the air was rushing out of the room.

Gently, he nudged clothes aside with his socked feet, making his way to her messy desk where he removed a pile of magazines from the chair, set them on a precarious stack of novels and pen boxes, and sat.

Clearing his throat, he seemed to struggle with how to begin. "You can start seeing Judy again if you like."

He had to be kidding. Mary had gone through months of therapy with Judy St. Claire, slogging through one-on-one sessions as well as joint sessions with her mother, but all that had ended once Cody began bouncing the family from town to town as though his career was more important than her mental health. Her mother, Kendra hadn't been able to keep up and eventually moved back to Sanbornton, choosing Judy over all of her daughters. As far as Mary could tell, the red carpet Cody had rolled out for them was fast retracted the second he had won Hannah's heart.

Whatever he was getting at with this offer wasn't for Mary's benefit, but his own.

"I don't want that," she said in a small voice. "My friends are all I need."

His question sounded more like a statement. "Roberta?"

"You have a problem with Roberta?" she challenged, dragging her algebra book off her lap and resting it on the bunched up comforter beside her so she could draw her knees to her chin as she leaned against the wall.

Cody rolled his chair a few inches forward to compensate, and planted his elbows on his knees.

She felt examined.

"I don't want you spending time with her anymore."

"Why?"

He narrowed his eyes, studying her, and for an anxious moment she thought he might detect her cocaine high. "She's a bad influence."

Mary snorted a weak laugh and shook her head. "I'm not giving her up. She gets me."

"Judy gets you," he countered.

"No, Judy analyzes me and recites psyche verbatim when the moment calls for it. Roberta knows the *real* me."

"I know how smart you are," he said frankly, his tone indicating a jump in topics.

Thrown, she decided to play dumb. "Is this about my grades?"

She was met with silence. Cody studied her, and she knew he wasn't going to let her get away with the innocent act she had mastered.

From out of nowhere he stated, "Roberta works at a place called Diamonds."

Stunned—*how the hell did he know?*—her heart started punching in her chest. She didn't blink, terrified that he would take the slightest movement as confirmation. Gradually, she told him, "Roberta works at a pizzeria called Tony's."

"She works at an escort service," he shot back.

In desperate hope of ending the conversation, she launched into a performance of shocked confusion. She conjured tears, as well, sticking to her *I'm innocent* routine. "I had no idea. You're right. She's a bad influence." His face wasn't softening like it should be, so she kept blathering on. "Seeing Judy might be a good idea. I can go after school. Maybe tomorrow?"

"Maybe," he allowed, but his tone had deepened as though he knew he had successfully cornered her. Setting the stage, he insisted, "Please don't use your intelligence to lie to me."

"I'm not."

He cut in with, "Stop."

A bead of sweat rolled down her neck, but she was too scared to blot it. She swallowed instead, wishing her mouth hadn't gone dry.

"I'm not going to be punitive," he began leveling with her. "I'm not going to assert tough love or walk you through the jail cells at the precinct so that the meth-heads and hookers can horrify you into acting your age. I also haven't told Hannah and I might be willing to keep it that way if you work with me."

Realizing she had been biting her lower lip, she pressed her mouth into a thin line.

"I saw the Diamonds website," he went on and the implication landed like a fist to her gut.

She wasn't merely in too deep because she had been stealing away to the lounge and running wild with extravagant, mysterious men, relishing their attention and the thrill of living a secret. The fact Cody had found out meant that he knew Rose Wythe had worked there, and he assumed that Mary would have insight as to who killed her. If he didn't know how Benjamin fit in, he soon would.

Her voice was a thread. "Please don't tell Hannah."

He exhaled loudly as though he couldn't make any promises. "You're not going back there. You're not leaving this house except to go to school. If I see any sign you've snuck off, I will tell her. But I'll only make this deal with you if you answer my questions."

"No."

He stared at her, astonished.

Though she was uncertain of her friend's involvement—she had lain awake at night puzzling over the dark affair that she had never been able to make sense of, choosing time and again to believe Roberta incapable of murder—doubts shadowed her thoughts. She knew she couldn't tell him anything without incriminating Roberta and that was something she refused to do.

"Do you understand that two people have been killed?" He took a moment to temper his anger and when he continued, he spoke so firmly that her hands began trembling. "You knew Rose Wythe to some degree, because you worked with her at Diamonds. Her son was taken while you were supposed to be watching him." He let out a rocky breath. "Mary, I know you. I know you're a good person. You didn't kill or or take the boy. That's not where I'm going with this. But I think you know a hell of a lot and I need you to start talking."

Stonewalling him, she shrugged. "All I can tell you is I'm a cliché. The sexually abused seek out sexual scenarios. It's very sad. I went to Diamonds for my own reasons. I am what I am."

"Don't give me that. You can't pin this on your past."

"What do you think I'm going to tell you?" she asked impatiently, her tone a bit biting even for her taste. "You think I know who killed Rose?"

"Who was she friendly with there? Who disliked her? Did she get into any fights?"

Mary snorted a laugh. "I have no idea."

Rolling towards her in his chair and cursing when the wheels got stuck on a tee shirt, Cody jabbed his finger to underscore his point. "Rose was paid off. That club gave her thousands of dollars not to come back and I need to know why."

"Roberta and I are at the bottom of the food chain," she insisted. "I can't tell you what I don't know."

"You know something. I can see it in your eyes." When she said nothing, he asked, "Did you like Rose?"

The question disarmed her and she was suddenly dying to answer him. She hadn't talked about Rose since the murder. Roberta had shut down the few attempts that Mary had made. The hard and fast truth was that she had liked Rose. She had even loved her. But she loved Roberta more and couldn't open that vault. Not without a hell of a lot of help.

She angled her stark blue eyes up at him, her lip curling. "I feel like having a beer."

Skeptically, he cocked his brow. "You're going to tell me everything for one beer?"

"I would bring the case, if I were you."

He seemed reluctant to get to his feet and glanced over his shoulder at her several times on his way to the door. As he wrapped his hand around the knob he pointed out, "You have school tomorrow."

"We both have something the other wants. Don't give me a reason not to talk."

Heaving a deep, apprehensive breath, he opened the door and told her this better be worth it.

As soon as she heard him padding down the hallway, she urgently scrambled for her cell phone, tossing the pillows off the bed, throwing the comforter aside, and hunting through her purse.

She found Roberta's number in her cell as quickly as possible, tapping the text message app, opening the thread she kept with her best friend, and hitting the Send icon.

Her stomach bottomed out after three rings and when Roberta's outgoing message blared in her ear instead of her friend's melodic voice, panic surged through Mary's veins like ice water.

Quietly, she rushed through her message. "He knows. Cody wants me to tell him everything. Why the hell aren't you picking up?" She groaned and concluded the call with, "You have to come up with something. Tell Ron... I don't know... this is going to blow back on us badly."

Hanging up, a swell of dread overwhelmed her, but she snapped out of it the second she heard Cody approaching the door. She tucked her cell phone into her purse and threw the comforter over it, as he rounded into her bedroom, his arms cradling a case of Miller Light.

She was impressed that he had brought the whole case like she had asked. Getting past Hannah had probably been a trick to pull off.

He eased the door shut with his elbow and high-stepped over her nest of clothes. As he slid the case onto her desk, the stack of magazines toppled to the floor and he muttered, *Damn.*

"No games," he warned, cracking the lid off one of the bottles and handing it to her.

Eagerly, she chugged the beer, tipping her head back and catching the drips from the corners of her mouth.

She caught him uttering, *Unbelievable,* and quickly set the bottle between her legs in response.

As soon as he settled in the chair, he said, "Let's not waste time."

"You don't want one?"

"Everything you know about Rose... conversations, arguments, start talking."

"I don't want to go to the station. I don't want to make a statement."

Asserting the condition had only piqued his interest.

She slugged the rest of the bottle, drinking it in record time, and then held her hand out, ready for her second. He looked alarmed, but cracked open another beer. The alcohol was offsetting the coke in her system so when he handed her the cold one, she didn't hesitate to chug it.

Setting the bottle between her legs, she reiterated, "Promise me you won't make me go to the police station."

"You have to trust me."

His ambiguity made her nervous, but she wrestled the feeling down into the pit of her stomach and poured beer on it.

"Roberta and I were hanging out at Proctor Preserve near the lake, just chilling and trying to talk to guys. This was right after the school year started."

She studied his reaction for a beat—the flexing cheeks, the narrowing eyes—which told her he didn't like straining to figure out how this connected to Rose Wythe.

"It matters because we didn't meet Rose first," she offered, not quite ready to come out with it.

"Who did you meet first?" he asked, prodding her along.

"Roberta saw a flashy car pull into the parking lot and it stole her attention. Her eyes were glued to the man stepping out of it. I knew she was going to talk to him, or try to. She always thought the senior boys were a waste of time, like she would entertain herself with them if no one better was around."

"Who was the man?" he asked impatiently.

It was difficult to get the name out, but she made herself say, "Benjamin."

Immediately, Cody pitched forward in his chair. She had never seen him so poised, and the thrilled glint in his eyes had her feeling suddenly self-conscious.

When she still hadn't elaborated, he asked, "She talked to Benjamin?"

"She didn't have to. He approached us. At first he seemed guarded and I thought he was going to try to sell us dope or coke or something. He looked slick like that, but also boyish. But then I noticed his tie was all crooked and loose around his collar. He looked, I don't know, like he was coming apart at the seams."

Drinking more beer, she reminded herself to omit Roberta as much as possible from the story.

"If you really want to know," she went on, but paused to get some air in her lungs. "It was like Benji could tell what Roberta wanted, like he could read her face or something. He didn't really look at me so much. He basically implied he was into her, you know, because she clearly wanted him. But he said he needed a favor."

Catching on, he guessed, "Benjamin put you guys up to working at Diamonds?"

"It's not his place, Diamonds. He doesn't work there or anything," she corrected. "He suspected that Rose was working there. He wanted us—or Roberta really and then she dragged me along—to try to get into the place and confirm his wife hung out there. You know, spy on her." Skipping over the parts where Roberta had engaged in an illustrious affair with the man, so that Cody wouldn't discover Roberta had been with Benjamin the night of his murder, Mary shifted gears. "I got to know Rose a little bit. She was tough, but so protective of us. Look," she said abruptly. "I didn't have to do what I did there. I didn't have to stay or keep going back. But I liked it."

She couldn't even look at him, she was so filled with shame.

As if to assure her that he wasn't judging, Cody placed his hand on her foot, but it only made the moment more awkward. Shying away, he said, "You don't have to grow up so fast."

She smiled but it felt like a grimace.

"We told Benji that Rose worked there," she went on. "And that was that, kind of."

"So you didn't see him again?"

Melding lies with the truth, she offered, "I saw him around."

"Was Rose a business partner at the club?"

Drinking more to work up the nerve—this was the question she didn't want to have to answer—Mary avoided eye contact and racked her brain for alternative versions of the truth.

But there weren't any.

Finally, she admitted, "Rose wasn't like the rest of the girls. She didn't have the same deal. The club takes fifty percent of whatever you make. You have to cash out after each shift. But Rose never cashed out. She was kind of paying rent to be there in a sense, but never disclosing what she pulled in."

"Why would she get a better deal?"

"I'm not sure it was better," she countered, lifting the bottle to her lips. She tipped it up, pouring beer down her throat.

"Do you know why she was paid off and kicked out?"

Cody cracked a beer open for himself, perhaps getting comfortable in case the conversation stretched into the wee hours.

Closing her eyes, she breathed, "Christ," and chugged the rest of her beer.

Cody was ready on the quick with her third, but she reached for it slowly, anything to buy time.

She gritted her teeth then blurted out, "It was because of one of her clients." Studying his reaction for signs she wouldn't have to divulge more, she drank and drank and drank then relented. "The owner didn't like the client. I'm not being clear." She sighed out a frustrated groan. "Rose wasn't paid off. She had pre-paid a ton of money on rent. The only way to get her to leave was to reimburse her, but Ron didn't have it. He had already spent it on, hell I don't know. So he convinced the girls to come up with the cash, which made them hate Rose. It was a Goddamn mess."

"Why would the girls do that? Why would they care if Rose stayed?"

"Because," she said, exasperated. "Everyone was scared of Rose's client." She really didn't want to have to go there and continue down this road so she straightened her shoulders and stretched her legs off the side of the bed. "If you want my take on Ron…"

"I do," he assured her.

For a moment Mary receded into deep thought, seeing Ron's face in her mind, the spit that had formed in the corners of his mouth, and his red face as he had raged through the lounge. Finally, she said, "He probably killed her. I mean them."

Cody hadn't touched his beer, which bothered her for some reason. Maybe because she would prefer him good and drunk if this conversation was heading in the direction she feared. It would give her hope he might not remember it.

"Who was the client?"

Damn, she thought. There would be no getting around it.

"Here's the thing," she began stalling, buying more time. "And I'll preface this by saying it took me a long time to put this together. But I'm pretty sure that by the time I worked there Rose only had one client. Like, she wasn't an escort anymore. And the whole rent arrangement with Ron was like… how do I even say this without saying it?" she asked herself.

Encouragingly, he told her, "Just say it."

"It was a front. Just a front."

"For...?"

"Her affair. She just needed a place she could go to screw this guy. And when Ron discovered this and found out who the guy was, he was livid."

Cody let out a carefully measured breath, but it didn't conceal how thrilled he was. "Again, who was the client?"

Touching eyes with him, remorse swallowing her whole, she said, "If I told you, you would never believe me."

CHAPTER TWELVE

THE CENTER HARBOR PD didn't exactly have a Digital Forensics department. It had a specialist and a room in the basement, both of which reminded Lucas of high school computer science, a course he had hated and failed—eggshell-white walls, steel shelving units holding monitors of varying sizes, fluorescent lights buzzing overhead, a bleary-eyed geek fumbling through explanations Lucas didn't understand.

"Less technical jargon, please," he requested, and Tim pushed his rimless glasses up his nose, staring blankly at him as though he couldn't put it in plainer terms.

"The footage was erased after the fact," he managed, as he rolled his chair towards the table where a 17" PC displayed a black wash, which should have been camera feed from the Wythe Resort's east hallway. "That's why there's fifty-eight minutes of nothing."

"Unlike Rose and Benjamin's house," he supplied. Their security footage had a jump-cut, indicating the killer had shut off the system before he shot Rose and then resumed recording after.

"The tape was wiped," said Tim in a clipped tone, as he typed what looked like computer code into a laptop beside the PC they had been focused on. "Which means I can recover the footage... theoretically."

Leaning back in his chair, though it barely gave, Lucas folded his arms. "How long will it take?"

"Hard to say." With gusto, Tim hit the Enter key and pitched forward in his chair, nose-to-monitor, but the screen didn't even blink where they had both expected an image to surface. He slumped and began gnawing on his thumb.

Thinking out loud, Lucas asked, "Why would the guy use different methods of covering his tracks?"

Tim didn't answer and that's what Lucas liked about him. They had been at it all morning, suffering through the painstakingly slow process of trying to resurrect erased footage. They had been combing through, frame-by-frame, as if an image might jump out. For the digital forensic specialist, it was a thrilling challenge. Lucas could see it in the man's eyes, in the tense flex of his cheeks every time a new idea struck him. Tim enjoyed the battle, but for Lucas it was agonizing.

He was being punished.

After a long night of driving aimlessly, slipping in and out of thoughts so deep that his surroundings often disappeared; and after waking up with the sun, feeling bound and uncomfortable only to realize he had slept in his coat and boots, and his gun digging into his ribs, because he hadn't removed his holster, Lucas had bolted upright and leapt from the bed. Coffee hadn't crossed his mind let alone breakfast.

Tucker Wythe was missing. Holly was gutted, maybe even terrified, and Lucas was determined to attack this thing from every possible angle in order to find the kid, restore some semblance of her life, and win her trust in the process, her heart perhaps since he sensed it contained his own.

But Cody had shut him down when Lucas had reached the lockers, ordering him to work with Tim before he had even said good morning. His partner hadn't looked him in the eye and it wasn't for lack of time.

While Cody was off pursuing leads, talking to Ron Conover and the escorts at Diamonds, getting what he could from Roberta King and, God willing, his girlfriend's younger sister, which had to be a bone-cringing endeavor, Lucas was exiled to the precinct basement where he felt like he was being babysat by a pockmarked, balding man who had made one too many excited references to snowshoeing—*Snowshoeing is a sport, you know!* and *Ski poles only slow me down!* and *These fifty-eight minutes would be more promising if they were snowy, get it?*—each comment punctuating a burst of frantic typing followed by his signature slump.

When Tim slurped coffee from a mug with the caption, *I trip over my wiener,* in bold under the image of a dachshund, Lucas realized he had been mentally drifting off again, lost in the possibility that Roberta King—the young woman he had seen leaving the resort, who was also one of the vixens posed in one of the risqué photos on the Diamonds website—might also be the female he had spoken with while standing over Benjamin Wythe's body.

His gut told him that she had had something to do with the murders.

"How technically savvy would a person have to be to erase the footage?" he asked Tim, who was tapping his thumb on the keyboard spacebar for no apparent reason other than to drive Lucas crazy.

"A device like this?" For a moment, he pondered the question. "They would have to be familiar with it in the first place or have the manual, but it's fairly straightforward. It's like double-deleting files off a hard drive. You can't just drag and drop a file into the trash bin. You have to know to empty the trash as well."

So the real question was, could Roberta gain access to both the Wythe's house and the security room at the resort?

The clincher was her motive, which wasn't jumping out at him. Why would the young girl want to kill the couple and kidnap Tucker days later?

It didn't make sense.

All he knew at this point was that according to the missing hour from the east wing's footage, Benjamin had been murdered after Rose.

If Roberta had done it, why hadn't she taken Tucker immediately after Rose had fallen through the ice?

In terms of motive, there didn't seem to be any clear-cut answer, but Lucas had researched Roberta King, her harrowing upbringing, the inhumane treatment and methodic cruelty she had endured—the demonic process of torturing a child into forgetting, into forming blank spaces where memories should be, and systematically erasing experiences. Forgetting was a defense mechanism, a way of coping and surviving, which Lucas had read up on extensively. The phenomenon of forgetting could potentially stretch into adulthood and mask aspects of the survivor's life.

Had Roberta's history warped her so completely that her heart had turned to tar, black and sticky, eroding her conscience and eventually compelling her to kill?

If that were the case, then the same could be said of Lucas—he had survived a soul-murdering upbringing as well—but as soon as he touched upon the dark possibility, the monitor that he had been vacantly staring at flickered gray.

"Did you see that?" he asked, nudging Tim who was picking a hair out of his coffee. Lucas hit the spacebar, freezing the feed. "Rewind the footage by a few frames."

Tim dried his fingers on his khakis and scrolled back frame-by-frame until the monitor turned gray.

Or so he thought it was gray. Upon closer examination, he realized he was looking at shadowy gradations. He rolled backwards in his chair, creating more and more distance and staring at the screen as if it were a Magic Eye poster. Soon the shape of a hallway, a figure—a woman?—emerged.

The woman had a child in her arms.

Lucas felt his throat tighten.

It was Holly Danes.

"Yeah, I think we got something here," Tim agreed, his fingers dancing over the keyboard.

Suddenly, the door swung inward, and Cody McAlister filled the doorway and booming out a curt, "Where're we at?"

Thinking fast—the last thing he wanted was for Holly to fall under worse suspicion—Lucas advanced as if to greet his partner, but intentionally clipped his knee on Tim's chair with such force that the specialist bumped into the table, the mug flying from his hand onto the keyboard, coffee spilling everywhere.

"Whoa," said Cody, motioning to help.

But Lucas was already sopping up the spill as an excuse to hit the spacebar. The footage rolled into black before Cody had a chance to glimpse Holly carrying Tucker towards Room 112. "Damn, buddy, sorry about that."

"Don't worry about it," Tim grumbled, but when Lucas yanked a cord from the outlet and the monitor cut out, he yelped, "No! Don't unplug it!"

"Don't unplug it?" he echoed like a moron, holding the plug in his hand.

Tim groaned, stripped his glasses off his face, and pinched the bridge of his nose, as Cody began asking, "What's wrong? Did we lose the footage?"

Lucas held his hands up, wincing apologetically for the accidental damage.

"No," Tim grumbled. "I'll just re-transfer the still image."

In praise, Cody clapped his hand against the specialist's shoulder. "You isolated a still image?"

"A second ago," he complained.

"Of?"

Tim glanced at Lucas, soliciting an answer, which meant he hadn't gotten a good look at the hazy image, thank God.

"Couldn't make it out," he supplied. "Shades of gray."

Tim stood from his chair, blotting coffee from his khakis, then let out a disgruntled sigh, grabbed his mug, and excused himself.

As soon as they were alone, the door clicking shut and Tim padding away from it on the other side, Lucas asked, "How did it go over at Diamonds?"

Grimacing, his partner shook his head, but there was something disingenuous about his expression.

"Ron had nothing to say? Does he have an alibi?" he pressed.

"I don't know how to say this," he began as if unwilling to relay any developments. "For the time being..." He trailed off, clenching his jaw and avoiding Lucas's gaze. "I'm going to go it alone on this one."

"What?"

Combatively, he stated, "I couldn't get a hold of you last night and this isn't acceptable." As Lucas stammered to respond, his mind suddenly reeling with his profound lack of recall—Cody had tried to get a hold of him?—Cody angled in, jabbing his finger at the floor and spitting words through his teeth. "I have been patient time and again. I've forgiven your administrative slips. I've given you time to get yourself straightened out. I've made excuses for you to the Sergeant, which puts my ass on the line. But when you don't pick up your phone and you don't return my calls—and I don't give a damn how late it is or if you're sleeping, this job is around the clock—then I start to question if my partner is reliable."

Running out of steam, Cody's eyes turned intense and he was breathing so hard his nostrils flared, but all Lucas could say was, "I didn't know you called-"

"What were you doing?"

"What?"

"Where were you?" he demanded.

Thrown, Lucas stumbled through his answer. "Out for a drive then home; I crashed the second I got in the door." It seemed likely, though Lucas had zero recollection.

"I'm going to ask you something and I want a god damned straight answer." He pressed his mouth into a hard line to compose himself. "Did you have a personal relationship with Rose Wythe?"

The question hit him like a pail of ice water to his face.

An eternity passed before Lucas mentally registered the accusation. When he did, Lucas exclaimed, "What the hell are you talking about?"

Cody was staring him down and the glint in his eyes told Lucas that his partner actually believed this.

"I didn't know Rose Wythe," he insisted. "Who the hell told you I did?"

"Doesn't matter."

"I'm off the case because you think I was involved with the victim?"

"Something like that," he said in a low tone.

It was gradually hitting Lucas what this would mean—if he wasn't on the case then he couldn't protect Holly. There was no way in hell he was going to allow his partner to pull him off the investigation. He winced, preparing to disclose a detail that would be a huge gamble in terms of persuading his partner. Ultimately, he didn't have a choice. It was Hail Mary time and with nothing left to lose, he said, "It wasn't Rose."

Cocking his head, suspicious yet curious, Cody's brow lifted as if to suggest—*Go on*.

"It was Holly," he admitted. "And it was years ago and it's over. It was one night." Reassuringly, he added, "It hasn't affected how I do my job."

Cody didn't look convinced, but Lucas couldn't tell which part hadn't landed quite right, that it had only been one night or that it wasn't affecting how he did his job.

"You don't believe me?" he challenged. "You don't buy that someone, perhaps someone who's all amped up watching the news and probably has delusions of grandeur that their statement will crack this thing wide open, could confuse two identical twins?"

Holding his ground, Cody said, "I trust my source."

"Who's the source?" Lucas closed the gap between them, but his partner edged away. Pissed, he yelled, "You're being fed fiction and you like the taste." He started for the door but turned on his heel before leaving. "Did you pass this garbage to the Sergeant?"

"I will when I get a formal statement-"

"From your delusional source," he supplied with a disgusted snort.

"Your administrative failures were enough to get you pulled."

Lucas stared at the man and gradually Cody met his gaze.

"Am I under suspicion?"

"If there's an explanation, I'll hear it," he offered.

"I can't explain something that didn't happen."

"Then explain where you were the night of the murders, or last night for God's sake, because right now I'm having a hell of a time not picturing you distracted by a three-year-old."

Without thinking, rage took hold and he advanced on Cody and grabbed him by the collar, shoving him into a shelving unit, its monitors rattling on impact.

"I didn't do this," he hissed, his knuckles turning white, fists balling the man's shirt, fire flooding his veins. Cody stood his ground but didn't shove him off or fight back, unwilling to escalate a bad situation like he was some kind of saint. "You need to drop this," he warned, forcing himself to release his partner, step away, and catch his breath.

He yanked the door open on his way out and when Tim asked, "Early lunch?" as their paths crossed in the stairwell, Lucas muttered a swear-filled *Good luck*.

He wasn't just off the case. Lucas was staring down the long barrel of being fired, stripped of his badge, and desecrated in the news if the accusation against him was strong enough to seal his fate. He didn't see how it could. He hadn't done anything, but Cody was smooth and calculating and had a reputation for pulling off miracles. Could his partner convince an entire department of his guilt when nothing could be further from the truth?

As he left the precinct, walking out into the frigid air—the whitewashed parking lot, sunlight refracting off windshields—the business card he had found in his locker flashed through his mind.

Diamonds.

Someone was setting him up. They had planted the business card in his locker. They had unearthed his long-ago night with Holly. They were fabricating a motive that Lucas had committed those crimes.

It was fair to assume that Cody had confronted Mary Cole last night after he had seen her soft-porn photo on the escort website. She must have told him that Lucas had been involved with Rose, but why on earth she would say that, he couldn't imagine. Cody must have called Lucas to follow through with the claim as dreamt up by the teenage girl. Mary could've easily stolen away to the locker room at the precinct and planted the Diamonds business card. He had seen her there a few times, stopping in after school to see Hannah.

There was only one explanation forming in his mind—that the girls were behind this—but he didn't have a shred of proof.

Ragged patches of ice were frozen to his windshield. After climbing into his Ford, he flipped the wipers on, but even the fastest setting wasn't clearing the glass so he strained for the backseat and grabbed a scraper.

As he scraped, the plastic scraper grinding off some ice flakes until huge chunks broke free, Lucas puzzled over how he might stop this freight train before it flattened him or Holly.

He shouldn't have admitted their one-night stand.

Satisfied he had cleared the glass well enough to drive, Lucas climbed in behind the steering wheel and got his Focus idling. After blowing on his fingers to get a little feeling back, he adjusted the vents so cold air wouldn't hit him and pulled his cell phone from his pocket, hoping Tammy would be willing to pull information for him and be discreet about it.

He called the receptionist's phone, as he squinted through the glare, angling to see her desk beyond the first floor windows.

When she greeted him with a sultry sigh—*York?*—having recognized his number on the caller ID, he made an honest effort not to roll his eyes. "Can you help me out with something?"

"I don't see why not."

He could hear the smile in her voice, a promising sign. "I need the name of the high school and address for a girl named Roberta King and if she's employed anywhere, I'll need that information also."

"When do you need it by?" she asked, but she was already typing, her manicured nails clicking across her keyboard.

"Now would be ideal."

"And how might you return this favor?"

He was tempted to remind her that this was her job for Christ's sake, but something told him not to get cocky. Cody could've pulled her aside already and instructed her not to help Lucas, implying he might not be working there much longer. So he went with, "I'm always up for a beer."

"Yeah?"

Crap. He forced a smile, "Sure..."

"Got a pen handy?"

At first, he assumed she was about to suggest a time and place for said beer, but when she barreled ahead with the high school address, he exhaled in relief, clamped his cell between his ear and shoulder, and found a pen and scrap of paper in the backseat.

"Looks like she also works at Tony's Pizzeria," Tammy added then grumbled, "too many calories..."

"What's the address?"

He jotted both down quickly, thanked her, and checked the clock on the dashboard, vaguely aware that Tammy was chirping something about Shiraz at Harbor Inn. It was just before noon, which meant Roberta should be in class. Catching her wasn't likely, but he started for the high school anyway, thanking Tammy again and setting his cell on the passenger seat after hanging up.

The drive south to the high school was arduous—crawling along Kelsea Ave, tires spinning over black-ice, the likelihood his Ford would career off the road increasing with every passing second.

Laconia High was an ominous brick structure that was one barbed-wire fence shy of a prison. Students were walking lazily towards the parking lot, their shoulders rounded against the wind. Lucas guessed they were upperclassmen, seniors with cars who would rather spend their lunch period in town.

Carefully eyeing each student as though he might get lucky, he drove slowly through the parking lot, tires crunching over dirty snow, slush spitting against mud-flaps every time his car rolled through a puddle. He came to a stop in-between two clunkers and pulled the key from the ignition.

This was a terrible idea.

Interviewing a teenager without her guardian present was a reprehensible offense, not to mention that if Roberta had been involved in the murders, then being seen with her in public wouldn't exactly be Lucas's smartest move. But talking to Mary Cole was out of the question. He would get nowhere confronting the girl who had cast suspicion on him, and even if he did, she would surely tattle to Cody.

Reasoning that things couldn't possibly get any worse for him, Lucas stepped into the snow and made his way towards the entrance.

But he didn't get far.

Behind him, a girl said, "Hey, Killer, you're not looking for me, are you?"

Lucas whipped around and found Roberta—those muddy green eyes that swallowed the light, a coy curl to her lip, her sandy-blonde hair wavering in the wind, her bohemian coat billowing open—eyeing him with the same familiarity he had come to despise.

She was enjoying this.

Advancing on her, he wasn't certain what he was doing until he had her by the upper arm and was forcing her towards his vehicle. She didn't so much resist as bat her lashes at him as if mildly curious about where he was going with this.

It set his teeth on edge.

When he had her braced against the passenger side of his car—Roberta grinning, daring him, Lucas breathing hard, his stomach lurching at his own impulsiveness—he glanced around, scanning the parking lot and entrance for any administrators who might misunderstand their exchange.

"Get in," he ordered, thrusting her away from his car and throwing the door open.

She shoved him off, straightened her coat, and lowered willingly into the seat, not at all intimidated as she shut the door.

He stared at her through the windshield as he rounded the hood. His thoughts raced for just what in the hell he was going to say to get her talking.

After triple checking that there were no prying eyes watching them, he climbed in behind the steering wheel and squared his shoulders at her.

"I know you don't like that name," she said easily. "But I like teasing you."

Frantically, his thoughts darted from, *How do you know about my nickname?* to *You were at the resort after Benjamin's murder* to *Were you the caller that morning?* But he tempered his urgency and became instantly annoyed when he realized she was looking through his glove box.

"Stop that," he said, slapping the compartment closed. "I know you work at Diamonds. I know you were at Benjamin's hotel room. Christ, I saw you leaving the resort. And I know you and your little friend are trying to set me up."

Playfully, Roberta tilted her face to the headrest and smiled at him. "I thought we went over this last night."

CHAPTER THIRTEEN

HOLLY'S HANDS WERE shaking as she stood over the toilet—the tarnished porcelain bowl, dingy water, a slew of ad hoc jewelers' tools scattered across the tank cover—and tore open the first plastic baggie. Cocaine puffed out, sprinkling down into the basin.

Her eyes felt dry and scratchy, she had cried so much in the last twelve hours. There was nothing left. She was drained.

Failing Tucker had split her in two. Emotions raw, terror and guilt at war inside her. She should never have let him out of her sight

She dropped the shredded bag into the waste bin and grabbed the next 8-ball out of the sink. Methodically, she emptied the contents in the same fashion, tearing the plastic, letting the drug rain down into the toilet, and tossing the limp bag in the trash.

She wasn't going to keep pretending she could slide into her sister's life no matter how close it made her feel to Rose.

This was the end of the line. Losing Tucker had woken her up as jarringly as a slap across the face.

Flushing the toilet, she keeled over, her shoulders rounding, as a silent sob escaped her. No tears came. She had already used them up. She pressed her eyes shut with her fingertips, reeling in her emotions, and then looked at herself in the mirror.

The black eyeliner rimming her lashes was smudged badly, but masked the puffiness of her eyelids. She had pulled her hair back in a low ponytail, though rosy-blonde strands had fallen around her ears. She seemed pale except for the bright lipstick she was wearing. Dressed in her own clothes, she had made every effort not to look like her twin—she had even stripped off her sister's necklace, hanging it that morning on the vanity—but Rose's likeness was inescapable.

The person staring back at her in the mirror looked like an apparition, Rose incarnate.

She wished she hadn't driven the BMW to Shackles, but resolved to stick to her own car as soon as she got home.

Home?

Rose's house was no home, but she hadn't been able to bring herself to pack up and leave, because she feared doing so would be an act of betrayal. There would be no carrying on until Tucker was found.

A shudder of dread rolled through her. Where was he? Who had him?

Was he alive?

She pushed the dark thought from her mind and ran the faucet. Ice water beat against the porcelain sink. She cupped her hands then splashed water on her face, knowing and not caring how badly her eyeliner would run. She felt like garbage, she might as well look like it.

Slapping the toilet lid down, it hit her how bizarre she felt having come to the store, which wasn't at all the sanctuary she had thought. It felt wrong. Everything felt wrong, but at least the bad weather was keeping customers away.

She shut off the faucet and sat on the toilet lid, giving herself a moment to breathe. But the mounting tragedies weighed on her too greatly, bending reality so badly that she felt lost, beside herself, suffocated in grief.

The idea of Lucas kept nagging her, his commitment to helping her, the glimmer of affection in his eyes—unconditional and unsettling because of it. It was only a matter of time before Cody would discover she had been at the resort that night, the security feed would prove as much. Her fabricated alibi—McCoy's—would soon be dismantled.

Part of her was screaming to accept his help despite the fact that it wasn't necessary. She was innocent, though she looked guilty. That was the problem—how it all looked. Why not accept Lucas's help? But a small voice in the back of her mind kept warning her against it—she had snuck out from that motel room all those years ago for a reason. Slipping through the door at the crack of dawn as he had slept, she had tried and failed to shake his disturbing confession. When he had told her, she had been too drunk to process it. It hadn't fully registered until she had sobered up, waking with a splitting migraine after only a few hours sleep.

His mother.

Lucas had been wasted, slurring his words, disjointed admissions shrouded in a dark tone, but still Holly had understood.

The woman who raised him had taken pleasure in destroying his life, his mind, and his heart—creeping into his bedroom at night, covering his mouth, pressing her palm hard until his lip split, the taste of blood in his mouth, terror washing over him that he couldn't breathe because her hand partially covered his nostrils, no air. Her cold fingers had found him under the covers—the part of his body a mother should never touch—in the nightly ritual that had been as agonizing as it was arousing.

It had filled him with shame and paralyzed him with shock. He had been unable to fight. The horror compounded when his father had entered the bedroom—he liked to watch then beat the memory out of Lucas the following day.

The abuse had gone on for years.

'*I didn't remember for the longest time*,' he had told her, lying beside her in bed, his eyelids heavy and jaw slack as though he was caught in a dream. '*There were all these holes in my memory, these black spaces where the nights should've been... Until one night it came back, all of it came rushing back and at the worst possible moment. With my girlfriend. Pumping into her. In darkness under the bleachers at school, as some terrible dance unfolded on the basketball court. I thought I would kill her, the sheer realism of what was coming back to me... I almost strangled her, I was so confused. But I didn't. I ran home, forgetting my car in the high school parking lot, I ran home...*' He had smiled, a shred of humor easing him towards the worst of it. Then his smile slipped off his face. *I killed them instead, both of them, my parents.*

Holly had stiffened in the bed, every muscle in her body tensing in response. But Lucas had seemed lost, drifting into sleep, and the strange justice of his story compelled her to kiss him.

'People don't know,' he had mumbled. *'They can't see it. They can look a kid in the eye and still be blind to what's really going on even though it's written all over my face—the kid's face.'* He had corrected himself. *'You go on suffering and the world goes on smiling, oblivious, all around you. I finished the Academy last week. I'm going to be a cop. I'm going to find my people, the ones who are just like me; killers. They don't have to be alone in it, suffering with their scars. I'm going to help them.'* His eyes had slowly opened and when he had looked at her, Holly felt truly seen. *'You're scarred too, aren't you?'* She hadn't responded, only stared at him, nerves ratcheting up her spine. *'I wish there was a way to save these kids... There has to be a way.'*

The doorbell rattled faintly, snapping Holly out of her time warp. Someone had entered the store. She touched her cheeks, which were dry, so she got to her feet.

After a quick glance in the mirror where she wiped mascara smears from under her eyes, she padded through her studio, the scent of pickles in the air, and rounded into the jewelry store where Sarah Wythe was frowning with disdain at a necklace resting on one of the pedestals.

When her cool eyes settled on Holly—dark and wide-set, crows-feet spanning her temples, her jaw taut from the latest surgery—she seemed cognizant, alive, and not at all like her usual, medicated self.

Sarah made a performance of stripping her leather gloves off and tucking them into the pocket of her expensive fur coat.

"I'm horrified," she declared, her aging tone deep and biting. "You didn't have the decency to call. I had to find out from that detective." She had spit out the consonants as though disgusted.

Holly felt raw and vulnerable. What could she say to a woman who already hated her, who had despised her sister for years, who had begged Benjamin not to marry a Danes—*Those girls are trash* Sarah had argued even though the twins had been within earshot, standing in the next room.

When she finally managed, "I'm sorry," her voice was a thread.

"You're sorry." Sarah was looking down her nose, her brows arching and her eyes glazing over. "Is that what you call it? Being sorry?"

"I've been a wreck over this-"

"You have no right to custody," she snapped. "Tucker never should've been with you. Warren and I were listed as his guardians should anything happen. I don't know how the hell you got that Will changed." She was seething. "Do you have any idea the shock we suffered hearing about that damned Will, and on top of learning our precious son had been killed no less? And now Tucker is gone?" Staring her down, her bottom lip betrayed her resolve, quivering until she pressed her lips together. "I doubt the kidnapper will contact you, but if he does, if this is about money and he hasn't the good sense to call Warren, you send him our way. I don't care what price he asks for, I am getting my grandson back."

Holly prayed it would be so simple and she agreed, swallowing hard and nodding, as her gaze fell to the floor. When she was sure she could get the words out clearly, she asked, "Who would do this?"

Sarah seemed taken aback and a strange smile came over her. "I'm not going to commiserate with you or indulge in your game of playing detective."

As Sarah ranted, building momentum and listing the many ways in which the Danes twins were horrible, Holly startled at the sound of the bell chiming over the entrance door.

She recognized the girl who was entering in an instant.

Mary's friend. A woman followed in after, her mother perhaps though they looked nothing alike—both bundled in winter garb.

The girl touched eyes with Holly as she swayed towards one of the velvet pedestals, her mother trailing behind her, keenly aware of the tension between Holly and the older woman.

"This is upsetting for all of us," Sarah went on, assertive though her tone had softened given their present company. Nearing Holly so as not to be overheard, she kept pressing her vicious point. "We are going to sit down with the attorney and we are going to rectify the Joint Will. I will never give up on my grandson. He will be found and when he is, he will live in a safe environment."

Holly stole a quick glance at her customers—the girl was examining a pendant, its silver chain dangling down, which her mother collected in her palm so it wouldn't accidentally fall to the floor—then Holly locked eyes with Sarah. "I'm not sure a Will can be altered after a death."

"You knew Warren and I would challenge you," she argued as though she had caught Holly red handed. "You did this, didn't you?"

Outraged, she had to fight herself not to yell and the result sounded guttural. "You think I kidnapped my own nephew? Why would I do that? I have custody."

The older woman seemed unmoved.

"With all due respect, Sarah, I have to ask you. Have you gone off your medication?"

She gaped, her mouth hanging open and soon a stuttering laugh jackhammered out.

The girl and her mother were migrating over to the glass counter and Holly sensed they would need assistance, but here she was, caught in a stormy confrontation with a woman whose mental health ebbed and flowed as roughly as an ocean.

Sarah angled in on her and though she spoke quietly, her tone didn't soften. "At least my medication is legal. Oh, you think I didn't know about Rose's little habit?" Her eyes shifted, as she studied Holly's face, her gaze darting from one telltale sign of addiction to the next—the dry eyes, her pale skin, nostrils chapped pink. "You think I can't tell that you're just like her in that regard? Mark my words, you will not get Tucker once he's found."

She felt eyes on her and glimpsed the girl staring. It didn't seem like she was frustrated, however. She didn't have the classic look of a customer disgruntled at being ignored. The girl seemed curious, maybe even intrigued.

"Are you listening to me?" demanded Sarah, stealing Holly's attention.

But before she could answer, Warren Wythe barreled into the store and quickly collected his wife, taking Sarah by the upper arm and shooting Holly an apologetic smile.

"I have every right to speak with her," she protested, but he was talking over her.

"We have reservations. Come now, let's not be late."

"Late for what?" she snapped. "Lunch is not more important than finding our grandson."

Warren grumbled, widening his eyes at Holly as though they were in this together. Then, much to her surprise, he told Holly, "You don't have to be a stranger," which Sarah immediately objected to—*Don't you dare invite her into our home!* But he already was. "You're welcome at the resort any time. We consider you a part of this family."

Holly had never heard him talk like that.

"And no one should be alone during this... difficult time," he added.

She uttered, "Thank you," as Warren began ushering his wife through the store. The bell chimed overhead as they left and it wasn't until they had disappeared down the sidewalk that Holly felt like she could breathe again.

"I'm so sorry about that," she said, rounding behind the counter where her customers had been eyeing a number of pendants.

The girl grinned darkly now that she had Holly's attention and introduced herself as *Roberta*. "Do you have poison rings?"

"I thought you wanted a necklace," said her mother, whose face screwed up at the term *poison*.

"I have a few," Holly told her, getting a strange feeling from the request. But she padded down the counter, slid a glass door aside, and grabbed a velvet tray, which displayed eight rings.

After returning to them and presenting the options, the woman, who Roberta had referred to as *Gerty*, asked, "What's a poison ring?"

Holly explained, "It's a ring that has a small pillbox under its bezel." She pinched one of the rings off the tray and used her fingernail to pop up its sapphire encrusted bezel, revealing a tiny compartment and then handed the ring to Gerty for examination. "Poison rings were popular in Europe during the sixteenth century. Women kept perfume and other keepsakes inside, but the style was also rumored to hold poison."

As she went on detailing the history, it wasn't lost on her that in this day in age people generally used poison rings to hide drugs, more often than not cocaine. She suddenly remembered Rose's stash and how she had left most of it with Benjamin that night. Perhaps Roberta wasn't merely curious about the style, but would have an actual use for the ring, assuming she had nabbed a baggie or two.

"You want a ring like that?" asked Gerty.

"I don't want a ring like that," she corrected. "I want a *necklace* like that. Do you make those?"

Holly smiled at her. "It's a possibility." Then, thinking fast on her feet—she didn't know if she would ever have another opportunity with the girl who was the last person seen with Benjamin, what did she know? What might the peculiar girl tell her if she could get her alone?—she asked, "I might have to build it from scratch, but if you would like to come with me into the studio, you can pick out a gemstone?"

"I thought you made them here," she interjected, her eyes gleaming in subtle challenge. "A friend of mine had one and I could've sworn she said she got it at Shackles."

The comment piqued Holly's interest. She never forgot a face and she would've remembered selling a pillbox necklace. Something about the girl, her self-assured smirk and the confident glimmer in her eye, made Holly want to jam her revolver down the girl's throat, but she kept her expression even, as she said, "I can make whatever you like." Shifting her gaze to Gerty, she asked, "What's the occasion?"

Proudly, the woman began commending her daughter. "Consistent grades even in math and she's been handling her responsibilities well, working at Tony's Pizzeria and meeting her curfew."

"Congratulations," Holly said dryly, touching eyes with the girl and feigning a smile, all the while pitying the woman. Clearly, Roberta had her completely snowed, which meant that Cody and Lucas hadn't paid Gerty a visit to grill or at the very least question the girl. Why hadn't they? She reasoned the detectives might not want to waste time arresting a burgeoning prostitute when there was a killer on the loose.

"Let's pick out the chain and the gemstone and I'll give you an estimate." Starting for the studio door, she added, "It's a bit messy, but-"

"I know what I want," Roberta said, stopping her. "A sterling silver cable link chain, a heart shaped pendant, also sterling silver. And it has to have a jagged opal, dead-center."

What the hell?

Roberta had just described her sister's necklace.

Holly tensed, slowly facing the girl. "What did you say?"

Angling her cat eyes on Holly, her chin tipping down, the light dimmed behind her eyes. "A necklace just like my friend's."

Her mouth went dry. "Ah, yeah," she managed, her chest tightening and her thoughts reeling with sudden and confusing revelations.

How well did she know Rose?

Gerty asked, "Do you have an idea of the price?" but Holly didn't even hear her, her heart was pounding so hard that her pulse throbbed in her ears.

Holly touched her collarbone, expecting to feel Rose's necklace, but it wasn't there. Fumbling for words, she stammered, "Yeah, ah, a price..." and returned to the counter in search of an estimate pad. She found one in a drawer near the cash register.

As she began jotting down materials and their cost, her brain not quite working, she sensed more than saw a man enter the store. When he reached the woman, he breathed a smile and kissed her cheek, and Gerty called him *Jake,* while Roberta milled off, wandering around the store.

They whispered to each other something about lunch or dinner, Holly had no concept of what time it was, and then Gerty asked if Holly could email the estimate and placed her business card on the counter.

"Sure, no problem," she said in a hollow tone, as the couple walked to the door, leaving their peculiar daughter behind.

Roberta was staring at her again. "How long will it take?"

"A day or two." The second Gerty and her husband—boyfriend?—disappeared   down   the sidewalk, she urgently asked, "How do you know about my sister's necklace?"

Roberta shot her a sly smirk as she weaved her way around the displays towards the entrance door. After pushing it open, she glanced over her shoulder, saying, "See ya in a day or two," then stepped into the wintry afternoon.

Holly's stomach bottomed out like a blade over an anvil.

Was Roberta taunting her? Had she asked for Rose's necklace to rattle Holly like this was some kind of sick game? Or was the cunning girl hinting at something much deeper and much darker?

Had she meant to imply that Rose's necklace was significant for some reason?

Holly could remember every detail of making that necklace for Rose, from molding the silver to pickling the pendant to setting the sparkling opal onto the bezel. There was no pillbox beneath.

But Roberta's confidence, the dark conviction that had underscored her breezy comments—*Opal dead-center,* and *Just like my friend's,* and *Could've sworn she got it at Shackles*—had Holly second guessing herself.

Had Rose modified her necklace?

"Damn," she breathed, ridding Roberta from her mind. She wasn't about to let a teenage girl get inside her head and mess with her like this.

What would it matter if her sister had altered the necklace? Rose had been an addict. She had turned every nook and cranny into a hiding place. It was what it was. So what if she had softened the pendant in the kiln, carved out a compartment, welded on hinges in order to create one more hiding place?

Holly locked the storefront and flipped the sign, needing a breather before the next customer wandered in. But as she padded into her studio fully prepared to suck it up and get started on Roberta's necklace, she couldn't deny the unsettling fact that the girl had succeeded in disturbing her. Roberta's comments were worming their way through her mind and she couldn't shake the terrible urge to drive to Rose's house and examine her sister's necklace.

Grumbling, "Crap," she bundled up at the backdoor after unplugging the space heater and Crock Pot—the last thing she needed was to burn her store down, she wasn't even certain she had been keeping up with the insurance payments.

Once outside, she locked up and carefully made her way over snow-dusted ice to Rose's BMW.

Climbing into the vehicle sober as a judge was surreal. The sheer class of the interior—black leather seats, a slick dashboard, technology that reminded her of a spaceship—seemed suddenly foreign. She clicked the gear shifter into Drive and as she drove through town towards her sister's house, the glaring incongruity between her sister's life and her own leapt out at her.

If Roberta had meant to insinuate that she knew Rose better than Holly, maybe she was right. Holly hadn't known her sister, not really, not since the estrangement.

Rose had lived in a world of designer drugs and seedy nightclubs. She had associated with men like Ron Conover, characters that wouldn't hesitate to shove a gun in her face, perhaps kill her, her husband, and take her son for God only knew what reason. She had forged unlikely friendships with teenage girls and received envelopes stuffed with cash, all while raising an infant into a toddler then into a reserved three-year-old with signs of developmental regression.

What other secrets had Rose Wythe kept and why was Holly filled with the terrible intuition that Roberta wanted her to open the necklace?

Why did Holly sense that if she did, the secret it contained—its hidden truths—would break her?

Pulling off Newman Road into the driveway, she decided to park the BMW in the garage where it belonged since she had resolved to drive her own car from now on.

She pressed the remote where it was clipped to the sun visor and the garage door jutted upwards, slowly feeding into the ceiling rack, as she eased on the gas.

As soon as she had parked the BMW bumper-to-shelving unit at the back of the garage, she turned the key, killing the engine, and forced a deep breath as if doing so might prepare her for what she was about to discover should the necklace actually open.

CLICK.

The sound was faint yet distinct, and when rhythmic clicks followed, coming from the garage ceiling like an eerie premonition, instinct spiked hard and fast in her veins.

Frantic, she twisted the key in the ignition and jerked the gear shifter into Reverse, stomping the accelerator to the floor, the engine roaring, tires squealing, burning rubber, as the BMW flew out of the garage. She gritted her teeth without a glimpse at the rearview mirror, focusing only on clearing the house.

The rear bumper slammed into her parked Saab and her head whipped back, bouncing off the headrest and rattling her teeth—

BOOM.

The explosion pitched her sideways, shattering her window. Glass rained like needles against her cheek, as shrapnel pelted the windshield and the hood.

Stunned, terrified, her head pounding with the swell of a concussion, she straightened up in her seat, her eyes widening at the sight of it—orange flames crackling and licking the side of the house where the garage used to be.

Whatever the killer's motive had been for murdering Rose and Benjamin and for taking Tucker, Holly was also on the killer's list.

And she didn't have a goddamn clue as to why.

CHAPTER FOURTEEN

CLUTCHING HER REVOLVER and standing in the snowy driveway, Holly watched flames devour the garage. Flurries fluttered down all around her in innocent contrast to the danger she sensed.

There wasn't a soul in sight, but she didn't trust that the killer wasn't lurking in the wintery forest.

She had called 911, cursing when the operator hung up after taking the address. She would've preferred staying on the line until help arrived.

Dazed—what if she had closed the garage door and stepped out of the BMW? She would've been obliterated—she had the impulse to run into the house and snatch Rose's necklace from the vanity upstairs. What if the fire got to it before firefighters could save the second floor? What if every last shred of her sister was incinerated?

She started for the entrance, but turned at the sound of a growling engine. A Ford Focus was hurling up the driveway, zigzagging through the drift as though there was no other way to conquer the incline.

Quickly, she jammed her revolver into her coat pocket.

When the vehicle rolled to a stop, parking at an awkward angle next to her sister's totaled BMW, Lucas jumped out and rushed to her with such urgency that he left his car door open.

Taking her by the shoulders, he demanded, "Are you alright?"

He was gripping her too tightly, his eyes searching hers invasively, his concern seeming too intense.

"I'm fine," she said, bewildered. "Where is everyone?" When he narrowed his eyes, she clarified, "I called the police. Where's the fire truck?"

Loosening his grip, his hands slid down her arms as if warming her up, and he shook his head, staring at the raging fire. "Dispatch didn't call me," he admitted, which had her momentarily thrown.

"You were nearby?"

"I was on my way to ask you about a few things and heard the explosion," he said, but when she looked at him expectantly, he didn't address what those things were. Instead, he eyed the scene—the garage in flames, the BMW's damage, the stunned grimace on Holly's face. "Did you see anyone?"

"No." She studied his expression for a beat and tried not to get distracted by his obvious appeal—the straight mouth, his pale lips, the crisp quality of his blue eyes, the light dusting of stubble along his jaw. Did he have any idea what the hell was going on? She couldn't get a solid read on him. "I need to get into the house."

"What? No, you can't. It's not safe."

"The house isn't on fire," she countered.

"It will be."

She pointed to one of the second floor windows, explaining, "I need to get into that room up there. I'll have time if I go now."

"What do you need?" he asked quickly. "I'll get it for you."

But it was too late. A fire truck followed by two police cruisers was flying along Newman, their sirens wailing and lights blazing.

As soon as the vehicles began plowing up the driveway, Lucas told her that Rose's BMW was in the way, the fire truck wouldn't be able to get close enough to the garage.

He jogged to his Ford, asking her over his shoulder, "Can you move the car? Will it drive?" He didn't wait for an answer, but jumped into his vehicle, which was blocking hers, and drove through fresh snow towards the woods, clearing the way for Holly to move the BMW.

She hopped into it and, following his cue, drove her sister's car next to the detective's and then joined Lucas at the wayside.

The fire truck immediately pulled forward and firefighters began jumping off. They didn't leap to action, but rather waited for their Chief to give the order. The Chief eyed the fire, the damage, and the overall situation, as he gathered his men. A moment later, he stalked through the snow towards them, shouting, "What set it off?"

She quickly supplied, "I heard a clicking noise."

He didn't seem satisfied with that. "Like a bomb?"

"I think when I drove into the garage, I tripped something," she explained.

The Fire Chief seemed to mull that over then stomped off towards his team, shouting directives. Without hesitation the firefighters sprang to action, tearing a hose from its coil at the side of the truck and angling the spigot at the base of the flames. It took two men to control the spray once the water was blasting.

"Did Ron do this?" she asked, but Lucas only clenched his jaw, watching firefighters battle the flames. "It has to be him, doesn't it? First, he killed Rose and then Benji, because, I don't know because maybe Benji threatened him? And he took Tucker then blew up the garage, because I went to Diamonds and stuck my nose where it didn't belong? Did you guys talk to him yet?"

Meeting her gaze, he said, "Cody did."

"And?"

"And... I haven't connected with him since." He seemed guarded, but before she could ask if Cody had gotten anywhere with Ron, he added, "For the time being, you need a safe place to live."

Holly stuffed her hands in her pockets, balling her fists for warmth. She could barely feel her fingers and her toes were no better. "I've got my house on the lake."

"Is it listed?"

"I'm not sure... probably-"

"Then it's not safe."

The way he was looking at her, she thought he might suggest that she stay at his place and the notion strangely comforted her.

"Maybe a motel," he said instead. "Pay with cash, don't give your real name."

Warren's offer came to mind, though she doubted she would be comfortable around Sarah.

"Okay," she said.

Another vehicle was rolling up the driveway, but it wasn't a police cruiser, rather a truck. Lucas's mood seemed to darken, as the truck pulled to a stop at a healthy distance behind the fire truck.

Holly caught sight of the driver—Cody McAlister—and her stomach dropped. She didn't have another lengthy interrogation in her if he wanted to question her again.

"Can you drive me?" she asked, grabbing Lucas's arm with a sense of urgency, "Now?" When he cocked his head, she leveled with him, "I can't do an hour of questions, I just can't."

"Yeah," he said understandingly. "Sure."

Wasting no time, she immediately ducked onto the passenger seat of the Ford, dodging Cody just as he was climbing out of his truck. In the side view mirror, she spied him nearing the Fire Chief, as police officers hurried over. Soon the men were huddled in what appeared to be some kind of briefing, which apparently didn't require Lucas's attendance. He was settling in behind the steering wheel and twisting the key in the ignition.

As Lucas backed out, swinging the Ford around, Cody caught sight of them and began jogging over, but Lucas threw the gear shifter into First, keen to avoid his partner for Holly's sake.

They weren't so lucky.

"Whoa!" shouted Cody, giving his partner no choice but to squeeze the brakes.

"Taking Holly to a motel," he explained.

Stooping so that he could look Holly in the eye, Cody asked, "You don't need to go to the hospital?"

"No, I'm fine."

He seemed skeptical of that, but addressed Lucas, "What are you doing here?"

As Lucas stammered, Holly blurted out a lie, "I called him. Please, I'm fine, but exhausted and I-"

"No problem," he quickly interrupted, surprising her. "Where are you headed?" When she didn't respond except to mention that she wasn't sure, he told her, "I'll need to talk to you later." He eyed Lucas for a beat, adding, "Both of you."

"Can I let you know?" she asked. "Once I've decided?"

Cody told her that would be fine, though he didn't sound pleased, and paced off towards the cluster of police officers.

It wasn't until Lucas took his foot off the brakes, tires crunching over compacted snow, that Holly felt the knot in her stomach loosen.

Driving along Newman, Holly stared through the windshield at the whitewashed landscape—the snow-dusted road, the icy lake to their left, a dense forest beyond the shoulder to their right.

The silence between them didn't feel uncomfortable, but she broke it anyway. "I know you've been looking out for me." Glimpsing him briefly to gauge his reaction, she caught sight of his mouth lifting into a subtle smile. "But it's not necessary."

"I know," he said quickly. "But I don't want the fact that you were at the resort that night to muddy the waters of this investigation."

"I don't either," she said.

Holding her gaze for a beat, he smiled and for a split second she was reminded of how deeply she had felt for him during their shared night all those years ago.

"You can take me to the resort, if you don't mind. Warren offered," she mentioned when his eyes had returned to the road.

In response, Lucas veered the car, turning left and hugging the lake as per her request.

"Thank you," she said quietly.

"For what?"

Everything? nothing? For hiding the bullet, for having her back, for not reminding her that she was carrying his darkest secret—a secret that both disturbed and enthralled her.

He had made himself vulnerable to her. He had trusted Holly. And she had never told a soul.

Their night had been so intimate, so heavy, and yet strangely freeing.

Why hadn't he tracked her down? Found her? Insisted that they were destined to be together?

Leaving had been her choice, but seated beside him in the car as they now were, driving with him through a winter wasteland, she realized she hadn't left because his dark confession had scared her. She had left because it hadn't.

How could she love a killer?

A man who had killed his own parents...

She told herself that a killer wasn't what he was anymore, and said, "I'm just thanking you in general."

After a moment of Lucas shifting his gaze from the road to her, he asked, "Holly, are you okay?"

She realized her eyes had misted over with tears. She wasn't okay. She was losing it, coming undone in ways she hadn't thought humanly possible. Despite this, she managed, "Just catch the son of a bitch, get my nephew back, and I'll be fine."

As she shielded her face with her hand, her elbow planted on the armrest, Lucas placed his hand on hers.

When she glanced down, feeling the warmth of his hand, seeing the tender way he was conveying that he was here for her, she said, "You never confronted me."

He gave her a little squeeze. "About?"

"About how I left you in that motel room without saying goodbye."

He needed his hand to turn onto Keewaydin Road, the Wythe Resort looming in the distance, so he released her in favor of turning the steering wheel hand over fist. Returning his hand to hers, he said, "I never questioned it, or you. I didn't need you to stay if that wasn't what you wanted."

She laced her fingers with his, uncertain as to why holding hands felt so good but unable to deny that it did. The energy between them was building in a way that both worried and excited her.

"Did you guys get anywhere with Mary Cole?" When she glanced at him, Lucas scraped his teeth over his bottom lip. "Christ, what the hell is she doing working there?"

"I doubt she works there anymore."

"Did she give you any insight on Ron?"

"If she did, Cody will pursue it." He let out a rocky breath, slowing and turning the vehicle into the resort parking lot where bulldozers still dominated the far end, the west wing draped in plastic, workers marching building materials from tarps to the construction site as though immune to the frigid temperature.

Lucas drove as close to the entrance as possible.

"Why didn't you stay at the house to investigate?" she asked, curious. Cody had seemed wary of him—*What are you doing here?*

But Lucas was relaxed despite her intuition that perhaps the detectives weren't getting along, and complained, "Cody's pigheaded. I don't think he wants a partner, not that I ever was one. He treats me more like a subordinate and I decided to stop fighting him."

Holly glanced at the entrance and groaned.

"I can take you somewhere else," he offered.

"Someplace else won't be free," she said with a sigh. "Warren and Sarah wouldn't dream of charging me. They would rather be generous and hold it over my head even though they've hated me from day one... Just like they did to Rose before."

Offhandedly, he mentioned, "You look good," and when she met his gaze, he defused the compliment, adding, "I know dealing with her death has been rough and that's an understatement," as though he could anchor his prior implication in the territory of how she was holding up rather than the obvious fact that he was still attracted to her.

Both made her smile. "Why do I want to invite you in right now?"

He let out a modest laugh then guessed, "Because the Wythes hate you and you don't feel like being alone with them?"

Boldly, he drove forward, clearing a few parked cars, and pulled into a vacant spot then killed the engine.

"I have time," he said, popping his seatbelt.

She kept her smile hidden as she stepped out of the car, wind whipping flurries at her sideways.

Lucas was quick to open the entrance door for her when they reached it and though he walked by her side to the front desk, he stepped forward to handle the clerk so she wouldn't have to expend any energy, explaining Holly was here to see Warren Wythe.

"Same old song and dance," he said over his shoulder after the young woman behind the counter had made several attempts to dissuade him from summoning the owners. As the clerk grumbled, clamping the desk phone between her ear and shoulder, Lucas asked, "Why do they hate you?"

She widened her eyes and sighed, "Long story."

As Lucas eyed her, perhaps waiting for her to elaborate, the clerk slapped the phone in its cradle and told them they could have a seat in the lounge if they liked.

Starting through the lobby, they didn't get far. Warren was already walking briskly from the lounge. He smiled like an emperor welcoming weary pilgrims, but to Holly the sentiment seemed disingenuous.

"Holly, I'm so glad you came." He clapped his hands together and as he continued it dawned on her that he hadn't greeted or even acknowledged Lucas. "I understand you would like a room."

"If it's too short a notice-"

"No, not at all," he obliged, motioning her towards the east wing. As they walked—Warren shepherding her, Lucas trailing behind—he disclosed, "We're booked solid. Bad weather is good for business, but I do have a room for you." He nodded a *Hello* to a maid as she passed pushing a cart down the hallway. "I pray you won't be offended."

Abruptly, Warren turned and she realized they had arrived at her room, but when she glanced at the door and the number *112* jumped out at her, her stomach dropped.

It was Benjamin's room.

"With the news reports and the rumors we wouldn't dare book our guests in here," he explained, fishing the room key from his pocket.

"It's fine," she breathed, unnerved. "I appreciate it."

"Well," he said, twisting the key into the lock and pushing the door inward. "Here you are. Anything you need, anything at all, don't hesitate to ask." As if suddenly remembering, he added, "Oh, and if you would like to join Sarah and me for an early dinner, we'll be in the restaurant in about ten minutes."

Holly watched him trail down the hallway, then she stepped apprehensively into the room, Lucas following after her and closing the door.

If she was uneasy about the idea of retiring in the room where her brother-in-law had been murdered, the feeling was magnified the second she rounded the bed and saw the carpet.

Though she could tell it had been steam-cleaned and possibly scrubbed with hydrogen peroxide and bleach, a dark stain remained—blood.

"Christ, I don't know if I can do this," she said, lowering to the edge of the bed and staring at the carpet.

Lucas angled around the bed and it didn't take him long to understand what the problem was. Decisively, he scanned the room then grabbed a pillow off the bed and laid it over the stain. His effort had been thoughtful but useless.

"I'm still going to know it's there," she said in a small voice, realizing his honest attempt had caused her heart to sink.

Lucas studied the pillow, the carpet, their alignment from all angles, and seemed to decide a second pillow would do the trick, but when he grabbed it, she quietly said, "Please, stop."

"Okay," he said, setting the pillow to the bed and sitting beside her.

"Why are you doing this?"

"Covering the stain?"

"Taking care of me," she corrected. "The necklace and the bullet, and I'm scared to find out about what else-"

"Your alibi at McCoy's," he supplied.

"You got me an alibi?"

"No, but I will." After a moment he added, "You're on the security footage here."

She cut in with, "I didn't do any of this."

"I know." He had said it before, but this time it really landed.

"Then why are you doing this?" When he didn't answer except to touch her hand, she quieted the side of herself that still didn't trust him and asked, "Is it because of what you said to me? Your reason for becoming a cop?"

He held her gaze. They both knew what she was referring to, but he didn't respond, though he seemed to be working up the nerve.

"You told me you didn't want them to feel alone, the killers out there, the ones who became warped and twisted because of how they were raised. Is that why you're doing this? *Helping* me? Is that what you think I am?"

As he searched her eyes in silence, she could almost see the words forming in his mind, but after a tense moment, he still hadn't come out with it.

"The way you explained it," she went on, keeping her tone even. "It sounded like you identify with... those people. Killers. But Lucas, I'm not one of them. I didn't do anything."

For the third time he told her, "I know."

"Then what is all of this? What are you doing?"

He couldn't look at her when he said, "I'm protecting you while I figure it out."

"But why?"

After another long moment, he finally began, "I do things..." but interrupted himself, swallowing hard and drawing in a deep breath. "I think we're being set up, and..." Trailing off, his eyes shifted as if some dark memory was taking hold.

Holly leaned in, squeezing his hand, poised to learn who was setting them up.

His shoulders rounded as he exhaled and after pinching his eyes shut, perhaps to ward off whatever memory was gripping him, he reclaimed his composure, but when he finally went on, she realized that the night they had shared had a far greater impact on him than she had thought.

"When I was with you that night..." He squared his shoulders to her, locking eyes. "I've never been so completely myself with another human being. Call me a romantic or a fool or just plain crazy, but I know you didn't kill Rose and Benjamin. I know you didn't take Tucker. You didn't nearly blow yourself up in that garage. So no, I'm not helping because I think you're a killer. I'm helping because whoever is setting us up has Cody completely fooled. He's been sniffing around you-"

"Even though you guys know about Ron Conover?"

"It looks that way. And I don't know why, but I feel responsible."

"Responsible for what?"

"For you," he said as if the fact puzzled him. "I can't explain it..." He took another long moment to gather his thoughts. "I feel so close to this thing, I feel like I'm breathing it. And I know I can stop it. I know I can figure it out and end it and get Tucker back. But I can't do it if I'm worried Cody is going to come after you."

He closed his eyes, his cheeks flexing with a hint of remorse, and when he ran his hands down his face, Holly sensed he was just as distraught as her. "One of the girls from the club has been messing with me. I found a business card for Diamonds in my locker," he said after lowering his hands to the bed. "Not Mary-"

"Roberta?" she guessed.

"You know her?"

"I think she's been messing with me, too."

Angered, he said, "Roberta knows my nickname. But I don't know how that's possible. I've never told anyone. She's been acting familiar with me, getting under my skin and into my head. When I confronted her the other day..." He trailed off as if disturbed. "She claimed we had an entire conversation... but we didn't."

His anger was gone and Lucas looked baffled, which compelled Holly to explain, "She was in Benji's room that night."

His blue eyes flared. "Why didn't you say something?"

"Because I couldn't admit that I was also in his room. But she was here. I came to drop Tucker off," she explained, omitting the quarter pound of cocaine she had also brought to drop off as well as the ugly fact that she had held Benjamin at gunpoint in attempts to get him talking. "They were having some kind of an affair."

His gaze lowered as he fell into deep consideration.

"But I don't see how a teenage girl would have the know-how to rig a bomb in the garage," she countered.

"Mary Cole is brilliant."

Skeptically, she said, "She's some kind of genius?"

"Literally," he confirmed, surprising her.

"Why would Mary do this?" she questioned, though she was eager to hear his theory.

"You said that you saw Roberta here with Benjamin?" he asked as if thinking out loud. "If Roberta was involved with him, having an affair, but also working with Rose, then she might have wanted to put an end to the love triangle. Maybe she killed Rose and then came here to tell Benjamin, thinking he would see his wife's death as good news. And when he didn't, when he fell into shock, she realized her error and killed him. And maybe Mary's involvement boils down to her loyalty to Roberta." After a beat, he added, "Mary told Cody..." but couldn't come out with his point. "She implied I had a motive to kill the Wythes."

"What did she say?"

"Doesn't matter... It's a complete lie."

If it was a complete lie, Holly couldn't imagine why Lucas seemed suddenly terrified of it. But in her mind nothing was more important than using their theory to find her nephew. "Why take Tucker?"

"I don't know, but Mary was babysitting when it happened."

Holly couldn't deny that he was making sense, but she couldn't wrap her head around the garage. "Why try to kill me?"

"You said it yourself. You had gone to the club, ruffled feathers. Maybe the girls were worried you would catch onto them. Maybe setting the explosion was their pre-emptive strike. Maybe they realized they shouldn't have taken Tucker, that you would come after them and therefore they needed to eliminate you."

It made the darkest kind of sense.

"How are you going to investigate this if you're off the case?" she asked and his eyes lit up as if surprised or perhaps impressed she knew. She smiled at him. "I'm not an idiot. It's obvious."

Tense silence followed—Holly's smile waning, Lucas's eyes shifting, both sinking into the quicksand of their crisis. If Lucas was off the case, then he wouldn't be able to exonerate Holly by investigating the girls. Cody would be in charge and likely wouldn't prosecute his girlfriend's younger sister because of it, even if he did find Tucker in their possession and uncovered further evidence against Mary Cole and Roberta King, linking them to the murders.

Gradually, Lucas met her gaze. Holding hands, their faces close, she thought he might lean in, the spark between them having been rekindled.

She startled at the sound of pounding on the door, but she wasn't going to let this moment pass. Swiftly, she kissed him, pressing her lips to his and showing him that they were in this together. She would follow his lead. She trusted him.

Pounding on the door again, Warren called out, "Holly? I apologize for the intrusion. It's..."

As she started for the door, she heard Cody's good-natured voice supply, "Detective McAlister!"

"A detective here for you," Warren said loudly. "Holly?"

When she opened the door, Warren stepped aside for the detective. The look on Cody's face, having caught sight of Lucas on the bed, was unsettling.

"I would like to go over what happened," he told her, no longer sounding good-natured.

She stepped into the hallway, easing the door closed behind her. "How did you know I would be here?"

"Was that private?" asked Warren apologetically before mentioning, "You're welcome to chat in the lounge," he said as he led them in that direction.

When they reached the lobby, however, Cody brought her to a set of sofa-chairs near the window, but they didn't get comfortable.

Standing, he said, "I'm going to cut to the chase." His tone was low and so serious that it set her teeth on edge.

She nodded companionably even though it was the opposite of how she felt.

"If I'm being honest with you, I'm still trying to wrap my head around the explosion."

He flicked his eyes at the lounge where an elderly couple was rounding through towards the east wing. He held his tongue while they passed then glanced at the front desk, cautious that no one would overhear him. The clerk seemed disposed, pressing the phone to her ear.

"I have you on surveillance footage here at the resort. You went into Benjamin's room." She said nothing and tried not to look terrified. "Your alibi at McCoy's doesn't check out either. You were never there."

"I can explain-"

"You might not have to," he cut in, dismissing her.

"I don't understand."

"You're not my prime suspect."

Relieved, she breathed, "Okay."

"I'm going to ask you a straightforward question and I won't accept anything other than a straightforward answer."

The statement pitched her into sudden dread all over again, but she agreed.

Angling in and speaking discreetly, he asked, "What can you tell me about Rose's affair?"

Roberta came to mind, but she asked, "What affair?" He was studying her, analyzing every breath, judging every blink, but she didn't trust him with the information. "Rose's affair with who?"

"Lucas York."

CHAPTER FIFTEEN

PRE-DAWN TWILIGHT, gray and misty, gradually lifted as golden light streamed through the eastern windows of the resort lounge, marking the sunrise. Holly was seated cross-legged on one of the sofa-chairs, pliers in her hand, her jewelry case at her feet, a silver chain dangling from her fingers.

At the far side of the lounge, the assistant hotel manager was crouched in front of the fireplace, angling a long matchstick between logs and waiting for the flame to catch. Holly considered moving closer. The draft rolling off the windows chilled her bones, but she reasoned that the fire, once crackling, would warm the room.

She hoped the guests would sleep in. The lounge was quiet and empty except for the assistant manager, who rose to her feet and paced backwards a few steps, marveling at the fire and a job well done. As she started for the lobby, she smiled exhaustively—*Coffee?*

Holly declined, and the young woman continued onward to the lobby.

She had slept badly, having gone to bed with wet hair after the long, disturbing evening.

Pinching the silver heart pendant between her thumb and forefinger, she squeezed a dab of bonding glue onto the bezel, set the tube on the lid of her jewelry case, and then used pliers to align the opal gemstone that Roberta had requested into its proper place.

Sunlight pierced through the window, as she set the pendant on the case so it could dry.

Lucas and your sister were having an affair, Cody had told her.

Holly had willed herself not to believe it. Mary Cole had fed the accusation to the detective, who believed it outright. The girls were cunning, calculating, and demonic.

And yet the accusation riddled Holly with doubts.

Had Lucas been lying to her this whole time? Did his affection for her, the fact that he had been drawn to her, amount to a perverse form of mourning? He couldn't have her sister, so he was angling for the next best thing?

Roberta had gotten into her head and had caused her to obsess over the necklace, and then last night, Cody insinuated he had the same effect, passing along Mary's unbelievable statement that Lucas York had been seeing her sister in secret at Diamonds.

She felt like her mind was splitting apart.

After weathering the conversation with Cody, she had returned to Room 112 and disclosed the development to Lucas, who had seemed pained, but had denied the affair.

She had wanted to believe him, but struggled through tongue-tied excuses getting him out of the hotel, stammering nonsense about needing to join the Wythes for dinner, because she needed time to think.

As soon as he had left, she had watched him through the glass entrance door—Lucas walking, his shoulders hunched in the biting wind. Holly hadn't taken her eyes off his Ford, as he drove slowly out of the parking lot and hooked onto Keewaydin. When she realized she was stranded—her Saab at Rose's house as well as the BMW, not that it was drivable—she had cursed. She had gotten one of the desk clerks to do her the favor of driving her to Shackles so she could collect her tools, some materials, enough to keep busy at the lounge even though she would've preferred to work and sleep in her studio, the one place that always felt safe.

Leaning forward, golden sunlight momentarily blinding her where it shafted through the window, she picked up the pendant and nudged the opal to test whether the glue had dried. It had adhered well enough, so she used her fingernail to lift the bezel, working some movement into the tiny hinge. It looked good, though the irony wasn't lost on her that she was making Rose's necklace for the girl who had likely murdered her.

Holly couldn't spend another minute wrestling with doubts. She wasn't going to let a pair of teenage girls manipulate her.

But she couldn't deny that she felt trapped. She had to find a way to convince Cody that Lucas was being set up, but feared the detective would never believe the girls were behind this. And what Lucas was going to do about it in the meantime, she didn't have a clue.

The sound of teacups rattling on a tray stirred her from deep thought. Warren was easing through the lounge, a silver platter in his hands, a French-press filled with dark roast and antique teacups atop. He managed a chipper, *Good morning* when he reached her, gingerly sliding the tray onto a nearby coffee table then taking up on the sofa-chair across from her.

As he poured the coffee, he asked if she was enjoying the room.

Politely, she said, "I appreciate your hospitality," and accepted the porcelain teacup he had offered.

"Cream?" he asked, motioning to a miniature pitcher on the tray. When she declined, he jiggled a sugar packet out of a container.

But she said, "Black is fine."

"Have you seen the breakfast menu?" He was settling onto his chair, crossing his legs and resting his own teacup in his lap.

"I'm fine for the time being." She took a sip of coffee and wondered why the Wythe Resort was two hundred a night. The dark roast looked good, but had a watery taste.

Warren studied her for an uncomfortable moment. "You must be petrified."

"I'm hanging in there-"

"You were almost killed." He must have been able to tell she was taken aback that he had heard, because he mentioned, "The explosion. Why didn't you say something yesterday? We had to hear it from the detective."

"The police are handling it," she told him as if that could possibly conclude this conversation.

"Are they?" he questioned, genuinely curious. "That's not the impression I've gotten." He scanned the wintery landscape outside, squinting through the glare and drinking his coffee in contemplative silence. "All that matters is Tucker. We must find him, get him back. I've been losing sleep over suspicions that the police are wasting time focusing on the murders."

For an intellectual man who had made millions, his observation was flawed. "Warren," she said, reminding herself to maintain a respectful tone so as not to offend him as she edged into her point. "The kidnapper is the killer."

"Perhaps," he said, even though he didn't seem convinced. The assistant manager was crossing through so he waved her over and when she reached them, he began listing, "Blueberry muffins, low carb pancakes with real maple syrup, and yogurt with fresh fruit."

"And for you, Ma'am?" she asked, turning to Holly.

But Warren cut her off, snapping, "That *is* for her. You know I don't eat breakfast."

Though clearly insulted, the assistant manager remained stoic, working up a brittle smile and holding her shoulders back, as she said, "Certainly," before rushing off towards the kitchen.

"I can't possibly eat that much."

Warren waved his hand as though it was of no consequence and refreshed his teacup.

"You don't trust the police either," he pointed out with remarkable intuition. "There's no shame in being skeptical. I walk around with a lump in my throat and a lead ball in my stomach over the fact that my own son was... *killed*, while I slept, while Sarah slept as though nothing was wrong. But Tucker is all that matters," he repeated with conviction. After sipping his coffee, Warren pitched forward in his chair. "Is there anything you can tell me?"

Apprehensively, she said, "I don't know what you mean."

"What have you told the police?" When she said nothing, he lowered his tone. "I have resources, Holly. I can hire a private eye, get someone who's truly focused and invested."

"I, um..."

"You want him back, too, don't you? Rose, God rest her soul, but Rose wasn't the doting mother she should've been and she didn't allow Sarah and I to spend as much time with our grandson as we would've liked. I am desperate." He seemed choked up, but he swallowed his emotions before repeating, "Desperate to get him back." Pleadingly, he went on, "You will never want for anything, I can promise you. I see a future, a family, all of us. If there's anything you know, if there's anything you've heard, even if only a shred of information, perhaps something you think is insignificant, I can assure you it is not."

Debating. Intrigued yet unnerved by his intensity, she finally asked, "Have you heard about Ron Conover and Diamonds?"

He frowned then asked, "What's Diamonds?"

"It's a club. I thought..." She checked herself, censoring how she had learned about the escort service. "I told the detectives, because it seemed relevant. But I wasn't sure they had done anything about it. I don't know for sure if they talked to Conover. I think a few of his girls could be behind this."

"Conover, you say?" Pondering, he sipped his coffee.

It didn't sound like a question.

The lounge was filling up, guests traipsing in and taking up on the various chairs and couches, their voices adding texture over the crackling fireplace.

Sarah Wythe floated in from the lobby, the stylish coif of her hair, her precise makeup, and the artful lines of her tailored dress clashing with the glazed-over vacancy in her eyes. Strangely, her hand was pitched in the air like Miss America. She looked lost gliding through the lounge, her gaze drifting aimlessly as though faces and furniture were one in the same.

Concerned, Warren rushed to her and in a coddling manner, brought her to his sofa-chair and eased her down. After kissing the top of her head, he offered her coffee and Holly tried not to stare at the woman who only yesterday had been lucid.

Sarah seemed delighted when she realized the teacup was in her hand, smiling as though awed by a treasure. "Remember when we bought these?" she asked her husband.

"Of course," he said curtly, but Sarah was already launching into the tale for Holly's benefit.

"We flew to China. A filthy, just terribly dirty country, wouldn't you agree?"

Warren's smile seemed embarrassed.

"We went to a market, a *bazaar*," she quickly corrected herself then laughed, "everyone smelled like rotting onions and I couldn't wait to get out of there, but I insisted we buy this tea set."

"It was the Yuyuan Bazaar in Shanghai and if I'm not mistaken, you enjoyed yourself," he said, directing the comment to Holly before giving his wife another pat on the head as though she were a child, after which he excused himself.

Holly would've felt awkward being alone with Sarah if the woman had retained even a fraction of her personality, but she was far gone, lolling in a world of memories.

"I got into a bit of trouble," she confessed as though they were close friends, setting down her teacup. "I'm supposed to apologize for showing up at your store unannounced."

Unsure of what to say, Holly went with, "Oh, that's okay," but soon realized she had misunderstood the woman's sentiment.

"I don't see why I have to like you," she said bluntly. "Benjamin didn't even like Rose towards the end. He kept it to himself, but a mother knows."

Was Sarah opening up? Or was this merely a flash of clarity, soon to be snuffed out when the next wave of her medication kicked in? Gambling—maybe the woman knew something about Benjamin and Roberta that Holly didn't, some fresh angle that had strained the marriage and would give her insight—she asked, "Why didn't Benji like Rose?"

"Oh, you girls," she cackled, startling Holly. "When a person isn't cut from the same cloth, they aren't cut from the same cloth." She shrugged as though at a loss for explaining it better. "And those blue eyes of his-"

"Benji had brown eyes," she pointed out, confused that the woman could be so far gone she had forgotten.

Leaning in, a knowing smile spreading across her face, she said, "Exactly." When she straightened her back, finding something interesting about the snow-lain landscape beyond the window, she stated, "Tucker has the wrong eyes."

Holly's stomach lurched, suddenly realizing what the woman was alluding to. The connection, which she had never before put together, stunned her.

"Poor Benji," she droned on. "He knew."

"What did he know?" She needed to hear it before she would let herself freak out. "Sarah?"

The woman lolled her eyes at Holly as if on the brink of falling asleep—her eyelids heavy, a lazy smile forming across her taut face. "We love Tucker. We didn't care about that test." Longingly, she breathed, "We love him, sweet Tucker. We want him back."

"Sarah." She shook the woman's leg to rouse her and Sarah's eyes popped open. "What test?"

"Don't tell Warren I told you. I'm already in trouble," she mumbled, slipping away.

Holly began racking her brain for the hospital where Rose had given birth to Tucker. Would Benjamin have ventured to the same hospital for a paternity test or get it done privately at a clinic?

She steadied her thoughts, though it was a struggle, reminding herself that Sarah was high on medication, as she quickly collected her tools and Roberta's necklace, shoving them into her jewelry case and snapping it shut.

Just as she was rising to her feet, a waiter approached with a massive tray of food and Holly mentioned, "Can you see to it that Mrs. Wythe gets to her room?" before padding off to her own room to deposit the case.

Speare Memorial in Plymouth was where Rose had delivered Tucker, she recalled as she barreled into Room 112 and dropped her jewelry case on the floor, her mind reeling with the shattering possibility that Benjamin might not have been Tucker's father.

After locking the door and rounding into the lobby, she told herself it would be crazy to jump to conclusions based on the drug induced ranting of an incoherent woman. Tucker could have blue eyes even though Rose's had been fawn-brown and Benjamin's had been dark as chocolate, couldn't he? A medical anomaly, fine, but it was possible, wasn't it? Their mother had light eyes, and Sarah's were green.

She reasoned she would go to the hospital anyway just to set her mind at ease.

"I need a vehicle," she told the desk clerk, whose response was bleary-eyed confusion.

"A taxi?"

"No. A car that I can drive. Warren told me this wouldn't be a problem," she lied.

Befuddled as he was at the unexpected demand, the clerk immediately consulted his coworkers, mumbling, *Mr. Wythe,* as though their employer might skin them alive if they didn't handle this swiftly and quietly.

As the clerks scrambled for a solution, pointing fingers and arguing about who among them couldn't spare their vehicle—*Not mine, there's barely any gas,* and *My tires are low,* and *This is some serious crap*—Holly devised she would first drive to Rose's house, collect her twin's identification, dress in her clothes, and then storm into the hospital to collect every last record archived under the name Wythe.

Grimacing, the clerk returned with a set of car keys and reluctantly handed them over. "It's the brown Volvo with the *I like lipstick around my dipstick* bumper sticker."

She cocked her head at that, but didn't waste time commenting. Instead, she rushed outside and began scanning the cars in the parking lot.

When she found the Volvo, which boasted a slew of tasteless bumper stickers—*Vagitarian* with two spread fingers for the V, and *Two beers and I'm gay*, and *It was me, I let the dogs out*—she discovered the door handle was encased in ice so she scraped her fingernails over the lock, inserted the key, and after whipping the door open, settled behind the steering wheel.

Some terrible AC / DC song blared through the speakers as soon as she turned the engine, but she lowered the volume, pulling around the parking lot and arching onto Keewaydin where she picked up speed.

When she reached the house, the blasted hole where the garage used to be was charred and jagged, and she could see clearly where flames had licked towards the unscathed side of the house.

She hurried to the front door and fit the key into the lock. The foyer smelled singed as she stepped inside and the scent became overwhelming when she padded towards the stairs. A quick glance down the hallway told her why. The fire had eaten the wall, leaving it black and destroyed—electrical innards, frayed and tangled as a rats nest, poked through broken sheetrock.

She started up the stairs and walked briskly to the walk-in closet where stale smoke scented the air.

The necklace was hanging on the vanity mirror. She had every intention of acting quickly, fastening the necklace on and changing her clothes, grabbing her sister's driver's license from the purse Rose had favored, which was resting on a shelf above the clothing rack. But when Holly had the pendant in her hand, she became distracted, examining it from all angles.

It didn't appear altered. Yet it looked slightly bulkier than she remembered, the opal more raised from the silver. Eyeing it closely, she discovered tiny hinges.

Using her thumbnail, she tried to lift the silver bezel, but it didn't want to pop open.

Frustrated, she fastened it around her neck, pulled her long hair out from under the chain, and changed quickly into a pair of designer jeans, a woolen sweater, and wedge-heeled boots then riffled through Rose's purse in search of her twin's ID.

Tucking the driver's license into her pocket as soon as she had found it, she returned the purse to its home. She felt indecisive about choosing a coat, but went with a tailored trench. After cinching the belt, she hung her own coat in the closet and made her way out of the house.

It wasn't until she was driving along Newman that a punch of anxiety hit her chest.

Benjamin wasn't Tucker's real father.

What if Rose and Benjamin's murders hadn't stemmed from Roberta's affair with her brother-in-law? What if the girls hadn't killed them?

What if this was all about Tucker? Had the killer taken Rose and Benjamin's life in order to get his hands on the boy?

Was Tucker's real father behind this?

And were Roberta King and Mary Cole in fact innocent?

Speare Memorial Hospital was a two-story brick structure and as Holly passed through the sliding glass entrance, she considered how she might go about this. Would she need the maternity ward or would the front desk be able to supply the test results? Should she have searched for Rose's insurance card? Was it even required in a situation like this?

Daunted, she placed Rose's driver's license on the counter and told the receptionist, "I'm interested in medical records. They could be in my husband's medical history or perhaps my son's, Tucker Wythe."

After eyeing Rose's ID, the woman behind the counter began typing. "Let's see."

Nervously, Holly explained, "There should be a paternity test."

"It might take a minute to pull it up," she said, her eyes glued to the monitor. "If you would like, you can have a seat."

Though she felt too anxious to sit, she couldn't afford to seem difficult—considering the receptionist clearly wasn't keeping up with the news, she would've known she was speaking to a dead woman otherwise, Holly didn't want to press her luck by hovering—she found an empty chair in-between a mother who was tending to her coughing child and an elderly man with a patch of psoriasis on his cheek.

Restlessly, she fidgeted with the heart pendant around her neck, flicking her thumbnail over the opal.

Behind the counter, a printer began whooshing out sheets of paper and Holly rushed over.

"It looks like we ran two tests," said the receptionist, doling out the first report. Holly scanned it, immediately catching the name *Benjamin Wythe* and the word *negative*. "That one shows Mr. Wythe is not the father, and this one," she said, placing the second report on the counter for Holly to read; "you ordered this yourself."

Holly stiffened. The receptionist was staring at her suspiciously. "Yes," she said, playing along. "But I didn't have a chance to swing by for the results." Skimming the report, she asked, "Why can't I find the father's name?"

"Because you didn't provide a name," she explained, her finger tapping a line on the report, mid-way down the sheet. "You provided a hair sample, which we confirmed belongs to Tucker's biological father."

Frustrated—if it had listed the father, then she would have a solid lead to bring to Cody, get him on the right track and off of Lucas's back, not to mention quell her own doubts—she turned from the counter, the reports in one hand, the pendant clutched in the other, the receptionist bristling at Holly's lack of manners, *You're welcome!*

She crossed through the lobby.

When she climbed in behind the steering wheel, she reviewed the dates on each test more carefully. Benjamin had discovered the truth three weeks ago, but the test Rose had ordered was dated two years back.

She was so close, she could feel it, but she had nothing, and because of it she wanted to scream and kick and tear her hair out.

Holly slammed her palms against the steering wheel and, jumping out of her skin, yanked the pendant off, splitting the chain and lacerating the nape of her neck.

Clawing at the bezel, her fingernails chipping, blood seeping from her nail-beds, Holly growling, determined to force it open, force Rose's secret out,

Roberta's implication bending her mind into agonizing angles...

The pendant popped open.

There in her palm, gazing up at her from the shallow pillbox was a small photo of Lucas York.

CHAPTER SIXTEEN

STANDING IN THE center of his living room, pivoting slowly, and glancing from one familiar object to the next—the cracked leather couch that had come with the apartment, the end table made of warped wood, the lamp on top, its shade dusty, the bookshelves, mostly empty, the kitchen islet that seemed to invade the living area—Lucas tried and failed to ground himself in his surroundings, desperate to reel in the panic that was threatening to split his mind apart.

He had no idea where he had been all day, what he had done, why he was only now coming to his senses and into his right mind, when night had long since fallen.

Tempering his breathing, forcing oxygen into his lungs to ward off the sudden swell of dizziness that was overcoming him, he forced himself to recall something, anything he had done that day. But his mind kept going blank.

He needed to start small, focus on one task that he had probably done today, and find it in his memory.

Did he remember yesterday?

Yes. The explosion, driving Holly to the resort and Cody interrupting them. It was all there.

But today wasn't.

How had he gotten into his apartment? Mentally retracing his steps, he tried to remember fitting his key into the lock, which he definitely would've done, he would've had to... But he sensed the recollection he was touching upon had been from another day.

He kept searching his memory for it—*the metal key scraping into the lock*—racking his brain, warding off white-hot panic that he was losing it. But again, his mind went blank.

Exhaling loudly, he plowed his fingers through his hair and began pacing, as he conjured a different memory, the last thing he truly could remember—waking up in bed that morning.

He had been lying on his side, his cheek pressed to the cool pillow. He had flexed his feet, working his calves into a good stretch.

This felt promising, he thought. He let out a carefully measured breath and sat on the couch, mentally reviewing the shower that he had taken that morning, the cup of coffee he had made, its weak taste. He had opened the apartment door, stepped into the carpeted hallway, then...

His mind went blank.

He tried again. Starting from the beginning, he mentally reviewed getting out of bed, showering, drinking coffee, opening the apartment door, seeing the hallway, then...

Tunnel vision swallowing his sense of sight, his hands and face turning numb, darkness falling all around him. No, not around him, inside of him... until he had vanished.

Lucas jumped off the couch then froze, petrified.

It had never been this bad before.

The blackouts. Losing time.

Zoning out during one menial task at the station.

Slipping away while driving.

A few minutes here.

An hour there.

Never a full day.

But what if he was wrong?

What if today wasn't the first ten-hours of blackness, his body functioning without him?

He began pacing, his chest breaking out into a cold sweat.

As if the thought of her might have the power to calm him, he turned his racing mind towards Holly.

Yesterday had felt so good, holding hands, talking in her hotel room, exploring their connection that ten years hadn't changed. But when she had returned to the room after speaking with Cody, a dark intuition took hold.

He had listened to her explain what he had already known, that Cody believed Lucas had indulged in an affair with Rose Wythe.

Lucas had denied it and Holly had believed him, but deep down he had sensed doubt gnawing at his gut—an affair he had never had or an affair he hadn't remembered?

Suddenly, Roberta's comment echoed through his mind—*I thought we went over this last night.*

Inside his parked car, students milling about through the snowy parking lot, he had grabbed her by the collar, his fists balling around the matted fur of her coat. Seething, screaming, *What did we go over? What? Tell me?* He had slammed her against the door, her head cracking into the car window.

She had looked like a wild animal—her eyes flaring and her mouth snarling, shoving him off, and overpowering him despite his rage. His hands had gone strangely numb, trembling, Lucas was horrified at himself, at his violence, his lack of control. But the glint in her eye, as he had breathed heavily in the driver's seat, had seemed bizarrely empathetic, *familiar*—why had she acted so familiar with him? Why had he felt she *was* familiar?

By the time she had climbed out of his car, taking powerful, deliberate steps, he had gotten no answers.

What if Cody was right about him?

Could he have killed Rose Wythe, driven to the resort and murdered Benjamin? Why would he do something like that?

Why?

He plummeted onto the couch, rejecting the idea, but soon the fact that he couldn't remember where he had been the night of the 12th consumed him.

He had gotten the call from dispatch that night, but he hadn't been home, though being home was the lie he told Cody. He had been in his car, flying along... some darkened road? Where had he been?

Struggling to see it in his mind, he began pacing the living room, the snowy road unfolding in his memory. He had been managing the phone call, navigating the slick terrain, his partner's directives barely registering, as he hooked right at an intersection.

He had noted the street signs.

They were Forbes Road and Keewaydin.

Lucas grimaced at the revelation. He had been driving along Forbes, away from Newman Road where Rose Wythe had lain dead and trapped under the ice. Forbes would've brought him to Keewaydin, to the resort.

Pinching his eyes shut, he ran his hands down his face.

He could remember every detail of investigating the crime scene—standing on the ice, watching the diver bob in the dark water, discovering Holly Danes on the couch inside the house.

He told himself the fact that he could remember working the crime scene was a good sign and barreled into the kitchen where he slapped a cabinet open, grabbed a bottle of whiskey and a glass from the shelf, and poured himself a stiff drink. But as he brought the glass to his mouth—alcohol stinging his nostrils—he realized his hand was shaking.

Where the hell had he gone after Cody had released him from the crime scene?

The team had planned on going to Shenanigan's, the only bar open until four in the morning, but Lucas had no memory of having gone there. He had called Roger, the M.E. from the foyer of the house to order a ten panel on Rose Wythe. He had humored Cody, following his partner's orders for another half hour—going through the office, stealing the Joint Will—before he had been released. He could recall walking out to his vehicle, driving off, then nothing, nothing whatsoever, until the following morning when he had woken up in his boots and coat, lying on top of the covers.

He shot the whiskey back, refilled the glass, and carried both into the living room where he sank onto the couch.

After swigging half the glass and praying the alcohol would soon flood his bloodstream and smooth out the jagged edges of his tortured thoughts, he began emptying his pockets—jacket, jeans—letting crumpled receipts flutter to the coffee table. He tossed his wallet down and raced into the kitchen where he pulled open drawer after drawer, grabbing receipts by the fistful, which he shoved on the counter.

Methodically, he worked his way through the apartment, collecting receipts—the evidence of his whereabouts at any given time—and when he was satisfied he had left no stone unturned, he returned to the couch and began flattening each one—receipts from gas stations, fast food joints, supermarkets, and drug stores.

Overwhelmed, he read the first receipt, studying it closely.

It was dated three weeks ago, time stamped just after eight in the evening. Exxon Mobil—a gas station—and the address was in Center Harbor.

He moved onto the next one, another benign purchase in Center Harbor.

Pulling a receipt from the bottom of the stack, he noted the date—October of last year, another Center Harbor gas station.

But it shouldn't have been, not when he had been living in Plymouth at that time.

Frantically, he checked five more receipts; all dated prior to his transfer, all detailing Center Harbor addresses.

Without warning, an image of Holly in red lingerie flashed through his mind. Before he could place where the memory had come from—she hadn't worn red in the motel room ten years ago—it was quickly replaced with another...

Wearing nothing but two strips of black lace, Holly held his hand, guiding him down a hallway and into a private room, red walls, a heart-shaped bed, something trashy about the establishment, yet the emotions in his heart were real.

But it wasn't Holly.

Her hair was different—shoulder length and carefully styled—he realized, straining to see her in his mind.

It was Rose.

And it had been real.

Rattled, he drew his GLOCK from his holster. His hands were trembling badly as he dislodged the clip, catching the magazine in his palm. Though he was afraid to look at it, terrified at the thought of discovering his police issued .48 caliber weapon might have two bullets missing, he forced himself to check anyway, but what he found only confused him.

The magazine was empty.

Coming undone, he stalked through the apartment, scanning for signs of Tucker. The three-year-old was a critical piece of the puzzle after all. Whoever had killed Rose and Benjamin had taken the child. He shuddered recalling how Holly had looked standing in the snow, watching flames devour the garage—the explosion another critical piece to the war against the Wythes.

Had he set off the bomb?

Why had he been so close to the house?

He couldn't remember.

Lucas thought he might be sick. Bile stung the back of his throat, but he swallowed hard, tearing his bedroom apart, searching desperately for evidence that he hoped like hell he wouldn't find, all the while flashes of Rose mentally assaulted him, filling his head with the dark possibility that his parents weren't the only ones he had killed.

Wrestling the mattress off the box spring, he rid the image of Rose—nude, legs spread, smiling in aroused anticipation of him lowering down, pressing into her—from his mind.

He lifted the box spring, angling it against the wall, but the floor beneath was bare.

How could he have possibly gotten involved with Rose when the woman he wanted, the woman he had been obsessed with for years, was her twin?

Or was the answer hiding in the very question? Had he been so torn up about losing Holly that he had chased a cheap imitation?

You found me, she had said, welcoming him into Diamonds, entwining her arm around his, and leading him to the bar. Lucas, stunned yet grinning, hadn't been able to take his eyes off her.

Holly? he had asked, drinking in the sight of her, disbelief commingling with a burning desire to hold her and never let her go.

The woman had pretended she was the love of his life, as they talked at the bar. She had known things about their long-ago night together. She had proved she was Holly...

And then she had laughed.

Her admission came through a cool smile. *No, I'm not Holly...*

No, I'm not Holly...

Like a slap across his face, *No, I'm not Holly...*

And Lucas's heart had bottomed out with soul-crushing disappointment, as a dark fog had clouded his mind.

I recognized you from the paper, those murders you solved in Plymouth. Holly's my sister, my twin actually and she offhandedly mentioned your night together when I showed her the article.

But Lucas could barely hear her, his mind rejecting Rose, rejecting that she wasn't Holly. Darkness had swallowed him, trapping him in a black hole—to preserve the fantasy, the lie, his need to find the woman who had gotten away.

For years.

He had been seeing Rose for years.

Having slipped into darkness where the fantasy of Holly went on living, he hadn't heard her offer, *Call me Holly if you like.*

He had driven to Diamonds to see her, eventually he had begun meeting her at her house—his mind wrapped around Holly, his body making love to her twin.

Every tryst, every rendezvous, recorded on gas station and liquor store receipts.

Lucas couldn't take it.

In desperate need of whiskey, he refilled his glass, his hands trembling, as he wracked his brain for why he had gone to Diamonds in the first place. What had possessed him to set foot in an escort service? Why risk his career as an investigator?

Beads of sweat had formed across his brow so he wiped his forehead dry with his shirtsleeve and swigged the glass back, alcohol sliding down his throat.

He hadn't risked his career, he suddenly remembered. He had gone to Diamonds on a hunch, unsatisfied that a case he had wrapped up wasn't truly over.

Lucas had been the centrifugal force in taking down a prostitution ring in Plymouth that had functioned under the guise of an escort service. Closing the case had earned him notoriety and a few articles in the local paper since the crime itself had been brutal, two under-aged girls murdered, their bodies dumped in the Pemigewasset River. Though Lucas had locked up the major players, another had walked. There hadn't been enough evidence against him. And when Lucas had heard that the man had opened a new establishment—Diamonds—he had been eager to investigate and bring Ron Conover to justice.

But he never got that far.

Instead, he had continued to see Rose in secret, slipping into a black hole every time, while some part of him relished the fantasy of being with Holly Danes.

This was maddening.

He plowed his fingers through his hair, pacing like a caged wolf—riled up, jumping out of his skin, panic rising into full blown horror, an incredible urge to see Holly splitting his mind apart.

Killer...

But he wasn't! He couldn't be! He had promised himself, never again!

He told himself to keep hunting through the receipts and find proof of his whereabouts the night of the 12th. He should sneak into the precinct, review the evidence, and strip it of anything incriminating.

Was this why he had felt responsible for Holly? Was this why he had gone to great lengths to protect her? Because she truly was innocent, because by some terrible stroke of bad luck the crimes he had committed were falling squarely on her shoulders?

He couldn't get any air into his lungs. Feeling light-headed and knowing it wouldn't help to swig whiskey straight from the bottle, he did anyway, tipping the bottle up vertically, pouring booze down his throat, determined not to stop drinking until he was certain his rationale had been restored.

He couldn't have done it, could he? He hadn't killed them. Had he?

By the time he was staring at the bottom of the empty bottle, he had gotten no closer to the truth.

But Roberta King was weighing heavily on his mind.

If anyone knew what had really happened...

Killer...

She would know.

Decisively, he started for the door, but when he threw it open, ready to barrel down the hallway and out to his car, Holly was staring him in the face.

"I have to talk to you," she said bluntly.

She looked furious and exhausted, and scowled at the scent of booze on his breath.

She also looked surreal—the one he had wanted all along.

His brain wasn't working and words wouldn't come, but he widened the door, welcoming her inside.

She breathed, "Damn," when she realized the mess—the torn apart couch, its cushions lain haphazardly across the floor, a blizzard of receipts everywhere, every cabinet and drawer in the kitchen ajar, the pots, pans, and recipe books from the pantry now strewn across the linoleum.

"Were the police here?" she asked, catching him off guard.

He shook his head. His chest felt tight, his instincts alerting him to the probability that she knew things he didn't, things that could shatter him even worse than the mind-bending conclusion he had already reached.

Expression hardening, she stated, "Cody was right. You were involved with Rose."

"I didn't know-"

"That you were involved with her? You didn't know?" she challenged, her eyes misting over with tears. Her voice was thin and trembling when she asked, "Did you kill my sister?"

He swallowed hard, choking down his emotions. "I don't know."

They stared at each other for a long moment—Holly's mouth twisting into a pained grimace as tears sprung from her eyes, Lucas quaking with an agonizing mix of remorse and panic.

Finally, he found the strength to whisper, "I thought she was you. And if I thought that, there's no way I could've killed her."

But Holly was deaf to him. "Where is Tucker?" she demanded, advancing on him.

"I don't know."

Angling up at him, holding herself back, she screamed, "Where the hell is he?" But all he could do was repeat, *I don't know, I don't know,* hoping her balled fists wouldn't fly.

They didn't.

She drew her revolver instead, aiming the gun at his chest, her arms locked, and her finger on the trigger.

"I'm not going to ask you again," she warned, her tone firm though her hands were shaking. "I know he's your son. I know the lengths you went to get your hands on him. I want him back."

Stunned, the information hit him like a sledgehammer to his chest, though there was something eerily familiar about it—Tucker was his son?—and he slowly raised his hands in surrender and said, "I don't know who I am."

CHAPTER SEVENTEEN

THE WIND HOWLED, ticking sleet against the windowpane, as Mary tip-toed through her bedroom, stepping over the ever-growing mess on the carpet, and opened the door a crack, listening.

The hallway was dim and quiet.

She heard the faint hum of the refrigerator downstairs and startled when the radiator behind her clanged to life.

Cody had been going to bed later and later, his schedule thrown thanks to developments in the case, developments he wouldn't have if not for her, and she had only gotten a measly handful of beers in exchange.

Determined that a rift not form between them, Hannah had adjusted to his late timetable, pulling even longer hours at the station—her work as a police officer unrelenting, in at dawn, home long after night had fallen, entrusting Mary to cook dinner, tend to the house, and act grateful.

Mary was certain they were asleep, their steadily murmuring conversation behind closed doors having dried up a good half-hour ago.

She was already in her jeans, a sensible sweater, lacy cheetah print lingerie hugging her every curve like a second skin beneath.

Pulling her boots on, her heart began punching so hard in her chest that she feared her rib cage might crack. It wasn't the mere anxiety of sneaking out undetected that had her pulse rate quickening, her cheeks flushed hot, dewy beads of perspiration dampening her back and running down her cleavage where the fabric of her garments couldn't catch it. The reason she was on pins and needles was Roberta. She hadn't seen or talked to her best friend in days, not since Tucker had gone missing. Her friend hadn't returned her phone call that night or responded to any of Mary's text messages, each more urgent than the last—*Why weren't you in school today?* and *Where the hell are you, why haven't you called?* and stifling a sob, *Don't do this, don't punish me for telling him, I had no choice.*

The anticipation of seeing Roberta had Mary rocketing into the stratosphere of thrilled terror.

She was dying to know what her friend had been up to.

After lacing up her boots, she eased the door open, which caused the hinges to whine. She winced—had the sound woken them? She paused, listening hard, but was met with the same epic stillness.

Slowly and soundlessly, she made her way through the hallway, shifting her weight carefully from one foot to the next and avoiding the areas where the floorboards tended to creak beneath the carpet. She began praying to a God she didn't believe in that she wouldn't get caught.

Cody had kept up his end of the deal. He hadn't dragged her into the precinct and more importantly, he hadn't told Hannah about Mary's moonlighting at the club. In exchange, Mary had been a model citizen and student, but it had been at the expense of the friendship she cherished the most. She had to see Roberta.

She let out a jagged breath, coming to their bedroom door, and gave herself a moment to work up the nerve. Experience told her the floorboards spanning this portion of the hallway were especially noisy and with her half-sister's renowned sleeping issues—what if Hannah was balled on the floor with her ear to the ground? The slightest creak could rouse her—Mary would have to rush light and fast on her feet towards the stairs, or else leap, the landing of which, its presumed thud, could pose problems.

Opting to rush, she gave one hard listen at the door. She would've liked to hear snoring, but silence would have to be good enough. She went for it and didn't stop until she was rounding into the kitchen.

As luck would have it, there were five beers in the refrigerator. Cool air poured out, the bright light in the fridge spilling into the kitchen, as she tucked one bottle under her arm and grabbed a second. She let the door close on its own in favor of checking the digital clock on the coffee maker. It was ten before midnight. In her eagerness, she had left her room too soon.

Reasoning to use her time wisely, she cracked one of the bottle's open, sucked in a fast sip, and set the bottle on the counter as quietly as humanly possible, and then padded into the foyer where her jacket was hanging in the closet.

It took her a few moments to get bundled up—bomber jacket, scarf, skullcap, and fingerless gloves—after which she peered out at the wintery darkness through a small window on the front door.

Roberta was a dismal failure at a great many things, but punctuality wasn't one of them. She was never late and by the same measure she was never, ever early.

Two beers wouldn't be enough.

If anything good had come out of her cringe-worthy conversation with Cody—Christ, the thought of him discovering her, that photo, topless and smiling, her legs spread around the back of a chair, made her want to crawl into a hole and die—it was the fact that Cody had forbid her to set foot in Diamonds.

She had been happy to obey.

She couldn't deny she had relished the thrill of it. She had come to look forward to the late nights, the doting attention, the powerful, dangerous feeling that the club had filled her with every time she had crossed the threshold. But ever since Rose's death, the place just didn't feel the same. The white furniture she had once found glamorous seemed cheap and sticky. The cocktails she had assumed were top-shelf tasted watery. And the clientele that had fawned over her, now met her with vacuous, lust-crazed glances, which tipped her off to a possibility she hadn't before considered, that they might expect her performance to escalate into debasing acts she wouldn't in her right mind volunteer for.

Diamonds was the last place she wanted Roberta to take her.

Chugging her beer and hoping Roberta's Audi would soon growl up the driveway, she figured Diamonds had always been seedy. It had taken the murder of someone she had loved to open her eyes.

She couldn't very well toss the empty bottle in the trash where Hannah would easily discover it, so she wedged it into her jacket pocket, stole another beer from the fridge, and rounded back into the foyer, double-fisting the daddy sodas that she hoped like hell would loosen her up enough to go through with another long night at Diamonds, her penance or so it felt for spending time with her best friend.

Peering out the window, its pane distorted with splintered ice, she scanned the dark, snowy driveway, the row of gnarly maples and bowing pines beyond lining the road, all traced in a razor's edge of moonlight.

Shadowy movement caught her eye. Turning up the driveway was the Audi, its headlights off. The vehicle lurched and bounced with the slick terrain and came to a stop well before reaching the house.

Quickly, Mary juggled her beers while unlocking the door and in the same fashion locked up as soon as she had stepped onto the icy landing.

Though her cheeks stiffened from the cold, Mary was smiling, as she jogged down the driveway, while Roberta maneuvered the Audi pulling a three-point turn.

She didn't lower onto the passenger seat so much as jump in, beaming ecstatically at her friend whose serious expression caught her off guard. She slammed her door shut and hissed, "Damn," in delayed reaction to the thud, her eyes locking on the house, scanning for signs Cody or her sister had heard. She wasn't out of the woods yet, she reminded herself. She couldn't let her excitement get the best of her, but she threw her arms around Roberta anyway, beer bottles clinking against the car window.

"Missed you too," Roberta said coolly, though she held the hug, her body saying what her tone couldn't. As they loosened their grip, she affirmed, "Seriously though, I missed you."

Smiling, Mary let out a relieved exhale and shifted on her seat, clamping one beer between her knees, setting the other in the cup holder on the dash, while fastening her seatbelt, after which Roberta stomped on the accelerator.

The Audi barreled down the driveway and when they reached the road, pulling left, Roberta flipped the headlights on.

It wasn't until Mary had cracked a beer open and sucked down a long haul that she noticed her friend's right cheek looked discolored—strangely blue under a caked sheen of foundation.

Alarmed, she breathed, "Damn," as she reached out to touch Roberta's face, but the serious girl batted her hand away. "Is that a bruise?"

"It's nothing," she said, brushing her fingertips over the injury, which only piqued Mary's curiosity to intolerable levels. Perhaps because Mary was staring at her, she added, "Back-handed slap. I took it like a champ."

"Ron?"

"Are you kidding me?" She gaped. "Conover wouldn't have a chance in hell of going on breathing if he ever smacked me, you know that."

Mary meant for her response, *damn straight* to be in agreement, but it felt brittle and wavered badly. Rumor had it that Ron Conover had lent a hand in murdering a few under-aged girls up north and since overhearing the gossip, Mary had dealt with him accordingly, but never without Rose's ferocious support. She wouldn't put anything past Ron, certainly not a backhanded slap to keep Roberta in line.

She feared to imagine how Ron would react when she returned to the club. He generally despised girls who flaked and didn't show up for their shifts, and Mary had been absent for more than a few.

"Who hit you?"

Roberta concentrated as she maneuvered the Audi through a cloverleaf, merging onto the Daniel Webster Highway. Once she straightened the vehicle out, settling into a whopping forty-five miles per hour, she mentioned, "We have a few things to talk about."

"I'm listening."

Roberta reached for the beer in the cup holder, but Mary took it instead.

After cracking the bottle open, she handed it to Roberta, whose gaze snapped to the rearview to quickly confirm there were no cops behind them. The coast was clear so she chugged half the bottle. When she handed it back and Mary returned the bottle to the cup holder, she stated, "Lucas has been *off*."

"Off?"

"I've seen it before, but not like this, and quite frankly, I messed up big time-"

"*Off* in what way? What have you seen before?" she asked, staring wildly at her friend.

Mumbling under her breath, she said, "I didn't see it. I just didn't see it."

Mary drank her beer, waiting patiently for her friend to make sense.

"You know how I told you about Gerty, and about how she didn't remember the worst of it? How she couldn't remember, like her brain filed those memories away in a place that she couldn't access?"

"Yeah," said Mary, feeling a sting of jealousy. She could remember every last disgusting second of her father's abuse. No amount of booze had been able to kill it, mask it, or even blur it into enough obscurity that she might forget. Months had passed and the memories, those harrowing flashes that surged through her mind at the worst times—in the shower, lying in bed, flirting with jocks on the football field—hadn't quit but seemed to grow stronger, more urgent, as though her subconscious was designed to never let her move on. Irony was a bitch and she hated to resent Dale for not beating her, torturing her, making things so bad that some miraculous psychological phenomenon would take root and bury all that she had endured. She grit her teeth at the thought, gaze locking on the darkness where the headlights failed to penetrate.

"When Gerty was in the pit, when things were happening to her, she was functioning from this other place, this zombie-autopilot place, like a second person was living inside her mind, present for the worst of it, gone whenever Gerty had to lead the normal aspects of her life."

If there was a connection, Mary wasn't getting it. "What does this have to do with Lucas?"

"Gerty didn't need to keep living that way once she got out. She was smart enough, her mind was strong enough, to wall off that second part of her. The person inside her who had gone through the abuse died, because she didn't need it anymore, that mode of functioning." Roberta looked as though she was trying to ward off a nauseous spell, but she finally said, "Lucas's second persona, the part of him that took on the brunt of his lousy upbringing... it never died."

"What?" she asked, stunned yet confused at the concept too that was haunting to trust.

"It takes him over," she explained. "It swallows him up and takes over his body and functions for him, and man," she snorted a strange laugh that sounded angry or frustrated or just plain pissed that she hadn't been smart enough to catch onto Lucas's multiplicity sooner. "I didn't recognize it. I didn't realize that the Lucas I've been dealing with was the dark side of him, the disturbed side. I should've known. All that information about *Killer*." It sounded like she was talking to herself all of a sudden. "Why would he open up to me about that if he was in his right mind? He wouldn't. Of course I was dealing with his dark side. I should've known."

Roberta snapped out of it in time to pull off the exit, squeezing the brakes and angling around the off-ramp. It wasn't until she veered onto the road that Mary caught sight of a street sign and realized they couldn't possibly be heading towards Diamonds.

"Where are we going?"

"The shed," Roberta said easily.

Not that Mary was disappointed, the shed was a paradise compared to the club especially since she dreaded facing Ron, but she asked, "Why?"

"It's just a pit stop. Gisele's cool with us showing up a bit late." She slowed the Audi, turning onto Union Ave, which would take them along the Opechee Reservoir. "I thought that Lucas was like me, like us, but he's not, not in the sense that he's been, essentially, someone else. But he caught on. He's been figuring it out. And today, he came to me for answers." She indicated the bruise on her face. "I thought he was going to kill me."

"Damn."

"He looked... I've never seen a person look so angry, the rage in his eyes, the hurt, like I had betrayed him. He only hit me once, but I could tell he was holding himself back. He doesn't know, though."

"Know what?"

Again Roberta squeezed the brakes, cutting the steering wheel, this time turning onto Messer Street.

Mary was about to launch into questions, but her friend broke off on a new tangent. "Whatever his mental disease... Mary, he thought Rose was really her twin."

"What?"

"All those times he came to the club, he thought Rose was Holly. I can't tell you how many times I hung out with him in his apartment, drinking-" The very mention prompted her to reach for her beer and after a long sip, she continued. "Doing cocaine and talking all night. And I had no idea he was off. I've even spent time with him since Rose and Benjamin were killed, but that's when I realized what was going on with him, when he asked me to help him find Holly. That other side of him doesn't know Rose is dead, because it doesn't know Rose exists at all. That other side of him just thinks Holly disappeared again, like he's reliving a nightmare from ten years ago."

Mary knew the story and hoped a man would never latch onto her so badly that he would dedicate his life to capturing her.

"I'm telling you, he's dangerous," she said, as the Audi rolled to a stop in front of the vacant Colonial house, the shed hidden in shadows beyond the tree line. "I brought you here because I trust you."

Her tone had shifted so Mary said, "Okay," though she didn't understand Roberta's sudden gravity.

"I did this for a reason," she said as though she had no clue how vague she was being.

Again, Mary reassured her with, "Okay."

"You have to trust me," she pressed. "You have to keep this secret."

Mary was getting a bad feeling. Her gaze locked on the dark lake in the distance, too unnerved to look at her friend. When she popped the passenger side door ajar, Roberta grabbed her arm tightly.

"Promise me," she insisted.

"You're hurting me-"

"Because I love you, promise."

Her eyes held such intensity that for a split second Mary didn't recognize her. Intimidated, she whispered, "I promise," and Roberta loosened her grip.

They walked to the shed in silence, crusty snow crunching under their boots, wind howling in off the water and stinging Mary's cheeks, the tip of her nose losing feeling, her hands stiff and cold, holding the beers.

As they neared the orange door, its paint peeling, its wooden surface warped from the harsh winter, Mary heard the distinct whir of the space heater inside.

Roberta paused with her hand on the door handle, looking at Mary over her shoulder. She shot her a fleeting smile and when Mary tried to reciprocate, it felt like a grimace.

For the second time her friend told her that she loved her, but it sounded like a bribe. Roberta pushed the door open and into the darkness they stepped.

She heard a young boy ask, "Mom?"

Roberta yanked a string dangling from the ceiling and a naked bulb flickered on, starkly illuminating the shed.

On the floor sat Tucker, his knees pulled up to his chin, the space heater whirling beside him. He looked frightened and gutted with sadness, his blue eyes round and studying the females that had entered, perhaps desperate to recognize his mother. Littering the floor around him were several empty pizza boxes and crumpled bags of Doritos, Chex Mix, and other junk food.

Rushing to him, Mary wanted to cry. She dropped to her knees, set the beers down, and wrapped her arms around him, exclaiming, "Tucker!" He felt cool and limp in her arms and his heavy head fell against her chest. "Oh, sweetie, remember me? I'm your babysitter. You're going to be okay."

When she glanced at Roberta, she could see the stone-heart of her friend gleaming through those dark, angled eyes.

"Are you crazy?" she hissed, holding herself back from yelling. Considering Tucker was trembling, she refused to blow-up at Roberta, which would only terrify him.

As though she had anticipated Mary's reaction, Roberta pulled a milk crate up and sat confidently, and planted her elbows on her knees so she could probe her calculating eyes down at them.

"No, I'm not crazy," she said coolly.

She had more to say, but Mary cut in with, "There are consequences, God damn it, serious consequences. You didn't think, Christ! Roberta, they think the killers took him, don't you get that?" She tempered her emotions, drawing in a deep breath and stroking Tucker's wispy hair. Whispering in his ear, she promised, "You're going to be okay," and then tried to drill some reason into her friend. "Look at Candice. Look at Quinton. Everyone thought they were too young for prison, but they weren't."

Roberta seemed unmoved, unaffected, and determined.

Mary hadn't struck a nerve with her, though her voice had trembled saying her younger sister's name. She had loved the angelic girl whose demonic mind had orchestrated their mother's abduction and tortured Kendra nearly to death. Quinton Avery was no better. Though he had been Roberta's closest friend, he had harbored the worst kind of secret, that he had killed her younger sister in a twisted attempt to spare Roberta from emotional pain.

"I can't lose you, Roberta," Mary declared, gripping the boy tightly in her arms, cradling him as though she might conjure her own sister's warmth. "After everything you've been through and everything I've been through, you really want to spend the rest of your life behind bars?"

Roberta didn't look convinced. She straightened her spine, glancing down her nose at Mary, and said offhandedly, "I sold the coke so he could have food, warm clothes, and diapers since apparently he needs them."

Witnessing her friend's subdued attitude had Mary's blood boiling in her veins, but she tricked some calm into her brain, helping Tucker off of her. It wasn't until she got to her feet and started advancing and angling over Roberta that she let her emotions fly.

"You stupid moron!" yelled Mary.

Roberta leapt to her feet, but it didn't stop Mary from barreling forth.

"You've been keeping him here, in a freezing shed with no supervision?"

They were standing nose-to-nose and breathing hard. Mary balled her fists.

Roberta looked like a wild animal readying to attack.

But Mary cut her off at the knees, spitting through her teeth, "And you thought your mother was bad."

Eyes flaring, her mouth stiffening, white-hot rage rolling off her skin, she seethed, "What did you just say to me?"

"You heard me-"

"I did. I was giving you a chance to correct yourself."

Overwhelmed, she demanded, "You came into the house when I was babysitting? They're going to think we kidnapped him together."

"No, I would never risk you," she stated with conviction, which seemed so bizarre to Mary that it made her itch to plant a second bruise on the girl's face. "Cody would never suspect you, and even if he did, he would never arrest you."

Mary had to pace away before she did something she would regret. Turning on her heel, she caught sight of Tucker. The boy's mouth was a tight O, his eyes wide, watching the argument. She hoped he wouldn't ask for his mother again, knowing it would rip her heart open if he did.

"You promised," Roberta reminded her, pointing firmly.

"You're going to trust the promise of a loser like me?"

"Can we be real for a second?" she challenged, her eyes suddenly so big that they caught the light—catlike and muddy and screaming self-destruction. "Lucas is psychotic. That's what he is, psychotic. In addition to being mentally unstable, he's Tucker's father. Yeah, that's right," she added when Mary's shock blossomed. "The second I found out, I took him, because sooner or later Lucas is going to realize he has a legal right to guardianship." She swallowed hard. "Lucas had... and I'm repulsed to say this, but he had an even worse childhood than I did or than you did. And he's a *man*," she stated so deeply that Mary's heart skipped a rocky beat. Roberta's ferocious eyes misted over, glassy with tears, as she continued. "I know what he's capable of. I know what he'll do if he's awarded custody. You might think it's only an assumption, that just because terrible things happened to Lucas growing up doesn't mean he'll do terrible things to his son, but I know better. And I refuse to let that happen to this kid. I am not going to let it happen, Mary." Her tone had arched up, flighty as though she were coming undone. "After Maude..."

Mary quavered. She knew what was coming but wasn't sure she could stomach it.

"There's only one thing I did right in my life," Roberta went on, choking back the tremble in her voice. "I never let them get to Maude. And I know you never let Dale get to Candice. I'm not about to give Lucas the benefit of the doubt on this. I'm saving Tucker. That's the end of it."

Roberta's conviction, the raw emotion in her frayed tone, the pain and misery and gut-wrenching hope in her expression told Mary that her friend might have done far worse than kidnap a little boy.

Digging deep, terrified of the answer even before she had asked the question, she locked eyes with Roberta and demanded, "Did you kill them?"

Roberta's eyes shifted.

Her voice cracking, she insisted, "Was it you all along?" Her hands were trembling. Why wasn't Roberta answering her? "Did you kill them so you could take Tucker?" Her vision blurred with tears. "I loved Rose. I thought you loved Benji."

"I don't love anyone," she said finally, but her tone was melodic and easy as though this was some other conversation. "My heart isn't real. There's no soul in this body. I thought you knew that."

Mary shook her head, terrified of where they might go from here.

"Lucas once told me..." She trailed off, her gaze resting on Tucker who was huddled in a ball of uncertainty on the floor, "He once told me how his heart works, or how it doesn't. What it is, what it's made of... He described it as tar. Thick and black and sticky liquid, not yet hardened into asphalt, the heart of a killer," she angled her eyes at Mary. "When he explained it, it sounded so much like me..."

"It's not you," she pleaded, desperate to hear that her friend hadn't killed them. "Please tell me, please, Roberta. Tell me it wasn't you."

"I have Tucker now," she said definitively as though that could possibly be the end of it.

It wasn't.

Mary saw herself screaming, *Tell me!* and though she was a breath away from acting out her impulse, she was derailed from freaking out when the faint sound of a cell phone vibrating hit her ears.

Roberta fished her cell out of her coat pocket and when she eyed the screen, she mentioned, "Gisele," and answered the call, "Yeah?"

Mary heard nothing but murmuring through the receiver, much too soft to make out, as Roberta listened stoically for a long moment.

When she finally lowered the phone, a look of stunned confusion came over her face. "There was a fire at the club... some kind of explosion set it off," she said in a stupefied, vacuous tone. "Ron Conover is dead."

CHAPTER EIGHTEEN

"IT'S BEAUTIFUL." Gertrude was eyeing the heart-shaped pendant, its opal bezel, the flecks of periwinkle and tangerine and lavender within the milky-white gemstone. She lifted the silver, cable link chain, asking, "This is the one she wanted?"

"Just like her friend's," Holly assured her, smiling from across the counter.

"It's thicker than I imagined," she said, passing the necklace.

"It's a sturdy chain. She can accidentally yank it and the links won't weaken. It also won't tangle easily," Holly explained, as she coiled the chain into a jewelry box, fit a sheet of cardstock inside, and set the pendant atop so that it was resting on the Shackles logo.

Before Holly could close the box, Gertrude asked, "How does it open?"

Demonstrating, she angled her thumbnail under the edge of the bezel and popped the pillbox open. "It snaps shut just as easily," she said, showing her, then she handed Gerty the open box.

The woman tried it herself a few times, eyeing the small compartment beneath. "What in the world does she think she can fit in there...."

Holly was tempted to guess cocaine, but it wouldn't be the best way to get Gertrude to open up about her daughter. Not that Holly had dared yet. She was still working up the nerve to ask the woman about what Roberta had really been up to.

"Would you like it gift wrapped?"

"Yes, please," she said, fishing her wallet out of her purse. "Do you take debit cards?"

"Sure do," said Holly, taking the card, which she swiped in the machine, then set on the counter. Next, she wrapped the necklace box with silver paper. By the time the receipt slip was jutting out of the credit card terminal, Holly had stuck a pointy red bow on the box and was placing it inside a Shackles bag. "Well I hope she likes the necklace," she said, dropping the receipt in the bag and handing it to Gerty, who thanked her again for having the necklace ready so soon.

As the woman started for the entrance door, Holly felt a lump form in her throat. She should ask the woman about Roberta. There was still time. She should stop her. She should run to the entrance door, block Gertrude from leaving, and demand to know where Roberta was, where her secret hiding places were, and ask if she had Tucker...

But she couldn't.

After watching Gertrude shuffle down the sidewalk where cars were parked against dirty snow banks under a cloudless sky, Holly went into the studio and began straightening up, returning spools of chain to their proper home on the shelf, collecting scattered gemstones from the table, and setting the Crock Pot in the sink basin at the back of the room.

Lucas was weighing heavily on her mind.

Their encounter disturbed her.

I don't know who I am.

She had aimed her revolver at him, kept her elbows locked, her tone firm and demanding that he tell her where Tucker was. She had threatened to shoot, to kill him if he refused to explain where he was keeping her nephew.

In that moment, staring at him, breathing heavily, enraged, his eyes had suddenly distracted her. She had never seen it before, never noticed it, but in that moment she had realized that Lucas's eyes were the same as Tucker's—round and blue, tumultuous, maybe even stormy, his pupils pinprick black.

He was Tucker's father.

He had engaged in an affair with her sister.

And she had every reason to believe he had her nephew.

She shouldn't have been standing so close to him, the barrel just shy of his chest. Her hands had been trembling badly and within a split second she had understood she was making the exact same mistake.

It was Benjamin all over again.

In the blink of an eye, Lucas had swiped the revolver from her grasp and pointed it at her head.

Her heart had pounded violently, her breath quickening, her gaze locking on the barrel—*will he go through with it?*

Did he kill Rose?

Staring at him—her life in his hands—she had seen honesty in his eyes. He had looked like a man who had reached his breaking point, who was in desperate need of being believed, and Holly had wanted to believe him.

She wanted to believe that he wasn't behind the murders, the abduction, and the explosion, which had destroyed the house and nearly taken her life.

But she couldn't believe him.

I don't know who I am.

What if Lucas was responsible for it all, but didn't remember any of it? What if he was so confused that he had done it all and forgotten?

I thought she was you.

As Holly wiped down her worktable, spraying Lysol and rubbing off the dust and grease with a rag, she tried to fathom the incredible secret Lucas had been keeping from himself.

Was it possible for a person to be involved in an affair and have no recollection of it whatsoever? She didn't think so. Lucas wasn't a zombie, he wasn't functioning in a drug haze. How could he hold down a job, one that required keen investigative skills, if he was plagued with some drastic version of dissociation? What was it called? She had heard the term years ago while watching a PBS special—multiple personality disorder. She didn't even think it was real, but rather a fabrication, pseudoscience used when floundering psychologists wanted to appear remarkable within their communities, or at least that had been what the TV special focused on—the fiction of desperate psychoanalysts, how they would groom their patients, and frame the disorder though it wasn't truly present.

Did he even know, did that other side of him that functioned in the black hole of his psyche understand that the woman he had fallen in love with, the real woman, *Rose*, was dead?

After stealing her revolver, training the sight on her forehead between her eyes, Lucas had screamed, spit flying from his mouth and tears spilling down his cheeks, *I don't know how to remember, but she knows! She has to know!*

Who? she had begged, terrified he might squeeze the trigger whether he meant to or not.

Roberta, he had growled. *She has to know. She has to.*

Without warning, he had thrown the revolver as if the weapon was suddenly a thousand degrees. Holly hadn't even understood where it had landed until it fired, a bullet zinging through the air after the gun had struck the wall. The bullet had left a blackened circular hole in the windowpane, glass splintering out like a spider's web all around it.

Thoughts hadn't entered her mind. Before she knew what was happening, she was sprinting for the door, throwing it open, barreling down the stairs, taking the treads two at a time. He hadn't come after her. There was no yelling or screaming from the apartment, as she ripped the Volvo door open, desperate to get the hell out of there.

Faintly, the doorbell chimed from the store so Holly padded to the black curtain and peered out to see who had walked in off the street. Her chest tightened.

It was Cody McAlister. He stalked confidently through the store and though he eyed the displays, he obviously had no interest in jewelry.

She feared to imagine why he was here and, breathing out the dread in her chest, she stepped into the store, cleared her throat, and offered a brittle greeting, "Detective, how are you?"

"Been better," he frowned, shooting her a commiserating glance, as he neared one of the velvet pillars. "Help me out here, Holly."

"Okay..."

"I swung by Speare Memorial," he began.

It knocked the wind right out of her.

"I was curious. Let's just say the affair between Rose and Lucas was much deeper than I originally assumed, but I'm sure you know that." He let that hang for a beat, studying her. "Imagine my surprise when the receptionist told me that your sister had, in fact, stopped by the other day."

Holly probably looked like a deer in headlights so she made herself say, "I'm just trying to find my nephew."

"Did you think he was at the hospital?" he asked with an air of sarcasm.

"No, of course not," she said nervously. "But I thought... I was looking into something." She pressed her mouth into a thin line, afraid to say more, and stared at him.

"You're interfering with a police investigation-"

"I wouldn't," she blurted out. "I didn't mean to-"

"You keep lying," he shot back. "Are you protecting him?"

"No," she asserted.

He tucked his hand in his pocket and for an anxious second, she expected him to draw out a pair of handcuffs and arrest her. "I'm waiting on a warrant," he said instead. "I'm sure I don't have to tell you about the paternity test your sister ordered. I think we both know who the father is, but it'll be a day or so before I get a court order allowing me to swab the inside of Lucas's cheek."

She wondered why he was telling her this. She could see Lucas in her mind, those huge, panicked eyes, his mouth twisting with remorse, not because he was guilty of murder, but because it killed him that he couldn't remember—he didn't know for sure he was innocent, but believed it. Without thinking, she stated, "You think he did it just because he's Tucker's real father?"

Cody's eyes flared at the challenge, as his eyebrows sprung to his hairline. "So you are protecting him?"

"No," she shot back. "All I care about is the truth and finding my nephew; and..." She knew what she was about to say would sound like she was in fact protecting Lucas, but she came out with it anyway, "I don't think he did it."

Cody began theorizing, "Lucas is the boy's father. When he discovered the fact, he gave Rose an ultimatum. Let's be a family or something to that effect. But she rejected him so he went after her, killed her then Benjamin, stole his son back, and tried to kill you to tie up loose ends..."

She wasn't sure she could argue against him or that she should. He obviously trusted his theory and Holly couldn't deny it made a hell of a lot of sense. But Cody hadn't seen Lucas the way she had. He hadn't looked into his partner's eyes, while Lucas wavered on the brink of madness, desperate to be believed. His resolve and his determination—the look in his eyes that no human on earth could fake—had finally rested all doubt, all suspicion from her mind.

"I don't know what to say," she said finally.

"I'm going to need you to come to the precinct," he told her. "We haven't spoken since Benjamin's murder and there's a lot of ground to cover."

"Now?" she gaped. "It's the middle of the afternoon and my store is struggling as it is."

Groaning, he planted his hands on his hips. "Can you make it in after you close up for the day?"

"Yes, it would be around nine, though..."

He didn't seem thrilled but agreed, stating, "Fine."

"You're going to arrest Lucas?"

He held her gaze, narrowing his eyes in a way she didn't like. "I'm moving slowly and carefully on this. I'll act on the warrant as soon as I get it. I'll need your statement. I'm not going to rush this. The case I hand over to the D.A. is going to be air-tight."

"And Tucker?"

"The paternity angle is the biggest lead I've had. I'll get him back, Holly, but I can't say that's going to happen until I bring Lucas down to the station and get my forty-eight hours out of him."

She clenched her teeth together, feigning a smile, and walked him to the entrance door, which she opened for him.

"I'll see you at nine tonight," she said, holding the door.

Cody held her gaze for a long moment before saying, "See you then," and stepped out onto the slick sidewalk.

From the glass door, Holly spied him trekking towards his truck, which was parked grill-to-snow bank. It wasn't until he reversed out of the spot and drove off that she stampeded through the store, plowing her fingers through her hair and fighting the terrible panic riling up her throat.

Things had gotten worse, much, much worse and not just for Lucas.

If she sat down with Cody, it would only be a matter of time before he discovered all of her lies. At this point, Cody believed his partner was behind this, but all that would change if he learned the many ways in which Lucas had covered for Holly—hiding the .32 caliber bullet, sabotaging the security feed of Holly outside Room 112, and pocketing the Joint Will, which Benjamin had altered.

She knew how it would look. Cody would believe she was just as guilty as Lucas and they would both be arrested.

And what killed her was that neither had done it. She had grappled with Lucas's guilt and innocence, but the fact of the matter was that she knew he hadn't done it. She had seen it in his eyes.

Holly needed answers, real answers. And she needed them before nine o'clock.

Suddenly, an idea struck her, but it was so insane, so far-fetched, so desperate... that it just might work.

Scrambling for her cell phone, she hoped like hell she wasn't losing her damn mind and dialed.

When the line opened up, she blurted out, "I have an idea, but you're going to think it's crazy."

CHAPTER NINETEEN

THE LAKES Motor Inn.

It wasn't ideal.

Diamonds would've been ideal, but when Holly had proposed the club as their rendezvous point, Lucas had grown tense, his tone deepening through the receiver as he had detailed the bizarre news that Diamonds, along with its sleazy owner, Ron Conover, had gone up in flames. No one had seen it coming, least of all the escorts who worked there, many of whom had been rushed to the hospital with second and first degree burns.

An explosion, Holly had asked, stunned from where she had been pacing in her store, visions of shattered glass raining over her.

Just like the garage, he had said, connecting the same dots.

Holly scanned the shallow motel lobby, its plastic chairs, the vending machine, and the stained carpet. The front desk was unattended so she tapped the bell on the counter a few times, having been prompted by the handwritten sign next to it—*Strike me twice and I'll be nice!*—then she glanced over her shoulder through the glass door where golden light was pouring through, a precursor to dusk.

Her bag felt heavy on her right shoulder so she slung it over her left and stared at the doorway behind the counter where she presumed the clerk would emerge.

She felt jumpy.

An anxious minute later, an orange-haired punk wandered in from the back room, twisting his nose ring and hiking up his baggy pants, just as the entrance door behind her banged open and Lucas stepped in from the cold.

She sensed more than saw him nearing her, as she awkwardly diverted her eyes, not quite being able to look at the punk clerk either.

"A room, please," she mumbled, thumbing through her cash.

The kid snickered and Holly didn't have to meet his gaze to know he was sizing her up as well as the tall, blue-eyed man who had stepped in beside her. "By the night or the hour," he asked?

She glared at him, struggling to admit that by the hour would be just fine.

"Thought so," he said so sure of himself as he punched the cash register keys. "I'll take fifty for the deposit and you can pay on your way out." Staring at him as if she wasn't amused was enough to get him to clarify, "It's twenty-eight an hour."

She was about to question the steep deposit but decided against it and handed him the exact amount. He smelled it for some reason—probably high off his ass—and plucked a pink, plastic dildo off the wall-rack, which she realized had a room key attached.

"Room 14, but it's on the second level," he explained. "Stairs are to your left outside."

Holly didn't know whether to grasp the metal key or the dildo, but the kid hadn't left her much choice. The key was pinched between his thumb and index finger so she grabbed the phallic tchotchke, avoiding Lucas's strangely optimistic gaze, as she walked to the glass door and slapped it open.

If it was cold outside—and it was frigid—the temperature didn't pull the hot flush from her cheeks as she started down the walkway towards the stairs, Lucas trailing behind her at a cautious distance.

Once they reached the second floor balcony and found Room 14, she fumbled fitting the key into the lock thanks to the weight of the dangling dildo, which worked against her.

"Asinine," she grumbled when the door finally opened.

It didn't smell quite like she had expected—nothing like stale cigarettes and bleach or the offensive pine scent of any given car freshener.

As she eased skeptically into the motel room, Lucas followed and locked them inside so no one could accidentally stumble into what they were about to do, Holly got the general impression that the Lakes Motor Inn was pretending to be a quaint bed and breakfast—paisley curtains lined the windows, the carpet cream though matted badly, the bed crisply made, its florally comforter pleasant enough.

When she peeked in the bathroom, flipping on the light, which caused the fan to shudder louder than a jet engine, she noted the sink and bathtub were spotless, papered soaps sat on the counter, and tiny bottles of shampoo covered the ledge in the shower stall. The toilet lid was down, which for some reason helped her to breathe a bit easier.

She turned for the bedroom and found Lucas staring at her. He seemed both exhilarated and terrified—his blue eyes widening, his face drawing long as though sickened with arousal.

Holly hadn't told him about Cody, the timeline, that the detective was angling to arrest him, that meeting Lucas here was a last ditch effort to clear his name, one she had little faith would work. Maybe she should've warned him and detailed the stakes, but convincing him to come had been difficult enough. He was still on edge—the dark result of Holly having threatened his life, of Lucas retaliating, of gunfire and Holly fleeing his apartment without so much as a glance over her shoulder.

"You think this will work?" he asked.

"Do you?"

They stared at each other for a beat until Holly mentioned, "Diamonds would've been better."

Lowering his gaze, he nodded. When his eyes snapped up again, he asked, "What if I can't control myself? I mean... if this works then I won't really be here."

"I know," she said quietly, wishing she had her revolver, which she had abandoned in favor of running from his apartment. "Is there anything..." she began, not entirely sure how to phrase her question. "Do you think there's anything I can say, anything you're so connected to that if I say it, it'll bring you back?"

Lucas thought hard, his mouth pressing into a thin line, and his eyes shifting. "I don't think I've lost any time on the job."

"I could say..." Trailing off, she wracked her brain. "What's a police code?"

"Tell me there's a One Eight Seven in progress."

She let out a nervous laugh. "Okay." Then, when it occurred to her, she asked, "What's a One Eight Seven?"

"A Homicide."

Her voice a whisper, she repeated, "Okay," and turned for the bathroom.

"I'm going to want you."

She cracked a smile. "Let's hope, or else this won't work."

Nodding, Lucas glanced at the floor, but again stopped her before she could slip into the bathroom. "Should I... I don't know, take my clothes off?"

Thrown, Holly tempered her reaction so he wouldn't feel awkward, and thinking fast on her feet, said, "Maybe you should leave your clothes on, give me some place to go in case you don't start talking right away."

"Right, good," he said, clearly embarrassed. "Good point."

She felt for him as she hovered in the doorway, not quite ready to slip into Rose's lingerie. "I don't know how this is going to go, and I don't know how it works, but..." Hunting for the right words, she came up with, "Try not to fight it?"

Turning for the bathroom, Holly paused for the third time when he asked, "If thinking I'm with you could cause me to... or this other part of me to... whatever switch takes place. Then why hasn't it happened when I've seen you? For instance, at your sister's house on the night of the murders and then at your store?"

Considering his question, which was more than valid, she pulled her bag off her shoulder. "We're out of options here, Lucas. You've been in the habit of sleeping with Rose and thinking she's me... we have to have some faith that this is going to work."

"Right, sorry," he said quickly and began slowly pacing the room, clapping his palm to his fist as if working up some kind of nerve.

Reassuringly, she told him, "I'll be out in a sec," and gently closed the bathroom door.

Taking her time, she began stripping down, tucking her boots beneath the sink, hanging her coat on the door rack, folding and stacking her clothes on the toilet. Nude, she studied her reflection in the mirror, straining to see her twin.

Though she looked exactly like Rose, Holly felt lost. She had no way of knowing for sure how her sister had behaved around Lucas—her prowess, confidence, attitude. If their aim was to get him to switch into some alter ego who knew about the affair and every dark deed that had transpired because of it, then Holly would have to embody Rose's vibe in order to coax Lucas's other self out.

Why did all roads lead to Holly becoming her sister?

She forced a smile, but it looked like a grimace, and then rummaged through her bag for the lingerie. She stepped into a gaudy, zebra print thong lined with magenta lace around the hips and sparkling rhinestones along the seam. The matching bra was even worse and as she pulled it on, she discovered it failed to cover her completely.

"Damn," she muttered, glancing down at the terrible garment. It wasn't that she was too busty for it. This was simply its trashy design. Why hadn't she examined the lingerie more closely at the house? Or at the very least packed a few more options?

Lastly, she swiped on Rose's lipstick—Almay's Ravenous Red—and fluffed her hair, dousing her locks with hair spray, also Rose's. She had found black eyeliner in her sister's closet as well, so she drew thin lines along her lashes and then stepped back to assess her overall appearance in the mirror.

She looked like a truck-stop hooker.

Perfect?

Taking a few deep breaths that did nothing to calm her nerves, she cracked the door open and locked eyes with Lucas, who was still standing at the foot of the bed like a lost child.

She hadn't exactly thought this far ahead. She felt the urge to say something—she should break the ice before this got painfully awkward, shouldn't she?—but nothing came.

As she widened the door, his gaze traveled the length of her and because of it her chest tightened self-consciously. Realizing she had begun to slouch—as if any posture could shield her shape—she willed herself to straighten her back confidently as she took a few shallow steps into the room.

As awkward as she felt, when Lucas's expression shifted subtly—assured arousal washing away trepidation—her anxiety faded as well.

Was he now the man who had spent countless nights with her sister?

Advancing on her, he breathed, "Holly," and found her hips, grazing his warm hands around her as if they had done this a million times.

Was it working?

She urged him back, shot him a coy smile, though it felt contrived, and suggested, "Let's get comfortable."

Impatient or perhaps misunderstanding, Lucas wrapped his mouth around her breast, stunning her.

After a frozen moment, she urged him off again, letting out a breathy laugh, and guided him to the bed where she shoved him to sit.

But he was tangling with her, his hands squeezing her waist, groaning as he glanced up the length of her, pulling her between his splayed legs.

Testing him, she said, "We've been seeing each other for awhile..."

"You haven't left him," he pointed out, which relieved Holly for no other reason than it confirmed she was talking to the part of Lucas who knew the answers they both needed.

"I'm working on it," she offered, wrapping her head around the fact that while Lucas believed he had been involved with Holly, he thought she was living her sister's life—married and with a son.

Turning cross, he challenged, "I don't think you are, not other than fantasizing about leaving Benjamin."

"Do you remember the night of the 12th?"

"Why?"

"Tell me about it," she prodded. "We weren't together that night or were we?"

"It was a long night."

Attempting to be firm as she leveled with him, she stated, "I know about your friendship with Roberta-"

"It's just a friendship."

"I know."

"You think I was with her that night?"

"I think you know something," she pressed, angling over him, Lucas responding by leaning back on his elbows. "I want to hear it."

He snorted a laugh as though he couldn't believe her. "I was headed to your house that night. We had plans, remember?"

"So, you drove over?" she questioned.

"Almost, but Roberta called me. Lie down."

Ignoring him, she asked, "What did she say on the call?"

Lucas was kneading her thighs so she shoved him playfully, but the attempt backfired. He pulled her onto him. The next thing she knew, she was straddling him, Lucas gazing up at her, his hands rushing over her body.

"She was a mess that night," he explained. "You're at fault, by the way. You gave her way too much."

"Drugs," she guessed. "Coke?"

"What else?" After he admired her figure for a beat, he went on, "She was worried about your father-in-law."

"Why?"

"Probably because she had been sneaking into Benji's room and Warren was catching on. I don't know, she wasn't making sense. She wanted me to go to the resort, but she wasn't talking straight. She thought you were there. She was acting crazy. So I rerouted, but didn't get that far."

Holly didn't have to ask why that was. Lucas had probably gotten a call about her sister's murder and had to rush off to the house.

"Did you circle back later that night?"

"I was planning to, but Roberta called me and said Benji had kicked her out of his room. She was in tears, a mess. She begged me to meet her at Diamonds to talk, but I kept telling her I would meet her at the shed. Ron Conover hates me. I don't have to tell you that. Meeting at Diamonds was just plain stupid, but she insisted."

Holly was studying his face, her mind latching onto the shed—what shed?—as Lucas went on about how Conover had immediately thrown him out of the club.

Interrupting him, she asked, "Tell me about the shed?"

He smiled playfully. "It's our place, the keeper of our secrets."

"Where is it?"

"Why?"

"I would like to know where it is," she said firmly. "We should go there."

His expression softened, as he squeezed her waist, saying, "I'll take you anywhere you want to go, but not until..." He drank in the sight of her chest, hooking his finger under her thong, and then met her gaze. "I'm aching for you."

When he reached for her, she caught his hands. "Why was she worried about Warren Wythe?"

"Same reason you are," he countered.

"Tell me."

He gaped at her as if frustrated. "What's your angle? You dress in the most amazing lingerie so we can engage in idle chit chat? Come on, Holly."

Appeasing him, she began hiking his sweater up and caressing his stomach. "What do you guys do in the shed?"

"Talk," he answered as he pulled his sweater off. "I would rather not incorporate Roberta into our foreplay, if you don't mind."

"Can we just talk now?"

"Are you messing with me?"

He looked angered so she cooed, "No, I'm not, sorry," and began unbuttoning his jeans.

He settled, but his frustration remained. "I've tried, Holly. I've done everything I can to open up to you, but you've always shut me down. And now you want to talk?"

She tried to smile, but it landed badly, and in response, he stared off in another direction as though he needed a moment to cool down.

"Can we meet Roberta at the shed?"

His face snapped back to her. "This is seriously what you want to do tonight?"

Uncertain, she nodded anyway.

He snorted a laugh, lifting up on the bed. "You're damn lucky I'm crazy about you."

"I know," she said kindly, as she climbed off him.

Though she turned for the bathroom, he caught her hand, rising to his feet. When he pulled her in, wrapping his arm around her lower back and angling in for a kiss, she didn't react.

She also didn't stop him.

As their lips met, she told herself to demand the location of the shed before pulling him out of his fog by saying, *One Eight Seven*. But she wasn't sure she wanted that yet.

Kissing him, feeling his hands grazing her hips, her waist, scooping her tightly, hungrily, she was suddenly sure they weren't going anywhere...

CHAPTER TWENTY

SHE HADN'T MEANT to fall asleep.

And she would like to think she hadn't meant to sleep with Lucas, that her idea of meeting him at the Lakes Motor Inn had been for no other reason than finding out what had truly happened for the purposes of clearing his name, getting a solid lead, and setting Cody in a worthwhile direction. But the moment she had allowed Lucas to cross the blurred line into intimacy, Holly realized part of her had wanted this all along—to merge with him, to wake up in his arms, to feel like she had ten years ago.

Maybe to inspire hope that her sister could go on living if only through her...

Dusky morning light pooled across the comforter and spilled over the far wall. Careful not to wake him, she shifted, rolling over so she could glimpse his sleeping face. Lucas was lying on his back, one hand beneath his head, the other arm hooked under her neck, the comforter snuggled up to his chin, though it did little to ward off the chill from the drafty windows.

During their frustrating and at times confusing conversation last night, he had called her Holly, which told her that during the affair Rose hadn't corrected him. She had allowed Lucas to believe she was her twin. There was something so dark and disturbing about that fact, Holly could barely process it.

Why use him like that? Rose couldn't have possibly loved him. Could a person love another yet lie to them? Had doing so been Rose's way of feeling connected to her twin just as Holly had flirted with cocaine and played dress up in her sister's clothes, exploring her sister's life?

What had pulled the twins so far apart that they had both felt the need to do so?

For Holly it had been the estrangement. It killed her not to know her twin, not to have Rose in her life. But for Rose there had to have been a different catalyst. Their estrangement began two years ago, but Rose had connected with Diamonds years prior. Tucker was three years old. He was Lucas's son, which meant that while Rose was working alongside Holly at Shackles, tending to the bookkeeping and pushing sales in the store, she had been stealing away at night, indulging in a second life that should've belonged to her twin.

As Holly studied Lucas, her gaze tracing the slight curve of his lashes and the slope of his nose, she listened to the soft rhythm of his breathing and thought back to three years ago then five.

When Rose had met Benjamin...

Why had she nurtured a secret life with Lucas when her marriage hadn't yet faltered?

She was honing in on something, a revelation perhaps, but it eluded her, as sunlight gradually brightened the room, so she gently shook his shoulder, the words *One Eight Seven* on the tip of her tongue. But she couldn't say them, not yet, not until he brought her to the shed where she prayed answers had been tucked away.

As Lucas blinked his eyes open, drawing in a deep breath and stretching beneath the comforter, Holly reminded herself to make sure their game was still in play.

"Hey," she said softly and, testing the waters, asked, "we had talked about that shed?"

He furrowed his brow and for a stunned moment she worried the real Lucas, the detective, the one who thought he had lost her a decade ago, was beside her in bed. But when he groaned, "I was hoping the impulse had passed," she breathed a sigh of relief.

"No, not passed, just postponed," she smiled, brushing his dark hair off his forehead and eyeing his messy cowlicks.

Did this man know his son was missing?

Did he know that he had a son, and that his son was Tucker?

"Let's get dressed," she suggested, but he quickly pulled her in for a long kiss.

It felt unfair. She didn't want to lie to him like Rose had, and didn't want to take advantage of his confusion any longer than necessary.

Getting him out of bed was as easy as her climbing out. As she shut the bathroom door, Lucas began pulling on his jeans and complaining his way around the room, collecting his socks and undershirt, boots and sweater.

If they drove separately, he might shift into his primary persona, so when they started for the parking lot, having paid for the room while ignoring the orange-haired punk's uncouth guesses as to how they had used their time, Holly offhandedly proposed they take his Ford.

"Since when do you and Roberta get along?" he asked after settling behind the steering wheel—engine idling and cold air blasting from the vents.

"I don't have a problem with her." When he shot her a skeptical glance, Holly said, "She has her affair and I have mine."

It seemed to satisfy him, but he still commented, "Showing up at the shed seems off to me."

"Don't you show up there?"

"I'm usually invited," he explained, as they drove into the street.

"What makes you guys so close?"

Suddenly on edge, he said, "We're damaged in the same way."

In silence, Holly watched fog slip over the windshield and it wasn't until they had merged onto the Daniel Webster Highway that she asked, "You were never caught... Your parents... You were never charged?"

He hesitated, stiffening in the driver's seat. "No."

"Were you suspected?"

Looking over at her to perhaps assess where she was coming from with all this, he stated, "No," then returned his eyes to the slick asphalt, the gray landscape, sky as dreary-white as the snow lining the highway.

Though it was only a guess, she said, "You never told me... how you did it."

"When I said I wanted you to be okay with me opening up... You need to know how I killed my parents?" he asked, his tone hitching up as if disturbed. He inhaled deeply as if doing so could steady his emotions.

Gently, her voice was like wind over reeds, she said, "I don't need to know," and they drove in silence until Lucas flipped on his turn-signal, veering down the off-ramp and passing a green road sign for Laconia.

After zigzagging on back roads until the Ford spilled onto Messer Street, he surprised her, disclosing in a hollow tone, "I shot them, first my father; back of the head. He was watching the evening news on TV." His brow furrowed as though he no longer saw the road ahead, but rather a disturbing image in his mind. "I don't know why I had to kill him first." After a tense minute, he went on. "My mother... It was ugly. Her running into the living room, screaming at the sight of my dad, me scrambling to cock the gun, misfiring at the coffee table, then another struggle to pull the slide and get a bullet into the chamber. She started racing through the house, upstairs not outside." He clenched his jaw and swallowed hard, turning to stone, his hands clasping the steering wheel in a white-knuckle grip. "I charged after her and shot her five times. I was just a child. A boy in a man's body. I wiped the gun clean and dropped it. It was my father's anyway. And then I ran."

Lucas angled the car up an unplowed driveway and soon a white, Colonial house came into view. At first, Holly tensed, scanning the windows, but realized no one lived there when a For Sale sign caught her eye. It was leaning in a snowdrift, nearly on its side, and so weathered—scarred with amateur graffiti—that she figured the house had been on the market so long that it might never be sold.

They rolled to a stop. Lucas pushed the gear shifter into Neutral and pulled the key from the ignition. The engine pinged and clanked as if refusing to die.

"Roberta is stronger than me. That's what I tell her when we meet, when we spend time together. Retaliating against those monsters who raised me wasn't a courageous act, though for years I told myself the world was a better place without them. I was weak. I couldn't go on living knowing they were alive."

She scanned the woods and saw the shed sitting within a cluster of birches covered in snow.

"But Roberta could?"

"She did. She held on. She saw light at the end of the tunnel." Lucas grabbed her arm, forcing eye contact. "You don't have to understand our friendship, but she's kept me sane in an insane world. I would've died without her. I would've killed myself. I can't explain what she means to me..."

He didn't have to say more. Not only did she understand what Roberta meant to him, she could feel it, which made what they were about to do, about to potentially discover, all the more harrowing.

She almost didn't want to say goodbye to this other side of Lucas whom she had gotten to know, which was why she kissed him, their lips pressing for a long moment. She pulled back, smiled at him, and without thinking, soft and fast and nearly holding her breath, recited, "Call from dispatch." Her voice was trembling, but she pressed on, "One Eight Seven in progress. Lucas, are you there?"

The light behind his eyes dimmed as his expression clouded over then in a snap his eyes brightened as though coming alive. The gasp that followed alarmed her and when his eyes widened, darting around, she placed her hand on his. He kept a lid on his panic as he struggled to get his bearings, his breath quickening until he ran his hand down his face.

"Lucas?" Touching his arm, she said, ""There's a shed through the woods. I think we should check it out." But she was moving too fast. He was grappling with the lost time, the black hole in his memory, struggling to process where he was and why he was here. "What's the last thing-?"

"I remember?" he supplied, catching on. "The motel... stepping inside... you disappearing into the bathroom." His eyes locked with hers. "Did it work?"

Nodding, she said, "Yeah," but when it seemed he might fire off a million questions, she stopped him by saying, "Come on."

Keeping at her heels as they trekked through the snow, ducking under frozen branches and stepping over spikes in the drift, he asked, "Where are we?"

She didn't want to lie to him or omit the truth, but she wasn't sure this side of Lucas would agree with his other half. Lucas harbored a unique love for Roberta. She didn't have the heart to admit they were moments away from finding evidence of the girl's guilt so she went with, "A shed."

"I can see that."

"I think the murder weapon might be here."

"Whose shed is it?"

She was already at the door and opening it was her excuse for not answering.

Stepping inside, her eyes gradually adjusted to the darkness. A stream of dusky light shafted through a tarnished window on the east wall.

Groaning, childlike and distressed, stunned her. She caught movement on the floor in the far corner of the room and though at first she was too anxious to process what she was seeing, soon she jolted with the realization that it was Tucker.

"Oh my God!" she exclaimed, rushing to him and dropping to her knees. She cupped his cold face in her hands, staring at him, as a strange mix of disbelief and heart pounding relief warmed her chest. His eyes lolled and she noticed snot running from his nose. He felt weak in her arms. "We have to get him out of here."

When she touched eyes with Lucas—shocked still, his mouth gaping—he looked like a concerned father.

His voice was a thread. "Holly, I'm so sorry."

"It's over," she said. "Let's get him home."

"Who did this? Whose shed is this?" he asked, as she hoisted Tucker into her arms, rising to her feet.

When she had him securely on her hip, she met Lucas's gaze. "Not now-"

"Not now? I'm going to arrest whoever took him."

"Lucas," she insisted. "He's sick. He needs to get to a hospital. After everything we went over last night, I have enough to convince Cody you didn't do this and I didn't either, and we will convince him of that, and Cody can proceed accordingly with this shed and the people responsible, but first Tucker needs help."

Tucker coughed in her ear, his head weighing heavily on her shoulder.

"Tell me who," he demanded.

"Last night you told me she was with you. She didn't kill Rose or Benjamin just like you and I didn't."

"Who was it, Holly?"

But she refused to tell him, strangely loyal to the man with whom she had shared a night. "You have to drive me to the hospital now."

CHAPTER TWENTY-ONE

LUCAS COULDN'T TAKE his eyes off her.

After the hospital, where a pediatrician had diagnosed Tucker as having a severe cold and then prescribed antibiotics, Holly had insisted that he drive her to the resort. She opted to sit in the backseat with her nephew, cradling him and at times meeting Lucas's gaze in the rearview mirror.

When they walked through the lobby—Lucas shepherding Holly as she carried the sleeping boy in her arms—Warren Wythe rounded the corner from the east wing. Astonished, a broad smile came over his face, seeing that his grandson had returned, and he spread his arms, wasting no time embracing her.

He exclaimed something about a miracle, but Lucas wasn't listening, his whole world was Holly.

A phenomenon had occurred in the hospital—one that Lucas had kept to himself.

Standing in the corner of the examination room and watching the pediatrician press her stethoscope between Tucker's shoulder blades, Lucas had been overcome with flashes of his night with Holly—her lingerie, the draft in the room, their entire conversation and everything that had followed surging to the forefront of his mind as though the two halves of his psyche were suddenly merging. After the initial burst of recall, other memories had bubbled up in rapid succession, all centering on one fact...

It wasn't a fantasy or an obsession.

He loved her.

Deeply.

As Warren helped Holly to settle on the couch in his private study at the back of the Wythe Resort, Lucas watched her and the older man's doting behavior, the glances he exchanged with his wife, who seemed elated though barely lucid enough to grasp the miracle at hand.

Tucker was kicking his little legs, smiling up at her and cackling, something hysterical about the children's book Sarah was starting to read.

Affectionately, the older man glanced over at his wife and took her hand, though Sarah seemed to loll in some hazy stratosphere, drugged up and grinning like a lost hyena.

"He's bouncing back beautifully," said Warren, tickling his grandson's feet.

"The fever's coming down," said Holly, setting the back of her hand against Tucker's forehead.

As Warren released his wife's hand in favor of turning the page for Sarah as she continued reading quietly to her grandson, a waiter shouldered into the room, careful to keep the tray of tea and coffee in his hands level.

Diverting his gaze from the waiter, Warren said through a tight smile, "Anything you need, Holly, to make your life here more comfortable, you won't hesitate to ask, will you?"

Before she could answer, Sarah chimed in. "You do want to live here, don't you?" Perhaps the drug-haze clouding her world had cleared enough for her to speak coherently. "You know the west wing is under construction. We can easily build you proper quarters. This can be your home, do you understand? We can be a family. I've always liked you, Holly."

She locked eyes with Warren before driving her point home.

"I didn't mean to come off as adversarial," he added.

Holly touched eyes with Lucas, her smile waning until she looked at Sarah and cleared her throat. "I wouldn't want to impose."

"Nonsense," said the older woman before Warren quieted her by clasping her shoulder.

Getting to his feet, he said, "If Holly needs to think about it..." He assisted the waiter by taking the French-press from the tray and pouring coffee into a mug. "Black if I remember correctly," he said to Holly and she nodded.

As he handed her the steaming mug of dark roast, he said, "Excuse me," then padded off towards the library.

Holly kept her bright eyes on Lucas as she sipped her coffee, and he could almost see what she was thinking—she loved him, too.

But they were no closer to discovering who had killed Rose and Benjamin.

Lucas didn't understand why Roberta had taken Tucker, though he had theories about how her dark past might have compelled her to save the boy in a mixed-up effort to prevent abuse, whether or not severe mistreatment was truly on the horizon.

One thing was clear, however. Roberta and Lucas had met at Diamonds at the time of Benjamin's murder, which meant she couldn't have killed him. Likewise, she hadn't killed Rose since she was holed up with the husband at the resort during that window of time. As seedy as Ron Conover was, he hadn't done it either. Whoever was behind this had attempted to take Holly's life by rigging explosives to a trip-wire in the garage, and an identical method had been employed to blow up Diamonds and kill Conover.

Lucas was puzzled. He agreed with Holly that the double homicide revolved around Tucker, but it couldn't be for reasons of paternity. Lucas hadn't killed the couple.

It seemed the further he got into this investigation, the farther from the truth he became.

Would Holly and Tucker ever be safe?

Sarah pulled Tucker into her lap and draped her shawl over him, juggling the children's book in her hand, which she resumed reading quietly.

When Lucas glanced at Holly, he noticed she looked suddenly exhausted—her eyelids heavy, her gaze soft, and her mouth flexed. Barely gripping her mug, which was resting at a precarious angle between her legs, her eyes drifted shut. After a moment, her brow lifted bringing with it her eyelids. She was drained, or so he thought until he reached for the mug, and realized she actually seemed disoriented.

The mug was empty, so he set it on the coffee table, as Warren returned.

Quietly, he said, "Holly?"

She murmured, *Hmm?*

"You look like you could use some rest."

"Oh, she's fine," said Sarah, waving him away.

It was odd.

"Detective," said Warren, and for a second Lucas thought the man was addressing him. When he turned, however, Cody was entering the private study.

After briefly greeting Warren with a firm handshake and offering Sarah a warm smile, he neared Lucas, but Holly stole his attention. "Long day?" he asked.

Speaking for her, Warren explained, "She needs to sleep," and began rousing Holly to her feet. "I'll help her to her room."

As he grasped her arm, she perked up enough to understand that she needed to get to her feet, and she began taking slow, rubbery steps on her own, though the older man tightly shadowed her through the room and out into the hallway.

"We need to talk," said Cody in a discreet tone, but Lucas was still staring at the door where Holly had disappeared, a bad feeling swelling in his chest. "Why didn't you call me the second you found Tucker?"

Brushing off his partner's complaint, he said, "We had to get him to the hospital."

"You should've kept me informed. I just got a call from Mr. Wythe. Hey," he barked to get Lucas's attention. "I drove over here like a bat out of hell the second I heard. And Warren couldn't even tell me anything because you didn't let him know where you had found Tucker?"

Sarah was staring at them, so Lucas turned his back, facing Cody.

"Because the fewer people who know the better or else our investigation could be compromised," he said quietly.

"No, not *our* investigation," he corrected. "*I've* been investigating. You're off this case."

"Fine," said Lucas to shut him up.

"I would prefer to do this quietly," he interrupted, as he lifted a pair of handcuffs out of his jacket pocket, just enough to make his point crystal clear.

Stunned, it took him a moment to jump-start his brain into working properly. "You've got to be kidding me."

"I had a talk with Holly yesterday. She was planning on coming in to make a formal statement. The next thing I knew, she was unreachable and it turned out she was with you."

Keeping his tone low wasn't enough to hide the aggression in his voice. "You think I took her against her will?"

"I think we have a number of things to talk about."

"Am I under arrest?" he challenged, but Cody didn't answer except to take him by the arm, which he quickly jerked free, starting for the door of his own volition.

As they crossed down the hallway—Lucas fuming, wracking his brain for what his partner could possibly be thinking, circumstantial evidence would ultimately get him nowhere and Cody had to know that—he slowed nearing Room 112.

"Let me check on Holly," he said but it wasn't a request.

Blocking him before he could knock, Cody said, "Don't make this hard."

He had to grit his teeth not to shove the man, but then he continued on, rounding the front desk when they reached the lobby, and pressing onward to the entrance door.

The frigid temperature outside wasn't enough to pull the heat from Lucas's face.

"I don't want to leave her," he stated, locking eyes with Cody as they started through the parking lot.

"I'm not going to get sidetracked with diversions."

Lucas felt eyes on him and glanced over his shoulder to find Roberta staring at him from the driver's seat of her idling Audi.

Impulsively, recklessly, insanely, he hooked his leg behind Cody's and shoved his chest hard. As his partner fell onto the snow, swearing and scrambling for his weapon, Lucas bolted towards the car and gripped the open windowsill when he reached it, out of breath and hunching out of his partner's view. "I remember."

As she held his gaze, he thought he saw a glimmer of remorse behind Roberta's eyes.

Her voice was a whisper when she asked, "You stole Tucker from me?"

The fact that she seemed hurt by this had him thrown, but there was no time.

"You can't do this," she said. "You can't be a part of his life. Your brain is wired all wrong. You'll hurt him and you'll hate yourself for it, and..." She locked eyes with him. "And I'll end up killing you."

"So you kidnapped him?" When she didn't respond, he asked, "I'll hurt Tucker but you won't? We have the same past."

"That's what I think, yes." She clenched her jaw, looking away and gripping the steering wheel.

Placing his hand on her shoulder, he squeezed until she met his gaze. "I'm not going to hurt him, not for any reason. Do you believe me?"

When she faced him, her eyes were misty. "I believe you. I believe you think that, but I don't trust it."

"Who killed them?"

She stared at him and the light behind her eyes went out. "Am I in trouble?"

"Answer me."

"Did you turn me in for taking Tucker?" she demanded, acting deaf to his question.

A swell of memories rushed back—Lucas hunched on his couch, sobbing, Roberta's arm draped around him, as she cooed into his ear, the secrets they swapped, the laughs they shared, her skill for warming the vast loneliness in his chest, for filling the dark hollows of his heart—and Lucas knew, in stark epiphany, he would never turn her in, never risk severing their connection, which was his lifeline.

"No, I would never," he admitted.

An appreciative smile spread across her face as she held his gaze. Quickly, he peeked over his shoulder at Cody who was starting after him. When he looked at her again, he insisted, "Tell me what you know?"

"Does Holly know I took him?"

"Stop being self-centered," he hissed impatiently, anxious that his partner would apprehend him in seconds. "I'm about to be arrested. You have to tell me what you know."

Roberta studied his face and the anticipation pitched Lucas into gut-clenching, heart-pounding panic. His vision dimmed, but he fought to stay in his right mind and remain himself, desperate not to slip into the dark prison that had stolen so much of his life. The words, "Who killed them?" seeped through his lips, Lucas hanging on by a thread that he feared was disintegrating. Pleading, he spit out, "You were there that night. Tell me."

An excruciating moment elapsed, but just as Roberta was about to answer, Cody clamped his hands on Lucas's shoulder.

BOOM...

Lucas didn't just hear it. He felt it—the asphalt rumbling under his feet—as he ducked. Cody had the same reaction, though he quickly straightened up, staring at the west end of the resort where shards of granite were raining over the snow, a plume of smoke rising from the blast.

It was a long moment before the dust settled then, calmly, one of the construction workers took charge, directing the team towards the freshly carved hole in the earth. He shouted orders and the workers began collecting the larger chunks of granite, dropping them into wheelbarrows, and carting them off.

CHAPTER TWENTY-TWO

HOLLY HAD NO WAY of knowing how much time had passed—*minutes, or had it been hours?*—by the time her eyes cracked open. The room was dim, or was that her mind? Her body felt like sand.

She was laying on a bed, the back of her head pressing hard against the wooden headboard, her shoulder blades digging into it as well, the pillow behind her doing little.

Her hands were resting, palms up on the comforter, her boots splayed. She felt heavy and numb like a corpse resurrected.

Her thoughts were slow and simple, childlike. It didn't occur to her that this was a reaction to the coffee she had drunk, and that she wasn't simply tired. Her thinking wasn't dynamic enough to understand that she had never in her life felt this degree of exhaustion, or that this wasn't exhaustion—the heavy eyelids, the slack jaw, the shallow clipped breathing that seemed to happen without her—but rather the serious dampening of her central nervous system.

She had been drugged…

…but didn't know it.

She was vaguely aware that she wasn't alone. The sound of papers faintly rustling compelled her to turn her head and she hazily spied knuckles brushing over wood—the desk?

It was Warren. Seated in profile, lamplight bathing him in a strange, amber glow, he was thumbing through some kind of document, but his very presence bogged her in dazed confusion.

Pressing her hands against the comforter, she tried to straighten up, but she was too punch-drunk delirious to exert the kind of effort that getting to her feet would require.

A heavy exhale escaped her and Warren shifted in his chair, delighted she was lucid the second he saw her.

Sarah Wythe came to mind, as he said, "My dear," but Holly had never seen the woman as inebriated as she currently felt. "How are you feeling?"

"Tired," she groaned.

Sitting on the bed beside her, Warren ran his fingers through her long hair, tucking the strands behind her ear.

"You're quite beautiful, you know," he said softly as though the compliment might soothe her.

Oddly, it did, yet some part of her knew she was in danger.

"I could let you rest," he offered and she found herself nodding heavily, her eyes floating shut, slipping away except for her sense of hearing. She listened to him chuckle, which came breathy and amused like a master in awe of his silly pet. He stroked her hair once more. "Or I could give you a pick-me-up."

She murmured, "Hmm?" lolling between wakefulness and sleep, though her stomach clenched, instincts warning her of what her rational mind couldn't.

"It must be hard," he said, his cold hand now resting on her thigh, his thick fingers draped between her legs, "being a mother."

Confusedly, she struggled to open her eyes and make sense of his comment by reading his expression, but his warm, knowing smile, the way his white eyebrows arched up sympathetically as he drank in the sight of her withering state, only muddled her grasp on what was happening.

What was happening?

She couldn't make sense of it.

Was it daytime, or night? The curtains allowed almost no light into the room—the hotel room. She was at the resort. She and Lucas had found Tucker. At the hospital she had been sharp and alert. The coffee should've kicked her into high gear...

Forcing her mouth to work, she corrected him. "I'm not a mother."

"No," he cooed in slick agreement. "You're not. Your sister wasn't much of a mother either."

On his feet, he was doing something at the desk she couldn't see since his back was to her, though she gathered he was tapping it—tapping something onto the desk, a familiar sound.

A plastic credit card tapping a hard surface to break up white cocaine powder.

Rose...

"I'm going to need you to be a bit more alert than you are, my dear." He was pivoting now, something in his hand, a flat surface—a mirror with lines of cocaine on top.

When he returned to the edge of the bed, Holly tried to ball her hands into fists, but her fingers felt like wet noodles.

He placed a rolled dollar bill to the glass. She hadn't even seen him take it out of his wallet.

As he offered her the drug, angling the bill towards her nostril, the mirror close behind, he said in a promising tone, "Trust me."

She thought she was asking, "You turned her into this?" But it came out as an uneven groan.

"Shhh," he whispered, pressing her other nostril closed.

Wanting to refuse, to spit in his face, and fight and punch and scream her way out of the room, some small voice in the back of her mind was screaming, *take the bump*.

It was her only way out.

If she wanted the strength to escape, she had to inhale.

So she did.

Brain stinging, eyes flaring wide, she lurched, bolting upright as cocaine ripped through her bloodstream. She saw stars, white specks flickering in her vision, as the feeling returned to her hands. The back of her head felt tingly and she knew she was totally out of it. Concentrating was so difficult that she didn't realize that Warren was laughing at her.

She took the mirror and helped herself to the second line then the third, all the while trying to steady her racing thoughts—had he been doing this to her sister, had he gotten her hooked, did he have some tenacious interest in Tucker, in them living here, what did it all mean?

Why did he want Tucker?

Why would he kill Rose?

Why would he murder his own son, Benjamin?

He was staring at her, but she couldn't meet his gaze. Bile stung the back of her throat, as she pieced it all together. She had to get out of here, get Tucker, drive to the precinct, and get help. Her skin was zinging. She didn't trust her legs.

She didn't trust that Cody and the Center Harbor police would believe her unless she brought them proof.

Remembering her cell phone in her back pocket, she whispered, "More," and handed him the mirror.

He seemed pleased with the request and slid off the bed.

As soon as he turned his back to her, preparing the next ounce of cocaine by tapping his credit card to break up chunks in the grains, Holly slipped her cell phone out of her pocket and fumbled pulling up the recorder app. Her hands were trembling and she felt an incredible pressure in her head—uppers and downers fiercely competing throughout every cell in her body.

He was turning towards her again, so she snuck her cell behind her back, easing it between the pillow and comforter, and blindly, she tapped the screen, hoping like hell she was hitting the Record icon.

"Holly, tell me," he began, passing the mirror to her along with the bill, "are you ready for motherhood?"

"Why do you want him?" she asked bluntly before snorting the first line.

Her strength was returning hard and fast. He was old, she thought, sizing him up on the sly. She could fight him if need be.

But she didn't need to get out of this resort as badly as she needed a recorded confession.

"I only want to be a part of his life," he said easily.

"Then what's that on the desk?"

"Do you feel cognizant enough to discuss it?"

She held his gaze as if debating.

"You're so much like your sister," he mused, his gaze traveling the length of her in a way that made her stomach lurch.

"Do you know why Rose stopped coming here? Do you know why she let you see Tucker less and less?"

He inhaled a deep breath giving her question careful consideration. "She had her secrets."

"Which you knew about," she supplied.

"I discovered them, yes."

"Not *them*, one," she corrected. "One secret you couldn't live with." When he said nothing, holding a plastic smile, she provoked him with, "You don't know who the father is, do you?"

His smile hardened into a grimace then receded until he was glaring furiously at her. "Benjamin is his father. Tucker is my grandson."

"He isn't. That's why Rose changed the Will. You hooked her on a drug that nearly destroyed her."

"Rose and I were very close."

"You were killing her from the start." Dismissing her, Warren sprang to his feet and grabbed the paperwork from the desk, but Holly didn't stop. "You found out Rose worked at Diamonds. You found out about the paternity test. You knew Rose was going to leave Benjamin for another man. Mothers always get custody. You probably pressured Benji to go after full custody, but he didn't care because he knew Tucker wasn't his. So you killed Rose and then you killed your own son. Why? Because Benji found out?"

He was cool and unaffected, turning around with the contract in his hands. "You have no idea what that boy means to me. Benji was a failure. I need Tucker. And the..." He cringed, his face turning red, quaking as if he could kill with his bare hands. "The insult I suffered. Your whoring sister, she thought she could lie to me! She tried to abandon the family and take Tucker away from me..." Warren clenched his jaw and ordered, "You are going to sign this and award me sole custody of Tucker."

Holly worked her way off the bed, her strength returning. "I won't."

"Then you will be forced to take a drug test, which you will fail. You will be exposed as an addict and you will lose guardianship." He extended the contract, offering a pen with his other hand. "Humiliation is not what I want for you."

"Clever."

"Be reasonable," he insisted.

"You tried to kill me." Stampeding for the door, she heard the distinct *click* of Warren cocking a gun and she froze, her heart punching up her throat, her hands rising in the air.

When she slowly turned, he stated, "I gave you an option."

Staring down the barrel of the gun that had killed her sister, the incredible weight of their likeness crushing her heart—there was no telling where Rose ended and Holly began, she had embraced every facet of her dead twin right up until this very moment, a mere breath away from dying, from her own murder—her voice was filled with conviction, as she pleaded, "I want to be running." Tears sprung from her eyes, rolling down her hot cheeks. Warren stilled as if intrigued. "When you kill me," she spat the words out. "I want to be running out onto the lake, onto the ice. I want to feel the bullet slice through my back. I want to fall and skid and plummet into the icy water. I want to die in the exact same way as Rose. Not here." She was sobbing now, trying to see through her tears. "Not like Benjamin. Like Rose."

He studied her for a long moment. "Why?"

Sobering up and reeling in her emotions, she whispered, "You wouldn't understand."

He seemed to consider her request, but then straightened his arms, holding the gun firmly.

There was no doubt in her mind this was the end.

"Killing Rose didn't solve your problems," she yelled, spit flying from her mouth. "And killing me won't either."

"I beg to differ."

"We filled out the paternity paperwork at the hospital," she yelled and Warren's face went slack. "Lucas York filed it with the State. He'll have his son no matter what you do to me."

The revelation struck Warren like a sandbag to his chest and he mulled the name over, "York?" as though he couldn't accept it.

Glaring at him, she stated, "Now you know who the father is," vaguely aware of the faint commotion coming from down the hall. It was muffled through the walls, but as she held the sick man's gaze, listening hard, she realized it sounded like boots stomping over carpet, men running down the hallway.

Lucas yelled, "Holly!"

Sensing an ambush, Warren snarled, his finger tightening over the trigger.

BANG.

The last thing Holly saw was Lucas spilling into the room, his eyes white all around with a look of stark panic on his face, as she dropped to the ground, the gunshot ringing in her ears.

Her chest was on fire, but it wasn't until her head bounced hard against the carpet that she realized she had been shot.

EPILOGUE

THE LATE WINTER sun peeked between clouds overhead, brightening the pale blue sky, the melting snow where tulips had emerged along the shore, and the iced-over lake that was safe to skate so long as Lucas and Tucker didn't venture out too far.

Holding his son's hands, Lucas glided backwards, his stance wide, zigzagging, while Tucker watched his skates, pushing off, left then right then left, getting a feel for the rhythm, flitting and drifting just like Daddy.

Lucas loosened his grip, releasing his son who wobbled, ass-out and ecstatic, into a rocky glide. Tucker shuffled his ice-skates until he came to a gradual standstill and applauded himself.

Lucas clapped as well, skating over then arching tight circles around him. He had never felt it before—pride. But that was how he felt every day with Tucker, every moment, proud to be his father, proud that Tucker was an extension of himself. The boy was timid and sweet and found humor in unsuspecting places. He also had a serious set of pipes, and when he writhed in tantrums, there was no mistaking who was really in charge. But for Lucas there was something deeply comforting even in those moments. Supporting his son through fits and helping him reconcile his emotions, filled Lucas's heart with meaning and purpose, so bright and profound that at times he thought his soul might burst.

Caring for his son had transformed him. His heart hadn't been made of tar, but coated in it, and as if by magic, loving Tucker had worn away the muck and mire, releasing him.

If not for Holly, he wouldn't be here, living this life, teaching his son to skate on a warm, breezy afternoon in mid-March—cedars dripping along the shore, blades of grass pressing through the snow, the essence of new beginnings blossoming all around him.

Barging into Room 112 too late and witnessing her take a bullet—Holly falling, the terrible slam of dead weight to the ground, her head smacking against the floor—haunted him.

The scene had unfolded in gut-splitting chaos—Lucas charging to her, plummeting to his knees, his hands pressing her upper chest, blood hot and thick seeping through his fingers where he applied pressure just below her clavicle; Cody spilling in, shouting at Warren to drop his weapon, aiming his own gun at the killer who had almost gotten away with it all.

Lucas's throat had gone raw screaming for an ambulance, as police officers swept in, apprehended the older man, forcing him to the ground and jerking his wrists together behind his back, Sarah looking on from the doorway in abject horror as though seeing her husband for what he truly was, had scrubbed away the drugs from her system.

It had felt like it was happening in slow motion, the epic delay before the medics arrived, Cody throwing blankets over Holly to keep her warm in the interim, insisting to Lucas that she was going to make it even though neither had been able to find a pulse. All the while, Lucas had wrestled his deepest fear, begging it not to come true—that he was losing her and this time it would be forever.

Tucker was yanking on his sleeve and when Lucas glanced down, his son challenged him to a race, indicating fifteen yards off where Roberta and Mary were dizzying themselves, skating circles while holding hands.

Lucas smiled at his son's ambition, but just as Tucker was readying to shout, *On your marks, get set...* He shouted, "Mom!" instead, shuffling as best he could towards the shore where Holly seemed unsure about setting her skates on the ice.

She threw her hands up, locking eyes with Lucas as if to say, *Will he ever believe us?* Lucas and Holly had sat Tucker down several times, eventually with the help of a child psychologist, to gently explain to him that his mother had passed away. Holly was his aunt. But the boy refused to accept it.

Lucas had to laugh. Reality wasn't always easy. Tucker would get there in his own time.

Holly didn't even skate an inch onto the ice. She was shuffling ass-out almost as precariously as her nephew, who neared her.

As Lucas glided over with the stealth of a hockey professional, the gratitude he felt for Holly's recovery—as prolonged, as touch-and-go that it had been—filled him.

In the hotel room that day, she had dove in the nick of time. The bullet meant for her heart had struck too high and too far to the right. According to the medics she had died more than once before reaching the hospital where doctors dug the bullet out and stabilized her. She had spent over a week in the I.C.U. Then after transferring into recovery, where she remained for two weeks, she was finally released. Lucas had spent every spare minute he had with her during those grueling weeks at the hospital, holding her hand, helping her eat, and complaining in private to the nurses when he was certain her room wasn't warm enough. He had brought Tucker with him as well when he thought he could handle it emotionally, and he tended to his son otherwise when at home.

Roberta and Mary had been helping out, though trusting the secretive girls had taken more effort than he thought he had in him. It was Roberta who had convinced him. The fact that Lucas hadn't turned her in or uttered so much as a word to his partner had gone a long way with Roberta. She had wanted to prove herself and Lucas would've been a fool to deny her help.

Taking Holly's hands and nearly tripping over Tucker, who had wrapped himself around her leg like a barnacle, Lucas nodded towards the backyard and said, "Looks like lunch is on."

"Already? I just got out on the ice," she said, quickly glancing over her shoulder at Cody and Hannah who were setting food on a picnic table.

Beyond them, Roberta's parents were chatting on the back porch of the house, but were soon called over to the table, Hannah waving at them and gesturing with a six-pack of beer.

Whatever friction Lucas and Cody had suffered during their first month as partners was now gone and since Holly's release from the hospital, the men had not only settled into a nice dynamic at the precinct, but had also become friends.

Tucker was yanking on Holly's arm so she shot Lucas a smile and pushed off, skating with her nephew towards the shore.

Lucas took in the sight of it all—Roberta and Mary messing around near the tulips, the adults circling the picnic table and cracking beers open, the house Lucas shared with Holly, modest and blue and almost too charming to be real, in the background.

But it was real. This was his life.

Warren Wythe was convicted for the murders of Rose and Benjamin, for killing Ron Conover, and for the two attempts on Holly's life. His wife, Sarah, was in counseling. She had filed for divorce and was now running the resort, her mind sharp and clear, no longer bogged down in the haze of her husband's drugs.

As he skated towards the shore, feeling the warm wind on his face and taking in the picturesque scene, friends and family enjoying the afternoon, he realized that with so many secrets unearthed, even the ones he had kept from himself, he was no longer afraid. There was no risk of slipping into the abyss of his other persona or losing control to his darker side, though he sensed it lying dormant within him.

He was free.

THE END

ALSO BY MIRA GIBSON

Thomas from the Sea

Who Killed Leeanne?

The Kensington Killers: The Complete Series
Lunatic (The Kensington Killers, Book One)
Crank (The Kensington Killers, Book Two)
Maniac (The Kensington Killers, Book Three)

The New Hampshire Mysteries: The Complete Series
Daddy Soda (A New Hampshire Mystery, Book One)
Rock Spider (A New Hampshire Mystery, Book Two)
Tar Heart (A New Hampshire Mystery, Book Three)

ABOUT THE AUTHOR

I write mystery novels, detective novels, sleuth mysteries, and psychological literary fiction! You can find me most days working on my computer in the sunshine of beautiful Long Beach, NY where I dream up small town characters and write dark mysteries that are filled with unsuspecting tenderness.

Find me on Facebook! **/MiraGibsonAuthor**

Visit MysteryRoyalty.com to learn more.

Copyright © 2015
Published by: Mira Gibson

All Rights Reserved. This book or any portion thereof may not be reproduced or used in any manner whatsoever without the express written permission of the publisher except for the use of brief quotations in a book review. All characters appearing in this work are fictitious. Any resemblance to real persons, living or dead, is purely coincidental.

For questions and comments about this book, please contact www.mysteryroyalty.com

www.ingramcontent.com/pod-product-compliance
Lightning Source LLC
Chambersburg PA
CBHW031542240626
47153CB00002B/352